THE HEART'S HIGHWAY

MORE WILDSIDE CLASSICS

THE HEART'S HIGHWAY

A Romance of Virginia in the Seventeenth Century

MARY E. WILKINS

WILDSIDE PRESS

THE HEART'S HIGHWAY

This edition published 2005 by Wildside Press, LLC.
www.wildsidepress.com

I

In 1682, when I was thirty years of age and Mistress Mary Cavendish just turned of eighteen, she and I together one Sabbath morning in the month of April were riding to meeting in Jamestown. We were all alone except for the troop of black slaves straggling in the rear, blurring the road curiously with their black faces. It seldom happened that we rode in such wise, for Mistress Catherine Cavendish, the elder sister of Mistress Mary, and Madam Cavendish, her grandmother, usually rode with us — Madam Judith Cavendish, though more than seventy, sitting a horse as well as her granddaughters, and looking, when viewed from the back, as young as they, and being in that respect, as well as others, a wonder to the countryside. But it happened today that Madam Cavendish had a touch of the rheumatics, that being an ailment to which the swampy estate of the country rendered those of advanced years somewhat liable, and had remained at home on her plantation of Drake Hill (so named in honour of the great Sir Francis Drake, though he was long past the value of all such earthly honours). Catherine, who was a most devoted granddaughter, had remained with her — although, I suspected, with some hesitation at allowing her young sister to go alone, except for me, the slaves being accounted no more company than our shadows. Mistress Catherine Cavendish had looked at me after a fashion which I was at no loss to understand when I had stood aside to allow Mistress Mary to precede me in passing the door, but she had no cause for the look, nor for the apprehension which gave rise to it. By reason of bearing always my burthen upon my own back, I was even more mindful of it than others were who had only the sight of it, whereas I had the sore weight and the evil aspect in my inmost soul. But it was to be borne easily enough by virtue of that natural resolution of a man which can make but a featherweight of the sorest ills if it be but put in the balance against them. I was tutor to Mistress Mary Cavendish, and I had sailed from England to Virginia under circumstances of disgrace; being, indeed, a convict.

I knew exceeding well what was my befitting deportment when I set out that Sabbath morning with Mistress Mary Cavendish, and not only upon that Sabbath morning but at all other times; still I can well understand that my appearance may have belied me, since when I looked in a glass I would often wonder at the sight of my own face, which seemed younger than my years, and was strangely free from any recording lines of experiences which might have been esteemed bitter by any one who had not the pride of bearing them. When my black eyes, which had a bold daring in them, looked forth at me from the glass, and my lips smiled with a gay confidence at me, I could not but surmise that my whole face was as a mask worn unwittingly over a grave spirit. But since a man must be judged largely by his outward guise and I had that of a gay young blade, I need not have taken it amiss if Catherine Cavendish had that look in her eyes when I set forth with her young sister alone save for those dark people which some folk believed to have no souls.

I rode a pace behind Mary Cavendish, and never glanced her way, not needing to do so in order to see her, for I seemed to see her with a superior sort of vision compounded partly of memory and partly of imagination. Of the latter I had, not to boast, though it may perchance be naught to boast of, being simply a kind of higher folly, a somewhat large allowance from my childhood. But that was not to be wondered at, whether it were to my credit or otherwise, since it was inherited from ancestors of much nobler fame and worthier parts than I, one of whom, though not in the direct line, the great Edward Maria Wingfield, the president of the first council of the Dominion of Virginia, having written a book which was held to be notable. This imagination for the setting forth and adorning of all common things and happenings, and my woman's name of Maria, my whole name being Harry Maria Wingfield, through my ancestor having been a favourite of a great queen, and so called for her honour, were all my inheritance at that date, all the estates belonging to the family having become the property of my younger brother John.

But when I speak of my possessing an imagination which could gild all the common things of life, I meant not to include Mistress Mary Cavendish therein, for she needed not such gilding, being one of the most uncommon things in the earth, as uncommon as a great diamond which is rumoured to have been seen by travellers in far India. My imagination when directed toward her was exercised only with the comparing and combining of various and especial beauties of different times and circumstances, when she was attired this way or that way, or was grave or gay, or sweetly helpless and clinging or full of daring. When, riding near her, I did not look at her, she seemed all of these in one, and I was conscious of such a great dazzle forcing my averted eyes, that I seemed to be riding behind a star.

I knew full well, though, as I said before, not studying the matter, just how Mistress Mary Cavendish sat her horse, which was a noble thoroughbred from England, though the one which I rode was a nobler, she having herself selected him for my use. The horse which she rode, Merry Roger, did not belie his name, for he was full of prances and tosses of his fine head, and prickings of his dainty pointed ears, but Mistress Mary sat him as lightly and truly and unswervingly as a blossom sits a dancing bough.

That morning Mistress Mary glowed and glittered and flamed in gorgeous apparel, until she seemed to fairly overreach all the innocent young flowery beauties of the spring with one rich trill of colour, like a high note of a bird above a wide chorus of others. Mistress Mary that morning wore a tabby petticoat of a crimson colour, and a crimson satin bodice shining over her arms and shoulders like the plumage of a bird, and down her back streamed her curls, shining like gold under her gauze love-hood. I knew well how she had sat up late the night before fashioning that hood from one which her friend Cicely Hyde's grandmother had sent her from England, and I knew, the first pages of a young maid being easy to spell out, that she wondered if I, though only her tutor, approved her in it, but I gave no sign. The love-hood was made of such thin and precious stuff that the gold of her head showed through.

Mistress Mary wore a mask of black velvet to screen her face from the sun, and only her sweet forehead and her great blue eyes and the rose-leaf tip of her chin showed.

All that low, swampy country was lush and green that April morning, with patches of grass gleaming like emeralds in the wetness of sunken places and unexpected pools of marsh water gleaming out of the distances like sapphires. The blossoms thrust out toward us from every hand like insistent arms of beauty. There was a frequent bush by the wayside full of a most beautiful pink-horned flower, so exceeding sweet that it harmed the worth of its own sweetness, and its cups seemed fairly dripping with honey and were gummed together with it. There were patches of a flower of a most brilliant and wonderful blue colour, and spreads as of cloth of gold from cowslips over the lowlands. The road was miry in places, and then I would fall behind her farther still that the water and red mud splashing from beneath my horse's hoofs might not reach her. Then, finally, after I had done thus some few times, she reined in her Merry Roger, and looked over her shoulder with a flash of her blue eyes which compelled mine.

"Why do you ride so far away, Master Wingfield?" said she.

I lifted my hat and bent so low in my saddle that the feather on it grazed the red mud.

"Because I fear to splash your fine tabby petticoat, Madam," I answered.

"I care not for my fine petticoat," said she in a petulant way, like that of a spoiled child who is forbidden sweets and the moon, and questions love in consequence, yet still there was some little fear and hesitation in her tone. Mistress Mary was a most docile pupil, seeming to have great respect for my years and my learning, and was as gentle under my hand as was her Merry Roger under hers, and yet with the same sort of gentleness, which is as the pupil and not as the master decides, and let the pull of the other will be felt.

I answered not, yet kept at my distance, but at the next miry place she held in Merry Roger until I was forced to come up, and then she spoke again, and as she spoke a mock-bird was singing somewhere over on the bank of the river.

"Did you ever hear a sweeter bird's song than that, Master Wingfield?" said she, and I answered that it was very sweet, as indeed it was.

"What do you think the bird is mocking, Master Wingfield?" said she, and then I answered like a fool, for the man who meets sweetness with his own bitterness and keeps it not locked in his own soul is a fool.

"I know not," said I, "but he may be mocking the hope of the spring, and he may be mocking the hope in the heart of man. The song seems too sweet for a mock of any bird which has no thought beyond this year's nest."

I spoke thus as I would not now, when I have learned that the soul of man, like the moon, hath a face which he should keep ever turned toward the Unseen, and Mistress Mary's blue eyes, as helpless of comprehension as a flower, looked in mine.

"But there will be another spring, Master Wingfield," said she somewhat timidly, and then she added, and I knew that she was blushing under her mask at her own tenderness, "and sometimes the hopes of the heart come true."

She rode on with her head bent as one who considers deeply, but I, knowing her well, knew that the mood would soon pass, as it did. Suddenly she tossed her head and flung out her curls to the breeze, and swung Merry Roger's bridle-rein, and was away at a gallop and I after her, measuring the ground with wide paces on my tall thoroughbred. In this fashion we soon left the plodding blacks so far behind that they became a part of the distance-shadows. Then, all at once, Mistress Mary swerved off from the main road and was riding down the track leading to the plantation-wharf, whence all the tobacco was shipped for England and all the merchandise imported for household use unladen. There the way was very wet and the mire was splashed high upon Mistress Mary's fine tabby skirt, but she rode on at a reckless pace, and I also, much at a loss to know what had come to her, yet not venturing, or rather, perhaps, deigning to inquire. And then I saw what she had doubtless seen before, the masts of a ship rising straightly among the trees with that stiffness and straightness of dead wood, which is beyond that of live, unless, indeed, in a storm at sea, when the wind can so inspirit it, that I have seen a mast of pine possessed by all the rage of yielding of its hundred years on the spur of a mountain.

When I saw the mast I knew that the ship belonging to Madam Cavendish, which was called *The Golden Horn*, and had upon the bow the likeness of a gilt-horn, running over with fruit and flowers, had arrived. It was by this ship that Madam Cavendish sent the tobacco raised upon the plantation of Drake Hill to England.

But even then I knew not what had so stirred Mistress Mary that she had left her sober churchward road upon the Sabbath day, and judged that it must be the desire to see *The Golden Horn* fresh from her voyage, nor did I dream what she purposed doing.

Toward the end of the rolling road the wetness increased; there were little pools left from the recedence of the salt tide, and the wild breath of it was in our faces. Then we heard voices singing together in a sailor-song which had a refrain not quite suited to the day, according to common opinions, having a refrain about a lad who sailed away on bounding billow and left poor Jane to wear the willow; but what's a lass's tears of brine to the Spanish Main and a flask of wine?

As we came up to the ship lying in her dock, we saw sailors on deck grouped around a cask of that same wine which they had taken the freedom to broach, in order to celebrate their safe arrival in port, though it was none of theirs. The sight aroused my anger, but Mary Cavendish did not seem to see any occasion for wrath. She sat her prancing horse, her head up, and her curls streaming like a flag of gold, and there was a blue flash in her eyes, of which I knew the meaning. The blood of her great ancestor, the sea king, Thomas Cavendish, who was second only to Sir Francis Drake, was astir within her. She sat there with the salt sea wind in her nostrils, and her hair flung upon it like a pennant of victory, and looked at the ship wet with the ocean surges, the sails stiff with the rime of salt, and the group of English sailors on the deck, and those old ancestral instincts which constitute the memory of the blood awoke. She was in that instant as she sat there almost as truly that ardent Suffolkshire lad, Thomas Cavendish, ready to ride to the death the white plungers of the sea, and send the Spanish Armada to the bottom, as Mary Cavendish of Drake Hill, the fairest maid of her time in the Colony of Virginia.

Then as suddenly that mood left her, as she sat there, the sailors having risen, and standing staring with shamefaced respect, and covertly wiping with the hairy backs of hands their mouths red with wine. But the captain, one Calvin Tabor, stood before them with more assurance, as if he had some warrant for allowing such license among his men; he himself seemed not to have been drinking. Mistress Mary regarded them, holding in Merry Roger with her firm little hand, with the calm grace of a queen, although she was so young, and all the wild fire was gone from her blue eyes. All this time, I being as close to her side as might be, in case of any rudeness of the men, though that was not likely, they being a picked crew of Suffolkshire men, and having as yet not tasted more wine than would make them unquestioning of strange happenings, and render them readily acquiescent to all counter currents of fate.

They had ceased their song and stood with heavy eyes sheepishly averted in their honest red English faces, but Captain Calvin Tabor spoke, bowing low, yet, as I said before, with assured eyes.

"I have the honour to salute you, Mistress," he spoke with a grace somewhat beyond his calling. He was a young man, as fair as a Dutchman and a giant in stature. He bore himself also curiously for one of his calling, bowing as steadily as a cavalier, with no trembling of the knees when he recovered, and carrying his right arm as if it would grasp sword rather than cutlass if the need arose.

"God be praised! I see that you have brought *The Golden Horn* safely to port," said Mistress Mary with a stately sweetness that covered to me, who knew her voice and its every note so well, an exultant ring.

"Yes, praised be God, Mistress Cavendish," answered Captain Tabor, "and with fine head winds to swell the sails and no pirates."

"And is my new scarlet cloak safe?" cried Mistress Mary, "and my tabby petticoats and my blue brocade bodice, and my stockings and my satin shoes, and laces?"

Mistress Mary spoke with that sweetness of maiden vanity which calls for tender leniency and admiration from a man instead of contempt. And it may easily chance that he may be as filled with vain delight as she, and picture to himself as plainly her appearance in those new fallalls.

I wondered somewhat at the length of the list, as not only Mistress Mary's wardrobe, but those of her grandmother and sister and many of the household supplies, had to be purchased with the proceeds of the tobacco, and that brought but scanty returns of late years, owing to the Navigation Act, which many esteemed a most unjust measure, and scrupled not to say so, being secure in the New World, where disloyalty against kings could flourish without so much danger of the daring tongue silenced at Tyburn.

It had been a hard task for many planters to purchase the necessaries of life with the profits of their tobacco crop, since the trade with the Netherlands was prohibited by His Most Gracious Majesty, King Charles II, for the supply being limited to the English market, had so exceeded the demand that it brought but a beggarly price per pound. Therefore, I wondered, knowing that many of those articles of women's attire mentioned by Mistress Mary were of great value, and brought great sums in London, and knowing, too, that the maid, though innocently fond of such things, to which she had, moreover, the natural right of youth and beauty such as hers, which should have all the silks and jewels of earth, and no questioning, for its adorning, was not given to selfish appropriation for her own needs, but rather considered those of others first. However, Mistress Mary had some property in her own right, she being the daughter of a second wife, who had died possessed of a small plantation called Laurel Creek, which was a mile distant from Drake Hill, farther inland, having no ship dock and employing this. Mistress Mary might have sent some of her own tobacco crop to England wherewith to purchase finery for herself. Still I wondered, and I wondered still more when Mistress Mary, albeit the Lord's Day, and the penalty for such labour being even for them of high degree not light, should propose, as she did, that the goods be then and there unladen. Then I ventured to address her, riding close to her side, that the captain and the sailors should not hear, and think that I held her in slight respect and treated her like a child, since I presumed to call her to account for aught she chose to do.

"Madam," said I as low as might be, "do you remember the day?"

"And wherefore should I not?" asked she with a toss of her gold locks and a pout of her red lips which was childishness and wilfulness itself, but there went along with it a glance of her eyes which puzzled me, for suddenly a sterner and older spirit of resolve seemed to look out of them into mine. "Think you I am in my dotage, Master Wingfield, that I remember not the day?" said she, "and think you that I am going deaf that I hear not the church bells?"

"If we miss the service for the unlading of the goods, and it be discovered, it may go amiss with us," said I.

"Are you then afraid, Master Wingfield?" asked she with a glance of scorn, and a blush of shame at her own words, for she knew that they were false.

I felt the blood rush to my face, and I reined back my horse, and said no more.

"I pray you have the goods that you know of unladen at once, Captain Tabor," said she, and she made a motion that would have been a stamp had she stood.

Calvin Tabor laughed, and cast a glance of merry malice at me, and bowed low as he replied:

"The goods shall be unladen within the hour, Mistress," said he, "and if you and the gentleman would rather not tarry to see them for fear of discovery —"

"We shall remain," said Mistress Mary, interrupting peremptorily.

"Then," said Captain Calvin Tabor with altogether too much of freedom as I judged, "in case you be brought to account for the work upon the Sabbath, *The Golden Horn* hath wings for such a wind as prevails today as will outspeed all pursuers, even should they borrow wings of the cherubim in the churchyard."

I was glad that Mistress Mary did not, for all her youthfulness of temper, laugh in return, but answered him with a grave dignity as if she herself felt that he had exceeded his privilege.

"I pray you order the goods unladen at once, Captain Tabor," she repeated. Then the captain coloured, for he was quick-witted to scent a rebuff, though he laughed again in his daredevil fashion as he turned to the sailors and shouted out the order, and straightway the sailors so swarmed hither and thither upon the deck that they seemed five times as many as before, and then we heard the hatches flung back with claps like guns.

We sat there and waited, and the bell over in Jamestown rang and the long notes died away with sweet echoes as if from distant heights. All around us the rank, woody growth was full of murmurs and movements of life, and perfumes from unseen blossoms disturbed one's thoughts with sweet insistence at every gust of wind, and always one heard the lapping of the sea-water through all its countless ways, for well it loves this country of Virginia and steals upon it, like a lover who will not be gainsaid, through meadows and thick woods and coarse swamps, until it is hard sometimes to say, when the tide be in, whether it be land or sea, and we who dwell therein might well account ourselves in a Venice of the New World.

I waited and listened while the sailors unloaded the goods with many a shout and repeated loud commands from the captain, and Mistress Mary kept her eyes turned away from my face and watched persistently the unlading, and had seemingly no more thought of me than of one of the swamp trees for some time. Then all at once she turned toward me, though still her eyes evaded mine.

"Why do you not go to church, Master Wingfield?" said she in a sweet, sharp voice.

"I go when you go, Madam," said I.

"You have no need to wait for me," said she. "I prefer that you should not wait for me."

I made no reply, but reined in my horse, which was somewhat restive with his head in a cloud of early flies.

"Do you not hear me, Master Wingfield?" said she. "Why do you not proceed to church and leave me to follow when I am ready?"

She had never spoken to me in such manner before, and she dared not look at me as she spoke.

"I go when you go, Madam," said I again.

Then, suddenly, with an impulse half of mischief and half of anger, she lashed out with her riding whip at my restive horse, and he sprang, and I had much ado to keep him from bolting. He danced to all the trees and bushes, and she had to pull Merry Roger sharply to one side, but finally I got the mastery of him, and rode close to her again.

"Madam," said I, "I forbid you to do that again," and as I spoke I saw her little fingers twitch on her whip, but she dared not raise it. She laughed as a child will who knows she is at fault and is scared by her consciousness of guilt and would conceal it by a bravado of merriment; then she said in the sweetest, wheedling tone that I had ever heard from her, and I had known her from her childhood:

"But, Master Wingfield, 'tis broad daylight and there are no Indians hereabouts, and if there were, here are all these English sailors and Captain Tabor. Why need you stay? Indeed, I shall be quite safe — and hear, that must be the last stroke of the bell?"

But I was not to be moved by wheedling. I repeated again that

I should remain where she was. Then she, grown suddenly stern again, withdrew a little from me, and made no further efforts to get rid of me, but sat still watching the unlading with a gravity which gave me a vague uneasiness. I began to have a feeling that here was more than appeared on the surface, and my suspicion grew as I watched the sailors lift those boxes which were supposed to contain Mistress Mary's finery. In the first place there were enough of them to contain the wardrobe of a lady in waiting, in the second place they were of curious shape for such purposes, in the third place 'twas all those lusty English sailors could do to lift them.

"They be the heaviest furbelows that ever maiden wore," I thought as I watched them strain at the cases, both hauling and pulling, with many men to the ends to get them through the hatch, then ease them to the deck, with regard to the nipping of fingers. I noted, too, an order given somewhat privately by Captain Tabor to put out the pipes, and noted that not one man but had stowed his away.

There was a bridle-path leading through the woods to Laurel Creek, and by that way to my consternation Mistress Mary ordered the sailors to carry the cases. 'Twas two miles inland, and I marvelled much to hear her, for even should nearly all the crew go, the load would be a grievous one, it seemed to me. But to my mind Captain Calvin Tabor behaved as if the order was one which he expected, neither did the sailors grumble, but straightway loaded themselves with the case raised upon a species of hurdles which must have been provided for the purpose, and proceeded down the bridle-path, singing to keep up their hearts another song even more at odds with the day than the first. The captain marched at the head of the sailors, and Mistress Mary and I followed slowly through the narrow aisle of green. I rode ahead, and often pulled my horse to one side, pressing his body hard against the trees that I might hold back a branch which would have caught her head-gear. All the way we never spoke. When we reached Laurel Creek, Mistress Mary drew the key from her pocket, which showed to me that the visit had been planned should the ship have arrived. She unlocked the door, and the sailors, no longer singing, for they were well-nigh spent by the journey under the heavy burdens, deposited the cases in the great room. Laurel Creek had belonged to Mistress Mary's maternal grandfather, Colonel Edmond Lane, and had not been inhabited this many a year, not since Mary was a baby in arms. The old furniture still stood in the accustomed places, looking desolate with that peculiar desolateness of lifeless things which have been associated with man. The house at Laurel Creek was a fine mansion, finer than Drake Hill, and the hall made me think of England. Great oak chests stood against the walls, hung with rusting swords and armour and empty powder-horns. A carven seat was beside the cold hearth, and in a corner was a tall spinning-wheel, and the carven stair led in a spiral ascent of mystery to the shadows above.

When the cases were all deposited in the great room, Mistress Mary held a short conference apart with Captain Calvin Tabor, and I saw some gold pass from her hand to his. Then she thanked him and the sailors for their trouble very prettily in that way she had which would have made every one as willing to die for her as to carry heavy weights. Then we all filed out from the house, and Mistress Mary locked the door, and bade good-bye to Captain Tabor; then he and his men took again the bridle-path back to the ship, and she and I proceeded churchward on the highway.

When we were once alone together I spurred my horse up to hers and caught her bridle and rode alongside and spoke to her as if all the past were naught, and I with the rights to which I had been born. It had come to that pass with me in those days that all the pride I had left was that of humility, but even that I was ready to give up for her if necessary.

"Tell me, Madam," said I, "what was in those cases?"

"Have I not told you?" said she, and I knew that she whitened under her mask.

"There is more than woman's finery in those cases, which weigh like lead," said I. "What do they contain?"

Mistress Mary had, after all, little of the feminine power of subterfuge in her. If she tried it, it was, as in this case, too transparent. Straight to the point she went with perfect frankness of daring and rebellion as a boy might.

"It requires not much wit, methinks, Master Wingfield, to see that," said she. Then she laughed. "Lord, how the poor sailor-men toiled to lift my gauzes and feathers and ribbons!" said she. Then her blue eyes looked at me through her mask with indescribable daring and defiance.

"Well, and what will you do?" said she. "You are a gentleman in spite — you are a gentleman, you cannot betray me to my hurt, and you cannot command me like a child, for I am a child no longer, and I will not tell you what those cases contain."

"You shall tell me," said I.

"Make me if you can," said she.

"Tell me what those cases contain," said I.

Then she collapsed all at once as only the citadel of a woman's will can do through some inner weakness.

"Guns and powder and shot and partizans," said she. Then she added, like one who would fain readjust herself upon the heights of her own resolution by a good excuse for having fallen — "Fie, why should I not have told you, Master Wingfield? You cannot betray me, for you are a gentleman, and I am not a child."

"Why have you had guns and ammunition brought from England?" I asked; but in the shock of the discovery I had loosened my grasp of her bridle and she was off, and in a minute we were in Jamestown, and could not disturb the Sabbath quiet by talk or ride too fast.

We were a good hour and a half late, but there was to my mind enough of preaching yet for my soul's good, for I thought not much of Parson Downs nor his sermons, but I dreaded for Mistress Mary that which might come from her tardiness and her Sabbath-breaking, if that were discovered. I dismounted, and assisted Mistress Mary to the horse block, and off came her black velvet mask, and she clapped a pretty hand to her hair and shook her skirts and wiped off a mud splash. Then up the aisle she went, and I after her and all the people staring.

I can see that church as well today as if I were this moment there. Heavily sweet with honey and almond scent it was, as well as sweet herbs and musk, which the ladies had on their handkerchiefs, for it was like a bower with flowers. Great pink boughs arched overhead, and the altar was as white as snow with blossoms. Up the aisle she flashed, and none but Mary Cavendish could have made that little journey under the eyes of the governor in his pew and the governor's lady and all the burgesses, and the churchwarden half starting up as if to exercise his authority, and the parson swelling with a vast expanse of sable robes over the Book, with no abashedness and yet no boldness nor unmaidenly forwardness. There was an innocent gayety on her face like a child's, and an entire confidence in good will and loving charity for her tardiness which disarmed all. She looked out from that gauze love-hood of hers as she came up the aisle, and the governor, who had a harsh face enough ordinarily, beamed mildly indulgent. His lady eyed her with a sort of pleasant and reminiscent wonder, though she was a haughty dame. The churchwarden settled back, and as for Parson Downs, his great, red face curved in a smile, and his eyes twinkled under their heavy overhang of florid brow, and then he declaimed in a hoarser and louder shout than ever to cover the fact of his wandering attention. And young

Sir Humphrey Hyde, sitting between his mother, Lady Betty, and his sister, Cicely, turned as pale as death when he saw her enter, and kept so, with frequent covert glances at her from time to time, and I saw him, and knew that he knew about Mistress Mary's furbelow boxes.

II

My profession has been that of a tutor, and it thus befell that I was under the necessity of learning as much as I was able, and even going out of my way to seek those lessons at which all the pages of life are open for us, and even, as it were, turning over wayside stones, and looking under wayside weeds in the search for them; and it scarcely ever chanced that I did not get some slight savour of knowledge therefrom, though I was far enough from the full solution of the problems. And through these lessons I seemed to gain some increase of wisdom not only of the matters of which the lessons themselves treated, such as the courses of the stars and planets, the roots of herbs, and Latin verbs and algebraic quantities, and evil and good, but of their bearing upon the human heart. That I have ever held to be the most important knowledge of all, and the only reason for the setting of those lessons which must pass like all things mortal, and can only live in so far as they have turned that part of the scholar, which has hold of immortality, this or that way.

I know not how it may be with other men, but of one branch of knowledge, which pertains directly to the human heart, and, when it be what its name indicates, to its eternal life, I gained no insight whatever from my books and my lessons, nor from my observance of its workings in those around me, and that was the passion of love. Of that I truly could learn naught except by turning my reflections toward my own heart.

And I know not how this also may be with other men, but love with me had a beginning, though not an end and never shall have, and a completeness of growth which makes it visible to my thought like the shape of an angel. I have loved not in one way, but in every way which the heart of man could conceive. There is no tone of love which the heart holds for the striking which I have not heard like a bell through my furthermost silences. I can truly say that when I rode to church with Mary Cavendish that morning in April, though I loved in my whole life her and her alone, and was a most solitary man as far as friends and kinsfolk went, yet not one in the whole Kingdom of Virginia had fuller knowledge of love in all its shades of meaning than I. For I had loved Mary Cavendish like a father and like a lover, like a friend and a brother, like a slave and like a master, and such love I had for her that I could see her good beyond her pain, and would have had the courage to bear her pain, though God knows her every pain was my twenty. And it had been thus with me near sixteen years, since I was fourteen and she was a little maid of two, and I lived neighbour to her in Suffolkshire. I can see myself at fourteen and laugh at the picture. All of us have our phases of comedy, our seasons when we are out of perspective and approach the grotesque and furnish our own jesters for our after lives.

At fourteen I was as ungainly a lad, with as helpless a sprawl of legs and arms and as staring and shamefaced a surprise at my suddenly realised height of growth, when jostled by a girl or a younger lad, and utter discomfiture before an unexpected deepness of tone when essaying a polite response to an inquiry of his elders, as was ever seen in England. And I remember that I bore myself with a wary outlook for affronts to my newly fledging dignity, and concealed all that was stirring in me to new life, whether of nobility or natural emotion, as if it were a dire shame, and whenever I had it in my heart to be tender, was so brusque that I seemed to have been provided by nature with an armour of roughness like a hedgehog. But, perhaps, I had some small excuse for this, though, after all, it is a question in my mind as to what excuse there may be for any man outside the motives of his own deeds, and I care not to dwell unduly, even to my own consideration, upon those disadvantages of life which may come to a man without his cognisance and are to be borne like any fortune of war. But I had a mother who had small affection for me, and that was not so unnatural nor so much to her discredit as it may sound, since she, poor thing, had been forced into a marriage with my father when she was long in love with her cousin. Then my father having died at sea the year after I was born, and her cousin, who was a younger son, having come into the estates through the deaths of both his brothers of smallpox in one week, she married her first love in less than six months, and no discredit to her, for women are weak when they love, and she had doubtless been sorely tried. They told me that my poor father was a true man and gallant soldier, and my old nurse used to talk to me of him, and I used to go by myself to think of him, and my eyes would get red when I was but a little boy with reflecting upon my mother with her new husband and her beautiful little boy, my brother John, a year and a half younger than I, and how my own poor father was forgotten. But there was no discredit to my mother, who was only a weak and gentle woman and was tasting happiness after disappointment and sorrow, in being borne so far out by the tide of it that she lost sight, as it were, of her old shores. My mind was never against my mother for her lack of love for me. But it is not hard to be lenient toward a lack of love toward one's self, especially remembering, as I do, myself, and my fine, ruddy-faced, loud-voiced stepfather and my brother John.

A woman, by reason of her great tenderness of heart which makes her suffer overmuch for those she loves, has not the strength to bear the pain of loving more than one or two so entirely, and my mother's whole heart was fixed with an anxious strain of loving care upon my stepfather and my brother. I have seen her sit hours by a window as pale as a statue while my stepfather was away, for those were troublous times in England, and he in the thick of it. When I was a lad of six or thereabouts they were bringing the king back to his own, and some of the loyal ones were in danger of losing their heads along his proposed line of march. And I have known her to hang whole nights over my brother's bed if he had but a tickling in the throat; and what could one poor woman do more?

She was as slender as a reed in this marshy country of Virginia, and her voice was a sweet whisper, like the voice of one in a wind, and she had a curious gracefulness of leaning toward one she loved when in his presence, as if, whether she would or no, her heart of affection swayed her body toward him. Always, in thinking of my mother, I see her leaning with that true line of love toward my stepfather or my brother John, her fair hair drooping over her delicate cheeks, her blue eyes wistful with the longing to give more and more for their happiness. My brother John looked like my mother, being, in fact, almost feminine in his appearance, though not in his character. He had the same fair face, perhaps more clearly and less softly cut, and the same long, silky wave of fair hair, but the expression of his eyes was different, and in character he was different. As for me, I was like my poor father, so like that, as I grew older, I seemed his very double, as my old nurse used to tell me. Perhaps that may have accounted for the quick glance, which seemed almost of fear, which my mother used to give me sometimes when I entered a room where she sat at her embroidery-work. My mother dearly loved fine embroideries and laces, and in thinking of her I can no more separate her from them than I can a flower from its scalloped setting of petals.

I used to slink away as soon as possible when my mother turned her startled blue eyes upon me in such wise, that she might regain her peace, and sometimes I used to send my brother John to her on some errand, if I could manage it, knowing that he could soon drive me from her mind. One learns early such little tricks with women; they are such tender things, and it stirs one's heart to impatience to see them troubled. However, I will not deny that I may have been at times disturbed with some bitterness and jealousy at the sight of my brother and my stepfather having that which I naturally craved, for the heart of a little lad is a hungry thing for love, and has pangs of nature which will not be stilled, though they are to be borne like all else of pain on earth. But after I saw Mary Cavendish all that passed, for I got, through loving so entirely, such knowledge of love in others that I saw that the excuse of love, for its weaknesses and its own crimes even, is such as to pass understanding. Looking at my mother caressing my brother instead of myself, I entered so fully into her own spirit of tenderness that I no longer rebelled nor wondered. The knowledge of the weakness of one's own heart goes far to set one at rights with all others.

When I first saw Mary Cavendish she was, as I said before, a little baby maid of two and I a loutish lad of fourteen, and I was going through the park of Cavendish Hall, which lay next ours, one morning in May, when all the hedges were white and pink, and the blue was full of wings and songs. Cavendish Hall had been vacant, save for a caretaker, that many a day. Francis Cavendish, the owner, had been for years in India, but he had lately died, and now the younger brother, Geoffry, Mary's father, had come home from America to take possession of the estate, and he brought with him his daughter Catherine by a former marriage, a maid a year older than I; his second wife, a delicate lady scarce more than a girl, and his little daughter Mary.

And they had left to come thither two fine estates in Virginia — namely these two: Laurel Creek, which was Mary's mother's in her own right, and Drake Hill; and the second wife had come with some misgiving and attended by a whole troop of black slaves, which made all our country fall agog at once with awe and ridicule and admiration. I was myself full of interest in this unwonted folk, and prone to linger about the park for a sight, and maybe a chance word with them, having ever from a child had a desire to look farther into that which has been hitherto unknown, whether it be in books or in the world at large. My lessons had been learned that morning, as was easily done, for I was accounted quick in learning, though no more so than others, did they put themselves to it with the same wish to have it over. My tutor also was not one to linger unduly at the task of teaching, since he was given to rambling about by himself with a book under one arm and a fish-pole over shoulder; a scholar of gentle, melancholy moving through the world, with such frequent pauses of abstraction that I used often to wonder if he rightfully knew himself whither he was bound.

But my mother was fond of him and so was my brother John, and as for my stepfather, Col. John Chelmsford, he had too weighty matters upon his mind, matters which pertained to Church and State and life and death, to think much about tutors. I myself was not averse to Master Snowdon, though he was to my mind, which was ever fain to seize knowledge as a man and a soldier should, by the forelock instead of dallying, too mild and deprecatory, thereby, perhaps, letting the best of her elude him. Still Master Snowdon was accounted, and was, a learned man, though scarcely knowing what he knew and easily shaken by any bout of even my boyish argument, until, I think, he was in some terror of me, and like one set free when he had heard my last page construed, and was off with his fish-pole and his book to the green side of some quiet pool. So I, with my book-lesson done, but my mind still athirst for more knowledge, and, maybe, curious, for all thirst is not for the noblest ends, crawled through a gap in the snowy May hedge, and was slinking across the park of Cavendish Hall with long, loose-jointed lopes like a stray puppy, and maybe with some sense of being where I should not, though I could not have rightly told why, since there were no warnings up against trespassers, and I had no designs upon any hare nor deer.

Be that as it may, I was going along in such fashion through the greenness of the park, so deep with rich lights and shadows on it that May morning that it seemed like plunging thought-high in a green sea, when suddenly I stopped and my heart leapt, for there sat in the grass before me, clutching some of it with a tiny hand like a pink pearl, the sweetest little maid that ever this world held. All in white she was, and of a stuff so thin that her baby curves of innocence showed through it, and the little smock slipped low down over her rosy shoulders, and her little toes curled pink in the green of the grass, for she had no shoes on, having run away, before she was dressed, by some oversight of her black nurse, and down from her head, over all her tiny body, hiding all save the merest glimmer of the loveliness of her face, fell the most wonderful shower of gold locks that ever a baby of only two years old possessed. She sat there with the sunlight glancing on her through a rift in the trees, all in a web of gold, floating and flying on the May wind, and for a minute, I, being well instructed in such lore, thought she was no mortal child, but something more, as she was indeed, but in another sense.

I stood there, and looked and looked, and she still pulled up tiny handfuls of the green grass, and never turned nor knew me near, when suddenly there burst with a speed like a storm, and a storm indeed it was of brute life, with loud stamps of a very fury of sound which shook the earth as with a mighty tread of thunder, out of a thicker part of the wood, a great black stallion on a morning gallop with all the freedom of the spring and youth firing his blood, and one step more and his iron hoofs would have crushed the child. But I was first. I flung myself upon her and threw her like a feather to one side, and that was the last I knew for a while. When I knew myself again there was a mighty pain in my shoulder, which seemed to be the centre of my whole existence by reason of it, and there was the feel of baby kisses on my lips. The courage of her blood was in that tiny maid. She had no thought of flight nor tears, though she knew not but that black thunderbolt would return, and she knew not what my ghastly silence meant. She had crept close to me, though she might well have been bruised, such a tender thing she was, by the rough fling I had given her, and was trying to kiss me awake as she did her father. And I, rude boy, all unversed in grace and tenderness, and hitherto all unsought of love, felt her soft lips on mine, and, looking, saw that baby face all clouded about with gold, and I loved her forever.

I knew not how to talk to a little petted treasure of life like that, and I dared not speak, but I looked at her, and she seemed not to be afraid, but laughed with a merriment of triumph at seeing me awake, and something she said in the sweetest tongue of the world, which I yet made poor shift to understand, for her baby speech, besides its incompleteness, had also a long-drawn sweetness like the slow trickle of honey, which she had caught from those black people which she had about her since her birth.

I had great ado to move, though my shoulder was not disjointed, only sorely bruised, but finally I was on my feet again, though standing rather weakly, and with an ear alert for the return of that wild, careering brute, and the little maid was close at my side, with one rosy set of fingers clinging around two of my rough brown ones with that sweet tenacity of a baby grasp which can hold the strongest thing on earth.

And she kept on jabbering with that slow murmur of sweetness, and I stood looking down at her, catching my breath with the pain in my shoulder, though it was out of my thoughts with this new love of her, and then came my father, Col. John Chelmsford, and Capt. Geoffry Cavendish, walking through the park in deep converse, and came upon us, and stopped and stared, as well they might.

Capt. Geoffry Cavendish was a gaunt man with the hectic colour of a fever, which he had caught in the new country, still in the hollows of his cheeks. He was quite young, with sudden alertnesses of glances in bright black eyes like the new colours in jewels when the light shifts. His daughter has the same, though her eyes are blue. Moreover, through having been in the royal navy before he got a wound which incapacitated him from further service, and was indeed in time the cause of his death, he had acquired a swift suppleness of silent movement, which his daughter has inherited also.

When he came upon us he stared for but one second, then came that black flash into his eyes, and out curved an arm, and the little maid was on her father's shoulder, and he was questioning me with something of mistrust. I was a gentleman born and bred, but my clothes sat but roughly and indifferently on me, partly through lack of oversight and partly from that rude tumble I had gotten. Indeed, my breeches and my coat were something torn by it. Then, too, I had doubtless a look of ghastliness and astonishment that might well have awaked suspicion, and Capt. Geoffry Cavendish had never spoken with me in the short time since his return. "Who may you be?" he asked, and his voice hesitated between hostility and friendliness, and my stepfather answered for me with a slight forward thrust of his shoulders which might have indicated shame, or impatience, or both. "'Tis Master Harry Maria Wingfield," answered he; then in the same breath, "How came you here, sir?"

I answered, seeing no reason why I should not, though I felt my voice shake, being still unsteady with the pain, and told the truth, that I had come thither to see if, perchance, I could get a glimpse of some of the black folk. At that Captain Cavendish laughed good-humouredly, being used to the excitement his black troop caused and amused at it, and called out merrily that I was about to be gratified, and indeed at that moment came running, with fat lunges, as it were, of tremulous speed, a great black woman in pursuit of the little maid, and heaved her high to her dark wave of bosom with hoarse chuckles and cooings of love and delight and white rollings of terrified eyes at her master if, perchance, he might be wroth at her carelessness.

He only laughed, and brushed his dark beard against the tender roses of the little maid as he gave her up, but my stepfather, who, though not ill-natured, often conceived the necessity of ill-nature, was not so easily satisfied. He stood looking sternly at my white face and my weak yielding of body at the bend of the knees, and suddenly he caught me heavily by my bruised shoulder. "What means all this, sirrah?" he cried out, but then I sank away before him, for the pain was greater than I could bear.

When I came to myself my waistcoat was off, and both men looking at my shoulder, which the horse's hoof must have barely grazed, though no more, or I should have been in a worse plight. Still the shoulder was a sorry sight enough, and the great black woman with the little fair baby in her arms stood aloof looking at it with ready tears, and the baby herself made round eyes like stars, though she knew not half what it meant. I felt the hot red of shame go over me at my weakness at a little pain, after the first shock was over, and I presumably steeled to bear it like a man, and I struggled to my feet, pulling my waistcoat together and looking, I will venture, much like a sulky and ill-conditioned lad.

"What means that hurt on your shoulder, Harry?" asked my stepfather, Col. John Chelmsford, and his voice was kind enough then. "I would not have laid such a heavy hand on thy shoulder had I known of it," he added. My stepfather had never aught against me that I wot of, having simply naught for me, and a man cannot in justice be held to account for the limitations of his affections, especially toward a rival's son. He spoke with all kindness, and his great ruddy face had a heavy gleam of pity for my hurt, but I answered not one word. "How came it so, Harry?" he asked again with growing wonder at my silence, but I would not reply.

Then Captain Cavendish also addressed me. "You need have no fear, however you came by the hurt, my lad," he said, and I verily believe he thought I had somehow caught the hurt while poaching on his preserves. I stood before them quite still, with my knees stiff enough now, and I think the colour came back in my face by reason of the resistance of my spirit.

"Harry, how got you that wound on your shoulder? Answer me, sir," said Colonel Chelmsford, his voice gathering wrath anew. But I remained silent. I do not, to this day, know why, except that to tell of any service rendered has always seemed to me to attaint the honour of the teller, and how much more when it was a service toward that little maid! So I kept my silence.

Then my stepfather's face blazed high, and his mouth straightened and widened, and his grasp tightened on a riding-whip which he carried, for he had left his horse grazing a few yards away. "How came you by it, sir?" he demanded, and his voice was thick. Then, when I would not reply, he raised the whip, and swung it over my shoulders, but I caught it with my sound arm ere it fell, and at the same time the little maid, Mary Cavendish, set up a piteous wail of fear in her nurse's arms.

"I pray you, sir, do not frighten her," I said, "but wait till she be gone." And then I waved the black woman to carry her away, and with my lame arm. When she had fled with the child's soft wail floating back, I turned to my stepfather, Col. John Chelmsford, and he, holding fiercely to the whip which I relinquished, still eyed me with doubt.

"Harry, why will you not tell?" he said, but I shook my head, waiting for him to strike, for I was but a boy, and it had been so before, and perhaps more justly.

"Let the lad go, Chelmsford," cried Captain Cavendish. "I'll warrant he has done no harm." But my stepfather would not heed him.

"Answer me, Harry," said he. Then, when I would not, down came the riding-whip, but only thrice, and not hard. "Now go you home," said my stepfather, "and show your mother the hurt, however you came by it, and have her put some of the cooling lotion on a linen cloth to it." Then he and Captain Cavendish went their ways, and I went toward home, creeping through the gap in the May hedge. But I did not go far, having no mind to show my hurt, though I knew well that my mother, being a woman and soft toward all wounds, would make much of it, and maybe of me on its account. But I was not of a mind to purchase affection by complaints of bodily ills, so I lay down under the hedge in the soft grass, keeping my bruised shoulder uppermost, and remained there thinking of the little maid, till finally the pain easing somewhat, I fell asleep, and was presently awakened by a soft touch on my sore shoulder, which caused me to wince and start up with wide eyes, and there was Catherine Cavendish.

Catherine Cavendish I had seen afar, though not to speak with her, and she being a year my senior and not then a beauty, and I being, moreover, of an age to look at a girl and look away again to my own affairs, I had thought no more of her, but I knew her at once. She was, as I said before, not a beauty at that time, being one of those maids which, like some flowers, are slow of bloom. She had grown so fast and far that she had outspeeded her grace. She was full of triangles instead of curves; her shyness was so intense that it became aggressiveness. The greenness and sallowness of immaturity that come before the perfection of bloom were on her face, and her eyes either shrank before one or else gleamed fiercely with the impulse of concealment. There is in all youth and imperfection a stage wherein it turns at bay to protect its helplessness with a vain show of inadequate claws and teeth, and Catherine Cavendish had reached it, and I also, in my different estate as a boy.

Catherine towered over me with her slender height, her sallow hair falling in silky ringlets over her dull cheeks, and when she spoke her voice rang sharp where mine would have growled with hoarseness.

"Why did you not tell?" said she sharply, and I stared up at her speechless, for I saw that she knew.

"Why did you not tell, and why were you whipped for it?" she demanded again. Then, when I did not answer: "I saw it all. I hid behind a tree for fear of the stallion. The child would have been killed but for you. Why were you whipped for a thing like that?" Then all at once, before I could answer, had I been minded to do so, she burst out almost with violence with a brilliant red, surging up from the cords of her thin neck, over her whole face. "Never mind, I like you for it. I would not have told. I will never tell as long as I live, and I have brought some lotion of cream and healing herbs, and a linen cloth, and I will bind up your shoulder for you."

With that, down she was on her knees, though I strove half rudely to prevent her, and was binding up my shoulder with a wonderful deftness of her long fingers.

When she had done she sprang to her feet with a curious multifold undoubling motion by reason of her great height and lack of practice with it, and I lumbered heavily to mine, and she asked me again with a sharpness that seemed almost venomous, so charged with curiosity it was, though she had just expressed her approbation of me:

"Why did you not tell?"

But I did not answer her that. I only thanked her, or tried to thank her, I dare say in such surly fashion that it was more like a rebuff; then I was off, but I felt her standing there close to the white-blooming hedge, staring after me with that inscrutable look of an immature girl who questions doubly all she sees, beginning with herself.

III

Although I was heir to a large estate, I had not much gold and silver nor many treasures in my possession. I never knew rightly why; but my mother, having control until I was come of age, and having, indeed, the whole property at her disposal, doubtless considered it best that the wealth should accumulate rather than be frittered away in trifles which could be of but passing moment to a boy. But I was well equipped enough as regarded comforts, and, as I said before, my education was well looked after. Through never having much regard for such small matters, it used to gall me not at all that my half brother, who was younger and such a fair lad that he became them like a girl, should go clad in silks and velvets and laces, with a ready jingle of money in his purse and plenty of sweets and trinkets to command. But after I saw that little maid it went somewhat hard with me that I had no bravery of apparel to catch her sweet eyes and cause her to laugh and point with delight, as I have often seen her do, at the glitter of a loop of gold or a jewelled button or a flash of crimson sheen from a fold of velvet, for she always dearly loved such pretty things. And it went hard with me that I had not the wherewithal to sometimes purchase a comfit to thrust into her little hand, reaching of her nature for sweets like the hands of all young things. Often I saw my brother John win her notice in such wise, for he, though he cared in general but little for small folk, was ravished by her, as indeed was every one who saw her. And once my brother John gave her a ribbon stiff with threads of gold which pleased her mightily at the time, though, the day after, I saw it gleaming from the wet of the park grass, whither she had flung it, for the caprices of a baby are beyond those of the wind, being indeed human inclination without rudder nor compass. Then I did an ungallant and ungenerous thing, for which I have always held myself in light esteem: I gathered up that ribbon and carried it to my brother and told him where I had found it, but all to small purpose as regarded my jealousy, as he scarce gave it a thought, and the next day gave the little maid a silver button, which she treasured longer. As for me, I having no ribbons nor sweets nor silver buttons to give her, was fain to search the woods and fields and the seashore for those small treasures, without money and without price, with which nature is lavish toward the poor who love her and attend her carefully, such as the first flowers of the season, nuts and seed-vessels, and sometimes an empty bird's nest and a stray bright feather and bits of bright stones, which might, for her baby fancy, be as good as my brother's gold and silver, and shells, and red and russet moss. All these I offered her from time to time as reverently and shyly as any true lover; though she was but a baby tugging with a sweet angle of opposition at her black nurse's hand and I near a man grown, and though I had naught to hope for save a fleeting grasp of her rosy fingers and a wavering smile from her sweet lips and eyes, ere she flung the offering away with innocent inconstancy.

Her father, Capt. Geoffry Cavendish, seemed to regard my devotion to his daughter with a certain amusement and good-will; indeed, I used to fancy that he had a liking for me, and would go out of his way to say a pleasant word, but once it happened that I took his kindness in ill part, and still consider that I was justified in so doing.

A gentleman should not have pity thrust upon him unless he himself, by his complaints, seems to sue for it, and that was ever far from me, and I was already, although so young, as sensitive to all slights upon my dignity as any full-grown man. So when, one day, lying at full length upon the grass under a reddening oak with a book under my eyes and my pocket full of nuts if, perchance, my little sweetheart should come that way with her black nurse, I heard suddenly Captain Cavendish's voice ring out loud and clear, as it always did, from his practice on the quarter-deck, with something like an oath as of righteous indignation to the effect that it was a damned shame for the heir and the eldest son, and a lad with a head of a scholar and the arm of a soldier, to be thrust aside so and made so little of. Then another voice, smoothly sliding, as if to make no friction with the other's opinions, asked of whom he spoke, and that smoothly sliding voice I recognised as Mr. Abbot's, the attorney's, and Captain Cavendish replied in a fashion which astonished me, for I had no idea to whom he had referred — "Harry Maria Wingfield, the eldest son and heir of as fine and gallant a gentleman as ever trod English soil, who is treated like the son of a scullion by those who owe him most, and 'tis a damned shame and I care not who hears me."

Then, before I had as yet fairly my wits about me, Mr. Abbot spoke again in that voice of his which I so hated in my boyish downrightness and scorn of all policy that it may have led me to an unjust estimate of all men of his profession. "But Col. John Chelmsford hath no meaning to deal otherwise than fairly by the boy, and neither, unless I greatly mistake, hath his wife." And this he said as if both Colonel Chelmsford and my mother were at his elbow, and for that manner of speaking I have ever had contempt, preferring downright scurrility, and Captain Cavendish replied with his quick agility of wrath, as precipitate toward judgment as a sailor to the masthead in a storm:

"And what if she be? The more shame to them that they have not enough wit to see what they do! I tell thee this poor Harry hath a harder time of it than any slave on my plantation in Virginia, I —"

But then I was on my feet, and, facing them both with my head flung back and my face, I dare say, red and white with wrath, and demanding hotly what that might be to them, and if my treatment at the hands of my stepfather and my own mother was not between them and me, and none else, and, boy as I was, I felt as tall as Captain Cavendish as I stood there. Captain Cavendish stared a moment and reddened and frowned, and then his gaunt face widened with his ever ready laugh which made it passing sweet for a man.

"Tush, lad," he cried out, "and had I known how fit thou were to fight thy own battles I had not taken up the cudgels for thee, and I crave thy pardon. I had not perceived that thy sword-arm was grown, and henceforth thou shall cross with thy adversaries for all me." Then he laughed again, and I stared at him still grimly but softened, and he and Mr. Abbot moved on, but the attorney, in passing, laid his great white hand on my black mane of hair as if he would bless me, and I shrank away from under it, and when he said in that voice of his, "'Tis a gallant lad and one to do good service for his king and country," I would that he had struck me that I might have justly hit back.

When they had passed back on the turf I lay with my boyish heart in a rage with the insults, both of pity and of praise, which had been offered me; for why should pity be offered unless there be the weakness of betrayal of suffering to warrant it, and why should there be praise unless there be craving for it, through the weakness of wronged conceit? Be that as it may, my book no longer interested me, and finally I rose up and went away after having deposited all my nuts on the grass in the hope that the little maid might chance that way and espy them.

It was both a great and a sad day for me when I came to go to Cambridge, great because of my desire for knowledge and the sight of the world which has ever been strong within me, and, being so strong, should have led to more; and sad because of my leaving the little maid without a chance of seeing her for so long a time. She was then six years old, and a wonder both in beauty and mind to all who beheld her. I saw much more of her in those days, for my mother, whose heart had always been sore for a little girl, was often with Captain Cavendish's wife, for the sake of the child, though the two women were not of the best accord one with another. Often would I notice that my mother caressed the child, with only a side attention for her mother, though that was well disguised by her soft grace of manner, which seemed to include all present in a room, and I also noticed that Madam Rosamond Cavendish's sweet mouth would be set in a straight line with inward dissent at some remark of the other woman's.

Madam Rosamond Cavendish was, I suppose, a beauty, though after a strange and curious fashion, being seemingly dependent upon those around her for it, as a chameleon is dependent for his colour upon his surroundings. I have seen Madam Cavendish, when praised by one she loved, or approached by the little maid, her daughter, with an outstretch of fair little arms and a coercion of dimples toward kisses, flash into such radiance of loveliness that, boy as I was, I was dazzled by her. Then, on the other hand, I have seen her as dully opaque of any meaning of beauty as one could well be. But she loved Captain Cavendish well, and I wot he never saw her but with that wondrous charm, since whenever he cast his eyes upon her it must have been to awaken both reflection and true life of joy in her face. She was so small and exceeding slim that she seemed no more than a child, and she was not strong, having a quick cough ready at every breath of wind, and she rode nor walked like our English women, but lay about on cushions in the sun. Still, when she moved, it was with such a vitality of grace and such readiness that no one, I suspect, knew how frail she was until she sickened and died the second year of my stay in Cambridge. When I returned home I found in her stead Madam Judith Cavendish, the mother of Captain Cavendish, who had come from Huntingdonshire. She was at that time well turned of threescore, but a woman who was, as she had always been, a power over those about her. She looked her age, too, except for her figure, for her hair was snowy white, and the lines of her face fixed beyond influence of further smiles or tears. My imagination has always been a mighty factor in my estimation of the characters of others, and I have often wondered how true to facts I might be, but verily it seemed to me that after Madam Cavendish arrived at Cavendish Court the influence of that great strength of character, which, when it exists in a woman, intimidates every man, no matter who he may be, made itself evident in the very king's highway approaching Cavendish Court, and increased as the distance diminished, according to some of my mathematical rules.

There were in her no change and shifting to new lights of beauty or otherwise at the estimation of those around her; she rather controlled, as it were, all the domestic winds. Captain Cavendish bowed before his superior on his own deck, though I believe there was much love betwixt them, and, as for the little maid, she tempered the wilfulness which was then growing with her growth by outward meekness at least. I used to think her somewhat afraid of her grandmother, and disposed to cling for protection and mother-love to her elder sister Catherine. Catherine, in those two years, had blossomed out her beauty; her sallowness and green pallor had become bloom, though not rosy, rather an ineffable clear white like a lily. Her eyes, at once shy and antagonistic, had become as steady as stars in their estimation of self and others, and all her slender height was as well in her power of graceful guidance as the height of a young oak tree. Catherine, in those days, paid very little heed to me, for her one year of superior age seemed then threefold to both of us, except as she was jealously watchful that I win not too much of the love of her little sister. I have never seen such love from elder to younger as there was from Catherine Cavendish to her half sister Mary after the little one had lost her mother. And all that the little maid did, whether of work or play, was with an eye toward the other's approbation, especially after the advent of her grandmother. Catherine had lovers, but she would have none of them. It seemed as if the maternal love of which most maids feel the unknown and unspelled yearning, and which, perchance, may draw them all unwittingly to wedlock, had seized upon Catherine Cavendish, and she had, as it were, fulfilled it by proxy by this love of her young sister, and so had her heart made cold toward all lovers. Be that as it may, though she was much sought after by more than one of high degree, she remained as she was.

For the last part of my stay at Cambridge I saw but little of her, and not so much as I would fain have done of her sister. I was past the boyish liberty of lying in wait in the park for a glimpse of her; she was not of an age for me to pay my court, and there was little intimacy betwixt my mother and Madam Cavendish. But I can truly say that never for one minute did I lose the consciousness of her in the world with me, and that at a time when my love might well be a somewhat anomalous and sexless thing, since she was grown a little past my first conception of love toward her, and had not yet reached my second.

But oh, the glimpses I used to catch of her at that time, slim-legged and swift, and shrilly sweet of voice as a lark, and as shyly a-flutter at the motion of a hand toward her, or else seated prim as any grown maiden, with grave eyes of attention upon her task of sampler or linen stitching!

My heart used to leap in a fashion that none would have believed nor understood, at the blue gleam of her gown and the gold gleam of her little head through the trees of the park, or through the oaken shadows of the hall at Cavendish Court during my scant visits there. No maid of my own age drew, for one moment, my heart away from her. She had no rivals except my books, for I was ever an eager scholar, though it might have been otherwise had the state of the country been different. I can imagine that I might in some severe stress have had my mind, being a hot-headed youth, diverted by the feel of the sword-hilt. But just then the king sat on his throne, and there was naught to disturb the public peace except his multiplicity of loves, which aroused discussion, which salted society with keenest relish, but went no farther.

I took high honours at Cambridge, though no higher than I should have done, and so no pride and no modesty in the owning and telling; and then I came home, and my mother greeted me something more warmly than she was wont, and my stepfather, Col. John Chelmsford, took me by the hand, and my brother John played me at cards that night, and won, as he mostly did. John was at that time also in Cambridge, but only in his second year, being, although of quicker grasp upon circumstances to his own gain than I, yet not so alert at book-lore; but he had grown a handsome man, as fair as a woman, yet bold as any cavalier that ever drew sword — the kind to win a woman by his own strength and her own arts.

The night after I returned, there was a ball at Cavendish Court, the first since the death of Madam Rosamond, and my brother and I went, and my stepfather and my mother, though she loved not Madam Cavendish.

And Mary Cavendish, at that time ten years old, was standing, when I first entered, with a piece of blue-green tapestry work at her back, clad in a little straight white gown and little satin shoes, and a wreath of roses on her head, from whence the golden locks flowed over her gentle cheeks, delicately rounded between the baby and maiden curves, with her little hands clasped before her; and her blue eyes, now downcast, now uplifted with utmost confidence in the love of all who saw her. And close by her stood her sister Catherine, coldly sweet in a splendid spread of glittering brocade, holding her head, crowned with flowers and plumes, as still and stately as if there were for her in all the world no wind of passion; and my brother John looked at her, and I knew he loved her, and marvelled what would come of it, though they danced often together.

The ball went on till the east was red, and the cocks crew, and all the birds woke in a tumult, and then that happened which changed my whole life.

Three weeks from that day I set sail for the New World — a convict. I will not now say how nor why; and on the same ship sailed Capt. Geoffry Cavendish, his mother Madam Judith Cavendish, his daughter Catherine, and the little maid Mary.

And on the long voyage Captain Cavendish's old wound broke out anew, and he died and was buried at sea, and I, when I arrived in this kingdom of Virginia, with the dire uncertainty and hardship of the convict before me, yet with strength and readiness to bear it, was taken as a tutor by Madam Judith Cavendish for her granddaughter Mary, being by education well fitted for such a post, and she herself knowing her other reasons for so doing. And so it happened that Mistress Mary Cavendish and I rode to meeting in Jamestown that Sabbath in April of 1682.

IV

Albeit I have as faithful a respect for the customs of the Church as any man, I considered then, and consider now as well, that it was almost beyond the power of any one to observe them according to the fashion of the times and gain therefrom a full edification of the spirit.

Therefore, that April morning, though filled in my inmost heart with love and gratitude toward God, as I had always been since I had seen His handiwork in Mary Cavendish, which was my especial lesson of His grace to meward, with sweetest rhymes of joy for all my pains, and reasons for all my doubts; and though she sat beside me, so near that the rich spread of her gown was over my knee, and the shining of her beauty warm on my face, yet was I weary of the service and eager to be out. As I said before, Parson Downs was not to my mind, neither he nor his discourse. Still he spoke with a mighty energy and a conviction of the truth of his own words which would have moved his hearers to better purpose had they moved himself as regarded his daily life. But beyond a great effervescence of the spirit, which produced a high-mounting froth of piety, like the seething top of an ale-tankard, there came naught of it. Still was there in him some good, or rather some lack of ill; for he was no hypocrite, but preached openly against his own vices, then went forth to furnish new texts for his sermon, not caring who might see and judge him. A hearty man he was, who would lend his last shilling or borrow his neighbour's with equal readiness, forcing one to a certain angry liking for him because of his good-will to do that for you which you were loth to do for him. Yet if there ever was a man in harness to Satan as to the lusts of his flesh and his pride of life, it was Parson Downs, in despite of his bold curvets and prances of exhortation, which so counterfeited freedom that I doubt not that they deceived even himself; and he felt not, the while he was expanding his great front over his pulpit, and waving his hands, on one of which shone a precious red stone, the strain of his own leash. But I have ever had a scorn which I could not cry down for any man who was a slave, except by his own will.

Feeling thus, I was glad when Parson Downs was done, and letting himself down with stately jolts of ponderosity from his pulpit, and the folk were moving out of the church in a soft press of decorously veiled eagerness, with a great rustling of silks and satin, and jingling of spurs and swords, and waving of plumes, and shaking out of stronger odours of flowers and essences and spices.

And gladder still I was when astride my horse in the open, with the sweet broadside of the spring wind in my face, and all the white flowering trees and bushes bowing and singing with a thousand bird-voices, like another congregation before the Lord. I had not the honour to assist Mistress Mary to her saddle. Sir Humphrey Hyde and Ralph Drake, who was a far-off cousin of hers; and my Lord Estes, who was on a visit to his kinsman, Lord Culpeper, the Governor of Virginia; and half a score of others pressed before me, who was but the tutor, and had no right to do her such service except for lack of another at hand. And a fair sight it was for one who loved her as I, with no privilege of jealousy, and yet with it astir within him, like a thing made but of claws and fangs and stinging tongue, to see her with that crowd of gallants about her, and the other maids going their ways unattended, with faces of averted meekness, or haughty uplifts of brows and noses, as suited best their different characters. Mistress Mary was, no doubt, the fairest of them all, and yet there was more than that in the cause for her advantage over them. She kept all her admirers by the very looseness of her grasp, which gave no indication of any eagerness to hold, and thus aroused in them no fear of detention nor of wiles of beauty which should subvert their wills. And, furthermore, Mary Cavendish distributed her smiles as impartially as a flower its sweetness, to each the same, though but a scant allotment to each, as beseemed a maid. I could not, even with my outlook, observe that she favoured one more than another, unless it might have been Sir Humphrey Hyde. I knew well that there was some confidence betwixt the two, but whether it was of the nature of love I could not tell.

Sir Humphrey kept the road with us for some distance after we had left the others, gazing beside the horse-block, all equally desirous of following, but knowing well that it would not be a fair deed to the maid to attend her homeward on the Sabbath day with a whole troop of lovers. But Sir Humphrey Hyde leapt to his saddle and rode abreast with no ado, being ever minded to do what seemed good to himself, unless, indeed, his mother stood in the way of his pleasure. Sir Humphrey's mother, Lady Clarissa Hyde, was one of those unwitting tyrants which one sees among women, by reason of her exceeding delicacy and gentleness, which made it seem but the cruelty of a brute to cross her, and thus had her own way forever, and never suspected it were not always the way of others.

Sir Humphrey was a well-set young gentleman, and he was

dressed in the farthest fashion. The broad back of his scarlet coat, rising to the trot of his horse, clashed through the soft gold-green mists and radiances of the spring landscape like the blare of a trumpet; his gold buttons glittered; the long plume on his hat ruffled to the wind over his fair periwig. Wigs were not so long in fashion, but Sir Humphrey was to the front in his. Mary Cavendish and Sir Humphrey rode on abreast, and I behind far enough to be cleared of the mire thrown by their horse-hoofs, and my heart was full of that demon of jealousy which possessed me in spite of my love. It is passing strange that I, though loving Mary Cavendish better than myself, and having the strength to prefer her to myself in all things, yet had not the power to do it without pain, and must hold that ravening jealousy to my breast. But not once did it get the better of me, and all the way was I, even then, thinking that Sir Humphrey Hyde might be good man and true for Mary Cavendish to wed, except for a few faults of his youth, which might be amended, and that if such be her mind I might help her to her happiness, since I knew that, for some reason, Madam Cavendish had small love for Sir Humphrey, and I knew also that I had some influence with her.

Behind us straggled the black slaves, as on our way thither, moving unhaltingly, yet with small energy, as do folk urged hither and yon only by the will of others and not by their own; but, presently, through them, scattering them to the left and right, galloped a black lad on a great horse after Sir Humphrey, with the word that his mother would have him return to the church and escort her homeward. Then Sir Humphrey turned, after a whispered word or two with Mistress Mary, and rode back to Jamestown; and the black lad, bounding in the saddle like a ball, after him.

I still kept my distance behind Mistress Mary, though often I saw her head turn, and caught a blue flash of an eye over her mask.

Then passed us, booted and spurred, for he had gotten his priestly robes off in a hurry, Parson Downs on the fastest horse in those parts, and riding like a jockey in spite of his heavy weight. His horse's head was stretched in a line with his neck, and after him rode, at near as great speed, Capt. Noel Jaynes, who, as report had it, had won wealth on the high seas in unlawful fashion. He was a gray old man, with the eye of a hot-headed boy, and a sabre-cut across his right cheek.

The parson saluted Mistress Mary as he passed, and so did Captain Jaynes, with a glance of his bright eyes at her that stirred my blood and made me ride up faster to her side.

But the two men left the road abruptly, plunging into a bridle-path at the right, and the green walls of the wood closed behind them, though one could still hear for long the galloping splash of their horse's hoofs in the miry path.

Mistress Mary turned to me, and her voice rang sharp, "'Tis a pretty parson," said she; "he is on his way to Barry Upper Branch with Captain Jaynes, and who is there doth not know 'tis for no good, and on the Sabbath day, too?"

Now Barry Upper Branch belonged to brothers of exceeding ill repute, except for their courage, which no one doubted. They had fought well against the Indians, and also against the Government with Nathaniel Bacon some half dozen years before. There had been a prize on their heads and they had been in hiding, but now lived openly on their plantation and were in full feather, and therein lay in a great measure their ill repute.

When my Lord Culpeper had arrived in Virginia, succeeding Berkeley, Jeffries, and Chichely, then returned the brothers Richard and Nicholas Barry, or Dick and Nick, as they were termed among the people; and as my Lord Culpeper was not averse to increasing his revenues, there were those who whispered, though secretly and guardedly, that the two bold brothers purchased their safety and peaceful home-dwelling.

Barry Upper Branch was a rich plantation and had come into full possession of the brothers but lately, their father, Major Barry, who had been a staunch old royalist, having died. There were acres of tobacco, and whole fields of locust for the manufacture of metheglin, and apple orchards from which cider enough to slack the thirst of the colony was made. But the brothers were far from content with such homemade liquors for their own drinking, but imported from England and the Netherlands and Spain great stores of ale and rum and wines, and held therewith high wassail with some choice and kindred spirits, especially on the Sabbath.

Not a woman was there at Barry Upper Branch, except for slaves, and such stories were told as might cause a modest maid to hesitate to speak of the place; but Mary Cavendish was as yet but a child in her understanding of certain things. Her blue eyes fixed me with the brave indignation of a boy as she went on, "'Tis a pretty parson," said she again, "and it would be the tavern, just as openly, were it on a week day."

I put my finger to my lip and cast a glance about, for it was enjoined upon the people under penalty that they speak not ill of any minister of the gospel. While I cared not for myself, having never yet held my tongue, except from my own choice, yet was I always concerned for this young thing, with her utter recklessness of candour, lest her beauty and her charm might not protect her always against undesirable results; and not only were the slaves within hearing of her voice, but none knew how many others, for those were brave days for tale-bearers. But Mary spoke again, and more sweetly and shrilly than ever. "A pretty parson, forsooth! And to keep company with a pirate captain! Fie! When he looks at me, I clutch my gold chain and turn the flash of my rings from sight, and Dick and Nick Barry are the worst rakes in the colony! Naught was ever heard good of them, except their following of General Bacon, but a good cause makes not always worthy adherents." This last she said with a toss of her head and a proud glance, for Nathaniel Bacon was to this maid a hero of heroes, and naught but her sex and her tender years, she being but twelve or so at the time, had kept her from joining his ranks. But, indeed, in this I had full sympathy with her, though chary of expressing it. Had it not been for my state of disgrace and my outlook for the welfare of the Cavendishes, I should most assuredly have fought with that brave man myself, for 'twas a good cause, and one which has been good since the beginning of things, and will hold good till the end — the cause of the poor and downtrod against the tyranny of the rich and great. No greater man will there ever be in this new country of America than Nathaniel Bacon, though he had but twenty weeks in which to prove his greatness; had he been granted more he might well have changed history. I can see now that look of high command which none could withstand, for leaders of men are born, as well as poets and kings, and are invincible. But it may be that the noble wave of rebellion which he raised is even now going on, never to quite cease in all time, for I know not the laws that govern such things. It may be that, in consequence of that great and brief struggle of Nathaniel Bacon, this New World will never sit quietly for long at the foot of any throne, but that I know not, being no prophet. However, this I do know, that his influence was not then ceased in Virginia, though he was six years dead, and has not yet.

Mistress Mary Cavendish had framed in black, in her chamber, a silhouette of this hero, and she wore in a locket a lock of his hair, by which she had come, in some girlish fashion, through a young gossip of hers, a kinswoman of Bacon's, from whose head I verily believe she had pilfered it while asleep. And, more than that, I knew of her and Cicely Hyde strewing fresh blossoms on the tide of the York River, in which Bacon had been buried, on the anniversary of his death, and coming home with sweet eyes red with tears of heroic sentiment, which surely be not the most ignoble shed by mankind.

"'Twas the only good ever heard of them," repeated Mistress Mary, "and even that they must need spoil by coming home and paying tithes to my Lord Culpeper that he wink at their disaffection. I trow had I been a man and fought with General Bacon, as I would have fought, had I been a man, I would have paid no price therefore to the king himself, but would have stayed in hiding forever."

With that she touched Merry Roger with her whip and was off at a gallop, and I abreast, inwardly laughing, for I well understood that this persistency on other and stirring topics, and sudden flight when they failed, was to keep me from the subject of the powder and ammunition unladen that morning from the "Golden Horn." But she need not have taken such pains, for I, while in church, had resolved within myself not to question her further, lest she tell me something which might do her harm were I forced, for her good, to reveal it, but to demand the meaning of all this from Sir Humphrey Hyde, who, I was convinced, knew as much as she.

V

Thus we rode homeward, and presently came in sight of the Cavendish tobacco fields overlapped with the fresh green of young leaves like the bosses of a shield, and on the right waved rosy garlands of the locust grove, and such a wonderful strong sweetness of honey came from it that we seemed to breast it like a wave, and caught our breaths, and there was a mighty hum of bees like a hundred spinning-wheels. But Mistress Mary and I regarded mostly that green stretch of tobacco, and each of us had our thoughts, and presently out came hers — "Master Wingfield, I pray you, whose tobacco may that be?" she inquired in a sudden, fierce fashion.

"Madam Cavendish's and yours and your sister's," said I.

"Nay," said she, "'tis the king's." Then she tossed her head again and rode on, and said not another word, nor I, but I knew well what she meant. Since the Navigation Act, it was, indeed, small profit any one had of his own tobacco, since it all went into the exchequer of the king, and I did not gainsay her.

When we had passed the negro huts, swarming with black babies shining in the sun as sleek as mahogany, and all turning toward us with a marvellous flashing of white eyeballs and opening of red mouths of smiles, all at once, like some garden bed of black flowers, at the sight of our gay advance, we reached the great house, and Mistress Catherine stood in the door clad in a green satin gown which caught the light with smooth shimmers like the green sheath of a marsh lily.

Her bare, slender arms were clasped before her, and her long, white neck was bent into an arch of watchful grace. Her face was the gravest I ever saw on maid, and not to be reconciled with my first acquaintance with her, thereby giving me always a slight doubt as of a mask, but her every feature was as clear and fine as ivory, and her head proudly crowned with great wealth of hair. Catherine Cavendish was esteemed a great beauty, by both men and women, which shows, perchance, that her beauty availed her little in some ways, else it had not been so freely admitted by her own sex. However that may be, Catherine Cavendish had had few lovers as compared with many a maid less fair and less dowered, and at this time she seemed to have settled into an expectation and contentment of singleness.

She stood looking at her sister and me as we rode toward her, and the sun was full on her face, which had the cool glimmer of a pearl in the golden light, and her wide-open eyes never wavered.

As she stood there she might have been the portrait of herself, such a look had she of unchanging quiet, and the wonder and incredulity which always seized me at the sight of her to reconcile what I knew with what she seemed, was strong upon me.

When her young sister had dismounted and had gone up the steps, she kissed her, and the two entered the hall, clinging together in a way which was pretty to see. I never saw such love betwixt two where there was not full sympathy, and that was lacking always and lacked more in the future, through the difference in their two temperaments gotten from different mothers.

Madam Cavendish was still in her bedchamber, and the two sisters and I dined together in the great hall. Then, after the meal was over, I went forth with my book of Sir William Davenant's plays, and sought a favourite place of mine in the woods, and stayed there till sundown. Then, rising and going homeward when the mist floated over the marshlands like veils of silver gauze, and the frogs chorused through it in waves of sound, and birds were circling above it, calling sweetly with fluting notes or screaming with the harsh trumpet-clang of sea-fowl, I heard of a sudden, just as the sun sank below the western sky, a mighty din of horns and bells and voices from the direction of Jamestown. I knew that the sports which a certain part of the community would have on a Sabbath after sundown, when they felt so inclined, had begun. Since the king had been restored such sports had been observed, now and then, according to the humour of the governor and the minister and the others in authority. Laws had been from time to time set forth that the night after the Sabbath, the Sabbath being considered to cease at sundown, should be kept with decorum, but seldom were they enforced, and often, as now, a great din arose when the first gloom overspread the earth. However, that night was the 30th of April, the night before May day; and there was more merrymaking in consequence, though May was not here as in England, and even in England not what it had been in the first Charles's reign.

But they kept up their rollicking late that night, for the window of my chamber being toward Jamestown, and the wind that way, I could hear them till I fell asleep. At midnight I wakened suddenly at the sound of a light laugh, which I knew to be Mary Cavendish's. There was never in the maid any power of secrecy when her humour overcame her. She laughed again, and I heard a hushing voice, which I knew to be neither her sister's nor grandmother's, but a man's.

I was up and dressed in a trice, and sword in hand, and out of my window, which was on the first floor, and there was Mistress Mary and Sir Humphrey Hyde. I stepped between them and thrust aside Sir Humphrey, who would have opposed me. "Go into the house, madam," said I to her, and pointed to the door, which stood open. Then while she hesitated, half shrinking before me, with her old habit of obedience strong upon her, yet with angry wilfulness urging her to rebellion, forth stepped her distant cousin Ralph Drake from behind a white-flowering thicket, and demanded to know what that cursed convict fellow did there, and had he not a right to parley with his cousin, and was her honour not safe with her kinsman and he an English gentleman? I perceived by Ralph Drake's voice that he had perchance been making gay with the revellers at Jamestown, and stood still when he came bullyingly toward me, but at that minute Mistress Mary spoke.

"I will not have such language to my tutor, Cousin Ralph," said she, "and I will have you to understand it. He is a gentleman as well as yourself, and you owe him an apology." So saying, she stamped her foot and looked at Ralph Drake, her eyes flashing in the moonlight. But Ralph Drake, whose face I could see was flushed, even in that whiteness of light, flung away with an oath muttered under his breath, and struck out across the lawn, his black shadow stalking before him.

Then Mistress Mary turned and bade me goodnight in the sweetest and most curious fashion, as if nothing unusual had happened, and yet with a softness in voice as if she would fain make amends for her cousin's rough speech, and fluttered in through the open door like a white moth, and left me alone with Sir Humphrey Hyde.

Sir Humphrey was but a lad to me, scarcely older than Mistress Mary, for all his great stature. He stood before me scraping the shell walk with the end of his riding whip. Both men had ridden hither, and I at that moment heard Ralph Drake's horse's hard trot.

"If you come courting Mistress Mary Cavendish, 'tis for her guardians, her grandmother, and elder sister to deal with you concerning the time and place you choose," said I, "but if it be on any other errand —"

"Good God, Harry," broke in Sir Humphrey, "do you think I am come lovemaking in such fashion, and with Ralph Drake in his cups, though I swear he fastened himself to me against my will?"

I waited a moment. Sir Humphrey had been much about the place since he was a mere lad, and had had, I believe, a sort of boyish good-will toward me. Not much love had he for books, but

I was accounted a fair shot, and had some knowledge of sports of hunting and fishing, and had given him some lessons, and he had followed me about some few years before, somewhat to the uneasiness of his mother, who could not forget that I was a convict.

I cast about in my mind what to say, being resolved not to betray Mary Cavendish, even did this man know what I could betray, and yet being resolved to have some understanding of what was afoot.

"A man of honour includes not maidens in plots, Sir Humphrey," said I finally.

Sir Humphrey stammered and looked at me, and looked away again. Then suddenly spake Mistress Mary from her window overhead, set in a climbing trumpet-vine, and so loudly and recklessly that had not her grandmother and sister been on the farther side of the house they must have heard her. "'Tis not Sir Humphrey included the maid in the plot, but the maid who included Sir Humphrey," said she. Then she laughed, and at the same moment a mock-bird trilled in a tree.

"Why do you not tell Master Wingfield that the maid, and not you nor Cousin Ralph, is the prime mover in this mystery of the cargo of furbelows on *The Golden Horn*?" said she, and laughed again.

"I shield not myself behind a maiden's skirts," said Sir Humphrey, grimly.

"Then," cried Mary, "will I tell thee, Master Wingfield, what it means. He cannot betray us, Humphrey, for his tongue is tied with honour, even if he be not on our side. But he is on our side, as is every true Englishman." Then Mary Cavendish leaned far out the window, and a white lace scarf she wore floated forth, and she cried with a great burst of triumph and childish enthusiasm: "I will tell thee what it means, Master Wingfield, I will tell thee what it means; I am but a maid, but the footsteps of General Bacon be yet plain enough to follow in this soil of Virginia, and — and — the king gets not our tobacco crops!"

VI

I have always observed with wonder and amusement and a tender gladness the faculty with which young creatures, and particularly young girls, can throw off their minds for the time being the weight of cares and anxieties and bring all of themselves to bear upon those exercises of body or mind, to no particular end of serious gain, which we call play and frivolity. It may be that faculty is so ordained by a wise Providence, which so keeps youth and the bloom of it upon the earth, and makes the spring and new enterprises possible. It may be that without it we should rust and stick fast in our ancient rivets and bolts of use.

That very next morning, after I had learned from Mary Cavendish, supplemented by a sulky silence of assent from Sir Humphrey Hyde, that she had, under presence of ordering feminine finery from England, spent all her year's income from her crops on powder and shot for the purpose of making a stand in the contemplated destruction of the new tobacco crops, and thereby plunged herself and her family in a danger which were hard to estimate were it discovered, I heard a shrill duet of girlish laughs and merry tongues before the house. Then, on looking forth, whom should I see but Mary Cavendish and Cicely Hyde, her great gossip, and a young coloured wench, all washing their faces in the May dew, which lay in a great flood as of diamonds and pearls over everything. I minded well the superstition, older than I, that, if a maid washed her face in the first May dew, it would make her skin wondrous fair, and I laughed to myself as I peeped around the shutter to think that Mary Cavendish should think that she stood in need of such amendment of nature. Down she knelt, dragging the hem of her chintz gown, which was as gay with a maze of printed posies as any garden bed, and she thrust her hollowed hands into the dew-laden green and brought them over her face and rubbed till sure there was never anything like it for sweet, glowing rosiness. And Cicely Hyde, who must have come full early to Drake Hill for that purpose, did likewise, and with more need, as I thought, for she was a brown maid, not so fair of feature as some, though she had a merry heart, which gave to her such a zest of life and welcome of friends as made her a favourite. Up she scooped the dew and bathed her face, turning ever and anon to Mary Cavendish with anxious inquiries, ending in trills of laughter which would not be gainsaid in May-time and youth-time by aught of so little moment as a brown skin. "How look I now?" she would cry out. "How look I now, sweetheart? Saw you ever a lily as fair as my face?" Then Mary, with her own face dripping with dew, with that wonderful wet freshness of bloom upon it, would eye her with seriousness as to any improvement, and bid her turn this way and that. Then she would give it as her opinion that she had best persevere, and laugh somewhat doubtfully at first, then in a full peal when Cicely, nothing daunted by such discouragement in her friend's eyes, went bravely to work again, all her slender body shaking with mirth. But the most curious sight of all, and that which occasioned the two maids the most merriment, though of a covert and even tender and pitying sort, was Mary's black serving-wench Sukey, a half grown girl, who had been bidden to attend her mistress upon this morning frolic. She was seated at a distance, square in the wet greenness, and was plunging both hands into the May dew and scrubbing her face with a fierce zeal, as if her heart was in that pretty folly, as no doubt it was. And ever and anon as she rubbed her cheeks, which shone the blacker and glossier for it, she would turn the palms of her hands, which be so curiously pale on a negro's hands, to see if perchance some of the darkness had stirred. And when she saw not, then would she fall to scrubbing again.

Presently up stood Mary and Cicely, and Cicely flashed in the sun a little silver mirror which she had brought and which had lain glittering in the grass a little removed, and looked at herself, and saw that her brown cheeks were as ever, with the exception of the flush caused by rubbing, and tossed it with her undaunted laugh to Mary. "The more fool be I!" she cried out, "instead of washing mine own face in the May dew, better had it been had I locked thee in the clothes-press, Mary Cavendish, and not let thee add to thy beauty, while I but gave my cheeks the look of fever or the smallpox. I trow the skin be off in spots, and all to no purpose! Look at thyself, Mary Cavendish, and blush that thou be so much fairer than one who loves thee!"

And verily Mary Cavendish did for a minute seem to blush as she cast a glance at herself in the mirror and saw her marvellous rose of a face, but the next minute the mirror flashed in the grass and her arms were about Cicely Hyde's neck. "'Tis the dearest face in Virginia, Cicely," said she, in her sweet, vehement way, and laid her pink cheek against the other's plain one. And Cicely laughed, and took her face in her two hands and held it away that she might see it.

"What matters it to poor Cicely whether her own face be fair or not, so long as it is dear to thee, and so long as she can see thine!" she cried as passionately as a lad might have done, and I frowned, not with jealousy, but with a curious dislike to such affection from one maid to another, which I could never understand in myself. Had Cicely Hyde had a lover, she would have said that fond speech to him instead of Mary Cavendish, but lover she had none.

But all at once the two maids nudged one another, and turned their faces, all convulsed with merriment, and I looked and saw that the poor little black lass had crept on hands and knees to where the mirror flashed in the grass, and was looking at her face therein with such anxiety as might move one at once to tears and laughter, to see if the dew had washed her white.

But Mary Cavendish ceased all in a minute her mirth, and went up to the black child and took the mirror from her, and said, in the sweetest voice of pity I ever heard, "'Tis not in one May dew nor two, nor perchance in the dews of many years, you can wash your face white, but sometime it will be."

Then the black wench burst into tears, and begged in that thick, sluggishly sweet tongue of hers to know if ever the May dew would wash her black away, and Mistress Mary answered as seriously as if she were in the pulpit on the Sabbath day that it would sometime most surely and she should see her face in the glass as fair as any.

Then the two maids, Mary Cavendish and Cicely Hyde, went into the house, and left me, as I said before, to wonder at that spirit of youth which can all in a minute disregard care and anxiety and risk of death for the play of vanity. But, after all, which be stronger, wars and rumours of wars or vanity? And which be older, and which fathered the other?

After the house door had shut behind the maidens, I too went out, but not to wash my grim man's face in May dew, but rather for a stroll in the morning air, and the clearing of my wits for reflection; for much I wondered what course I should take regarding my discovery of the night before. I went down the road toward Jamestown, and struck into the path to the wharf, the same that we had taken the day before, but there were no masts of *The Golden Horn* rising among the trees with a surprise of straightness. She had weighed anchor and sailed away over night, and possibly before. The more I reflected the more I understood that Mistress Mary Cavendish, with her ready wit and supply of money through her inheritance from her mother, might have concocted the scheme of bringing over ammunition from England to enable us to make a stand against the government; but the plot in the first of it could not have been hers alone. Assuredly Ralph

Drake was concerned in it, and Sir Humphrey Hyde, and no one knew how many more. The main part for Mistress Mary might well have been the furnishing of the powder and shot, for Ralph Drake was poor, and lived, it was said, by his good luck at cards; and as for Sir Humphrey Hyde, his mother held the reins in those soft hands of hers, which would have been sorely bruised had they been withdrawn too roughly.

I sat me down on a glittering ridge of rock near the riverbank, and watched the blue run of the water, and twisted the matter this and that way in my mind, for I was sorely perplexed. Never did I feel as then the hamper of my position, for a man who was held in such esteem as I by some and contempt by others, and while having voice had no authority to maintain it, was neither flesh nor fowl nor slave nor master. Madam Cavendish treated me in all respects as the equal of herself and her family — nay, more than that, she deferred to me in such fashion as I had never seen in her toward any one, but Catherine treated me ever with iciness of contempt, which I at that time conceived to be but that transference of blame from her own self to a scapegoat of wrong-doing which is a resort of ignoble souls. They will have others not only suffer for their own sin, but even treat them with the scorn due themselves. And not one man was there in the colony, excepting perhaps Sir Humphrey Hyde and Parson Downs and the brothers Nicholas and Richard Barry, which last were not squeamish, and would have had me as boon companion at Barry Upper Branch, having been drawn to me by a kindred boldness of spirit and some little passages which I had had with the Indians, which be not worth repeating. I being in such a position in the colony, and considering the fact that Madam Cavendish and Catherine were staunch loyalists, and would have sent all their tobacco to the bottom of the salt sea had the king so ordained, and regarded all disaffection from the royal will as a deadly sin against God and the Church, as well as the throne, and knowing the danger which Mary Cavendish ran, I was in a sore quandary. Could I have but gone to those men whom I conceived to be in the plot, and talked with them on an equal footing, I would have given my right hand. But I wondered, and with reason, what hearing they would accord me, and I wondered how to move in the matter at all without doing harm to Mistress Mary, yet feared greatly that the non-movement would harm her more. As I sat there I fell to marvelling anew, as I had marvelled many times before, at that yielding on the part of the strong which makes the power of those in authority possible. At the yielding of the weak we marvel not, but when one sees the bending of staunch, true men, with muscles of iron and hearts of oak, to commands which be manifestly against their own best interests, it is verily beyond understanding, and only to be explained by the working of those hidden springs of nature which have been in men's hearts since the creation, moving them along one common road of herding to one common end. As I sat there I wondered not so much at the plot which was simply to destroy all the young tobacco plants, that there be not an over supply and ruinous prices therefor next year, as at the fact that the whole colony to a man did not arise and rebel against the order of the king in that most infamous Navigation Act which forbade exportation to any place but England, and load their ships for the Netherlands, and get the full worth of their crops. Well I knew that some of the burgesses were secretly in favour of this measure, and why should one man, Governor Culpeper, for the king, hold for one minute the will of this strong majority in abeyance?

I reasoned it out within myself that one cause might lie in that distrust and suspicion of his neighbour as to his good-will and identical interest with himself which is inborn with every man, and in most cases strengthens with his growth. When a movement of rebellion against authority is on foot, he eyes all askance, and speaks in whispering corners of secrecy, not knowing when he strikes his first blow whether his own brother's hand will be with him against the common tyrant, or against himself.

Were it not for this lamentable quality of the human heart, which will prevent forever the perfect concerting of power to one end, such a giant might be made of one people that it could hold all the world and all the nations thereof at its beck and call. But that cannot be, even in England, which had known and knows now and will know again that division of interest and doubts, every man of his brother's heart, which weaken the arm against the common foe.

But, reflecting in such wise, I came no nearer to the answer to my quandary as to my best course for the protection of Mary Cavendish.

I sat there on that rock glittering like frost-work in the May sunlight and watched the river current until it seemed to me that my rock and all Virginia were going out on the tide to sea and back to England, where, had I landed then, I would have lost my head and all my wondering with it, and my old astonishment, which I had had from a boy, was upon me, that so many things that be, according to the apparent evidence of our senses are not, and how can any man ever be sure that he is on sea or land, or coming or going? And comes there not to all of us some day a great shock of knowledge of the slipping past of this world, and all the history thereof which we think of so much moment, and that we only are that which remains? But then verily it seemed to me that the matter of the tobacco plot and Mary Cavendish's danger was of more moment than aught else in the century.

"Master Wingfield," said a voice so gently and sweetly repellent and forbidding, even while it entreated, that it shivered the air with discord, and I looked around, and there stood Catherine Cavendish. She stood quite near the rock where I sat, but she kept her head turned slightly away as if she could not bear the sight of my face, though she was constrained to speak to me. But I, and I speak the truth, since I held it unworthy a man and a gentleman to feel aught of wrath or contempt when he was sole sufferer by reason of any wrong done by a woman, had nothing but that ever recurrent surprise and unbelief at the sight of her, to reconcile what I knew, or thought I knew, with what she seemed.

I rose and stepped from my rock to the green shore, and she moved a little back with a slight courtesy. "Good-morning, Mistress Catherine," I said.

"What know you of what my sister hath done and the cargo that came yesterday on *The Golden Horn*?" she demanded with no preface and of a sudden; her voice rang sharp as I remembered it when she first spoke to me by that white hedge of England, and I could have sworn that the tide had verily borne us thither, and she was again that sallow girl and I the blundering lout of a lad.

"That I cannot answer you, madam," said I, and bowed and would have passed, but she stood before me. So satin smooth was her hair that even the fresh wind could not ruffle it, and in such straight lines of maiden modesty hung her green gown — always she wore green, and it became her well, and 'twas a colour I always fancied — that it but fluttered a little around her feet in the marsh grass, but her face looked out from a green gauze hood with an expression that belied all this steadfastness of primness and decorum. It was as if a play-actress had changed her character and not her attire, which suited another part. Out came her slim arm, as if she would have caught me by the hand for the sake of compelling my answer; then she drew it back and spoke with all the sharp vehemence of passion of a woman who oversteps the bounds of restraint which she has set herself, and is a wilder thing than if she had been hitherto unfettered by her will.

"I command you to tell me what I wish to know, Harry Wingfield," said she, and now her eyes fixed mine with no shrinking, but a broadside of scorn and imperiousness.

"And I refuse to tell you, madam," said I.

Then indeed she caught my arm with a little nervous hand, like a cramp of wire. "You shall tell me, sir," she declared. "This much I know already. Yesterday *The Golden Horn* came in and was unladen of powder and shot instead of the goods that my sister pretended to order, and the cases are stored at Laurel Creek. This much do I know, but not what is afoot, nor for what Mary had conference with Sir Humphrey Hyde and Ralph last night, and you later on with Sir Humphrey. I demand of you that you tell me, Harry Wingfield."

"That I cannot do, madam," said I.

She gave me a look with those great black eyes of hers, and how it came to pass I never knew, but straight to the root of the whole she went as if my face had been an open book.

Such quickness of wit I had often heard ascribed to women, but never saw I aught like that, and I trow it seemed witchcraft. "'Tis something about the young tobacco plants," quoth she. "The king would not pass the measure to cease the planting, and the assembly of this spring broke up with no decision. Major Beverly, who is clerk of the assembly, hath turned against the government since Bacon died, and all the burgesses are with him, and Governor Culpeper sails for England soon, and what, is the lieutenant-governor to hold the reins? There is a plot hatching to cut down the young tobacco plants." I could but stare at her. "There is a plot to cut down the young tobacco plants as soon as the governor hath sailed," she said, "and my sister Mary hath sent to England for arms, knowing that the militia will arise and there will be fighting."

I still stared at her, not knowing in truth what to say. Then suddenly she caught at my hands with hers, and cried out with that energy that I saw all at once the fire of life beneath that fair show of maiden peace and calm of hers, "Harry, Harry Wingfield, if my grandmother, Madam Cavendish, knows this, my sister is undone; no pity will she have. Straight to the governor will she go, though she hobble on crutches to Jamestown! She would starve ere she would move against the will of the king and his representative, and so would I, but I will not have my little sister put to suffering and shame. God save her, Harry Wingfield, but she might be thrown into prison, and worse — I pray thee, save her, Harry! Whatever ill you have done, and however slightingly I have held you for it, I pray you do this good deed by way of amends, and I will put the memory of your misdeeds behind me."

Even then my bewilderment at her mention of my misdeeds, when I verily considered that she, as well as I, knew more of her own, was strong, but I grasped her two little hands hard, then relinquished them, and bowed and said, "Madam, I will save your sister at whatever cost."

"And count it not?" said she.

"No more than I have done before, madam," said I, and maybe with some little bitterness, for sometimes a woman by persistent goading may almost raise herself to the fighting level of a man.

"But how?" said she.

"That I must study."

"But I charge you to keep it from Madam Cavendish."

"You need have no fear."

"May God forgive me, but I told Madam Cavendish that *The Golden Horn* had not arrived," said she, "but what have they done with the rest of the cargo, pray?"

I started. I had, I confess, not given that a thought, though it was but reasonable that there was more beside those powder casks, if the revenue from the crops had been so small.

But Catherine Cavendish needed but a moment for that problem. "'Twill return," said she. "Captain Tabor hath but sailed off a little distance that he may return and make port, as if for the first time since he left England, and so put them off the scent of the Sabbath unlading of those other wares." She looked down the burnished flow of the river as she spoke, and cried out that she could see a sail, but I, looking also, could not see anything save the shimmer of white and green spring boughs into which the river distance closed.

"'Tis *The Golden Horn*," said Catherine.

"I can see naught of white save the locust-blooms," said I.

"Locusts stand not against the wind in stiff sheets," said she. "'Tis the sail of *The Golden Horn*; but that matters not. Harry, Harry Wingfield, can you save my sister?"

"I know not whether I can, madam, but I will," said I.

VII

Mistress Catherine and I returned together to Drake Hill, she bearing herself with a sharp and anxious conciliation, and I with little to say in response, and walking behind her, though she moved more and more slowly that I might gain her side.

We were not yet in sight of Drake Hill, but the morning smoke from the slave cabins had begun to thrust itself athwart the hon-eyed sweetness of blossoms, and the salt freshness of the breath of the tidal river, as the homely ways of life will ever do athwart the beauty and inspiration of it, maybe to the making of its true har-mony, when of a sudden we both stopped and listened. Mistress Catherine turned palely to me, and I dare say the thought of Indians was in her mind, though they had long been quiet, then her face relaxed and she smiled.

"'Tis the first day of May," said she. "And they are going to set up the May-pole in Jarvis Field."

This did they every May of late, because some of the gover-nors and some of the people had kept to those prejudices against the May revelries which had existed before the Restoration, and frowned upon the May-pole set up in the Jamestown green as if it had been, as the Roundheads used to claim, the veritable heathen god Baal.

Jarvis Field was a green tract, clear of trees, not far from us, and presently we met the merry company proceeding thither. First came a great rollicking posse of lads and lasses linked hand in hand, all crowned with flowers, and bearing green and blossomy boughs over shoulder. And these were so swift with the wild spirit and jollity of the day that they must needs come in advance, even before the horses which dragged the May-pole. Six of them there were, so bedecked with ribbons and green garlands that I marvelled they could see the road and were not wild with fear. But they seemed to enter into the spirit of it all, and stepped highly and daintily with proud archings of necks and tossings of green plumed heads, and behind them the May-pole rasped and bumped and grated, the trunk of a mighty oak yet bristling with green, like the stubble of a shaggy beard of virility. And after the May-pole came surely the queerest company of morris dancers that ever the world saw, except those of which I have heard tell which danced in Herefordshire in the reign of King James, those being composed of ten men whose ages made up the sum of twelve hundred years. These, while not so ancient as that, were still of the oldest men to be come at who could move without crutches and whose estate was not of too much dignity for such sports. And Maid Marion was the oldest and smallest of them all, riding her hobbyhorse, dressed in a yellow petticoat and a crimson stomacher, with a great wig of yellow flax hanging down under her gilt crown, and a painted mask to hide her white beard. And after Maid Marion came dancing, with stiff struts and gambols, old men as gayly attired as might be, with garlands of peach-blossoms on their gray heads, bearing gad-sticks of peeled willow-boughs wound with cowslips, and ringing bells and blowing horns with all their might. And after them trooped young men and maids, all flinging their heels aloft and waving with green and flowers, and shouting and singing till it seemed the whole colony was up and mad.

Mistress Catherine and I stood well to one side to let them pass by, but when the morris dancers reached us, and caught sight of Catherine in her green robes standing among the green bushes, above which her fair face looked, half with dismay, half with a quick leap of sympathy with the merriment, for there was in this girl a strange spirit of misrule beneath all her quiet, and I verily believe that, had she but let loose the leash in which she held herself, would have joined those dancing and singing lasses and been outdone by none, there was a sudden halt; then, before I knew what was to happen, around her leapt a laughing score of them, shouting that here was the true Maid Marion, and that old John Lubberkin could now resign his post. Then off the hobbyhorse they tumbled him, and the lads and lasses gathering around her, and the graybeards standing aloof with some chagrin, would, I believe, in spite of me, since they outnumbered me vastly, have forced Catherine into that rude pageant as Maid Marion. But while I was thrusting them aside, holding myself before her as firmly as I might, there came a quick clatter of hoofs, and Mistress Mary had dashed alongside on Merry Roger. She scattered the merry revellers right and left, calling out to her sister to go homeward with a laugh. "Fie on thee, Catherine!" she cried out. "If thou art abroad on a May morning dressed like the queen of it, what blame can there be to these good folk for giving thee thy queendom?"

Catherine did not move to go when the people drew away from her, but rather stood looking at them with that lurking fire in her eyes and a flush on her fair cheeks. Mistress Mary sat on her horse, curbing him with her little hand, and her golden curls floated around her like a cloud, for she had ridden forth without her hood on hearing the sound of the horns and bells, eager to see the show like any child, and the merrymakers stared at her, grinning with uncouth delight and never any resentment. There was that in Mary Cavendish's look, when she chose to have it so, that could, I verily believe, have swayed an army, so full of utter goodwill and lovingkindness it was, and, more than that, of such confidence in theirs in return that it would have taken not only knaves, but knaves with no conceit of themselves, to have forsworn her good opinion of them. Suddenly there rose a great shout and such a volley of cheering and hallooing as can come only from English throats. A tall lad cast a great wreath over Mistress Mary's own head, and cried out with a shout that here, here was Maid Marion. And scores of voices echoed his with "Maid Marion, Marion!" And then, to my great astonishment and dismay, for a man is with no enemy so much at a loss as with a laughing one, since it wrongs his own bravery to meet smiles with blows, they gave forth that I was Robin Hood; that the convict tutor, Harry Wingfield, was Robin Hood!

I felt myself white with wrath then, and was for blindly wrestling with a great fellow who was among the foremost, shaking with mirth, an oak wreath over his red curls making him look like a satyr, when Mistress Mary rode between us. "Back, Master Wingfield," said she, "I pray thee stand back." Then she looked at the folk, all smiles and ready understanding of them, until they hurrahed again and rang their bells and blew their horns, and she looked like a blossom tossed on the wave of pandemonium.

I had my hand on her bridle-rein, ready to do my best should any rudeness be offered her, when suddenly she raised her hand and made a motion, and to my utter astonishment the brawling throng, save for some on the outskirts, which quieted presently, became still. Then Mistress Mary's voice arose, clear and sweet, with a childish note of innocence in it:

"Good people," said she, "fain would I be your Maid Marion, and fain would I be your queen of May, if you would hold with me this Kingdom of Virginia against tyrants and oppressors."

I question if a dozen there grasped her meaning, but, after a second's gaping stare, such a shout went up that it seemed to make the marshes quiver. I know not what mad scheme was in the maid's head, but I verily believe that throng would have followed her wherever she led, and the tobacco plants might have been that morning cut had she so willed.

But I pulled hard at her bridle, and I forgot my customary manner with her, so full of terror for her I was. "For God's sake, child, have done," I said, and she looked at me, and there came a strange expression, which I had never seen before, into her blue eyes, half of yielding as to some strength which she feared, and half of that high enthusiasm of youth and noble sentiment which threatened to swamp her in its mighty flow as it had done her hero Bacon before her. I know not if I could have held her; it all passed in a second the while those wild huzzas continued, and the crowd pressed closer, all crowned and crested with green, like a tidal wave of spring, but another argument came to me, and that moved her. "'Tis not yourself alone, but your sister and Madam Cavendish to suffer with you," I said. Then she gave a quick glance at Catherine, who was raising her white face and trying to get near enough to speak to her, for her sister's speech had made her frantic with alarm, and hesitated. Then she laughed, and the earnest look faded from her face, and she called out with that way of hers which nobody and nothing could withstand, "Nay," she said, "wait till I be older and have as much wisdom in my head as hath the Maid Marion whom you have chosen. The one who hath seen so many Mays can best know how to queen it over them." So saying, she snatched the wreath with which they had crowned her from her head and cast it with such a sweep of grace as never I saw over the head of flax-headed and masked Maid Marion, and reined her horse back, and the crowd, with worshipful eyes of admiration of her and her sweetness and wit and beauty, gave way, and was off adown the road toward Jarvis Field, with loud clamour of bells and horns and wild dancing and wavings of their gad-sticks and green branches. Mistress Mary rode before us at a gallop, and presently we were all at the breakfast table in the great hall at Drake Hill, with foaming tankards of metheglin and dishes of honey and salmon and game in plenty. For, whatever the scarcity of the king's gold, there was not much lack of food in this rich country.

Madam Cavendish was down that morning, sitting at table with her stick beside her, her head topped with a great tower of snowy cap, her old face now ivory-yellow, but with a wonderful precision of feature, for she had been a great beauty in her day, so alert and alive with the ready comprehension of her black eyes, under slightly scowling brows, that naught escaped her that was within her reach of vision. Somewhat dull was she of hearing, but that sharpness of eye did much to atone for it. She looked up, when we entered, with such keenness that for a second my thought was that she knew all.

"What were the sounds of merrymaking down the road?" said she.

"'Twas the morris dancers and the May-pole; 'tis the first of May, as you know, madam," said Mary in her sweet voice, made clear and loud to reach her grandmother's ear; then up she went to kiss her, and the old woman eyed her with pride, which she was fain to conceal by chiding. "You will ruin your complexion if you go out in such a wind without your mask," she said, and looked at the maiden's roses and lilies with that rapture of admiration occasioned half by memory of her own charms which had faded, and half by understanding of the value of them in coin of love, which one woman can waken only in another.

For Catherine, Madam Cavendish had no glance of admiration nor word, though she had tended her faithfully all the day before and half the night, rubbing her with an effusion of herbs and oil for her rheumatic pains. Yet for her, Madam Cavendish had no love, and treated her with a stately toleration and no more. Mary understood no cause for it, and often looked, as she did then, with a distressful wonder at her grandmother when she seemed to hold her sister so slightingly.

"Here is Catherine, grandmother," said she, "and she has had a narrow escape from being pressed as Maid Marion by the morris dancers." Madam Cavendish made a slight motion, and looked not at Catherine, but turned to me with that face of anxious kindness which she wore for me alone. "Saw you aught of *The Golden Horn* this morning, Master Wingfield?" asked she, and I replied truthfully enough that I had not.

Then, to my dismay, she turned to Mary and inquired what were the goods which she had ordered from England, and to my greater dismay the maid, with such a light of daring and mischief in her blue eyes as I never saw, rattled off, the while Catherine and I stared aghast at her, such a list of women's folderols as I never heard, and most of them quite beyond my masculine comprehension.

Madam Cavendish nodded approvingly when she had done. "'Tis a wise choice," said she, "and as soon as the ship comes in have the goods brought here and unpacked that I may see them." With that she rose stiffly, and, beckoning Catherine, who looked as if she could scarcely stand herself, much less serve as prop for another, she went out, tapping her stick heavily on one side, on the other leaning on her granddaughter's shoulder.

VIII

I looked at Mistress Mary and she at me. We had withdrawn to the deepness of a window, while the black slaves moved in and out, bearing the breakfast dishes, as reasonably unheeded by us as the cup-bearers in a picture of a Roman banquet in the time of the Cæsars which I saw once. Mistress Mary was pale with dismay, and yet her mouth twitched with laughter at the notion of displaying, before the horrified eyes of Madam Cavendish, those grim adornments which had arrived in *The Golden Horn*.

"La," said she, "when they come a-trundling in a powder-cask and I courtesy and say, 'Madam, here is my furbelowed and gold-flowered sacque,' I wonder what will come to pass." Then she laughed.

"My God, madam," said I, "why did you give that list?" She laughed again, and her eyes flashed with the very light of mischief.

"I grant 'twas a fib," said she; "but I was taken unawares, and, la, how could I recite to her the true list of my rare finery which came to port yesterday? So I but gave the list of goods for which my Lady Culpeper sent to England for the replenishing of her wardrobe and her daughter's, and which is daily expected by ship. I had it from Cicely Hyde, who had it from Cate Culpeper. The ship is due now, and may be even now in port, and so I worded what I said, that 'twas not, after all, a fib, except the hearer chose to make it so. I said, 'Such goods as these are due, madam.'" Then she gave the list anew, like a parrot, while Catherine, who had returned, stood staring at her, white with terror, though Mary did not see her until she had finished. Then, when she turned and caught her keenly anxious eyes, she started. "You here, Catherine?" said she. Then, knowing not how much her sister knew already, she tried to cover her confusion, like a child denying its raid on the jam pots, while its lips and fingers are still sticky with the stolen sweet. "What think you of my list, sweetheart?" cried she, merrily. "A pair of the silk stockings and two of the breast-knots and a mask and a flowered apron shall you have." Then out of the room she whisked abruptly, laughing from excess of nervous confusion, and not being able to keep up the farce longer.

Then Catherine turned to me. "She has undone herself, for Madam Cavendish will see those goods when *The Golden Horn* comes in, or ferret the mystery to its farthest hole of hiding," said she. Then she wrung her hands and cried out sharply, "My God, Harry Wingfield, what is to be done?"

"Madam Cavendish would surely never betray her own flesh

and blood," said I, though doubtfully, when I reflected upon her hardness to Catherine herself, for Madam Judith Cavendish was not one for whom love could change the colour of the clear light of justice, and she would see forever her own as they were.

"There is to her no such word as betray except in the service of the king," said Catherine. Then she added in a whisper, "Know you the story of her youngest son, my uncle Ralph Cavendish, who went over to Cromwell?"

I nodded. I knew it well, and had heard it from a lad how Ralph Cavendish's own mother had turned him from her door one night with the king's troops in the neighbourhood, though it was afterward argued that she did not know of that, and he had been taken before morning and afterwards executed, and she had never said a word nor shed a tear that any one saw.

"When *The Golden Horn* comes in she will demand to see the goods," Catherine repeated.

"Then — *The Golden Horn* must not come in," said I.

Catherine looked at me with that flash of ready wit in her eyes which was like to the flash of fire from gunpowder meeting tinder. Then she cried out, "Quick, then, quick, I pray thee, Harry Wingfield, to the wharf! For if ever I saw sail, I saw that, and the tide will have turned 'm. Quick, quick!"

She waited not for any headgear, but forth into the May sunlight she rushed, and I with her, and shouted at the top of my lungs to the slaves for my horse, then went myself, having no mind to wait, and hustled the poor beast from his feedbin, and was on his back and at a hard gallop to the wharf, with Mistress Catherine following as fast as she was able. Now and then, when I turned, I saw her slim green shape advancing, looking for all the world to my fancy like some nymph who had been changed into a river-reed and had gotten life again.

When I reached the wharf, with my horse all afoam, there was indeed *The Golden Horn* down the river, coming in. The tide and the wind had been against her, or she would have reached shore ere now. Then along the bank I urged my horse, and in some parts, where there was no footing and the tangle of woods too close, into the stream we plunged and swam, then up bank again, and so on with a mighty splatter of mire and water and rain of green leaves and blossoms from the low hang of branches through which we tore way, till we came abreast of *The Golden Horn*. Then I hallooed, first making sure that there was no one lurking near to overhear, and waved my handkerchief, keeping my horse standing to his fetlocks in the current, until over the water came an answering halloo from *The Golden Horn*, and I could plainly see Captain Calvin Tabor on the quarter-deck. The ship was not far distant, and I could have swam to her, and would have, though the tide was strong, had there been no other way.

"Halloo," shouted Captain Tabor, and two more men came running to the side, then more still, till it was overhung by a whole row of red English faces.

"Halloo!" shouted I.

"What d'ye lack? What's afoot? Halloo!"

"Send a boat, for God's sake," I shouted back. "News, news; keep where ye be. Do not land. Send a boat!"

"Is it the convict tutor, Wingfield?" shouted the captain.

I called back yes, and repeated my demand that he send a boat for God's sake.

Then I saw a great running hither and thither, and presently a boat touched water from the side of *The Golden Horn* with a curious lapping dip, and I was off my horse and tied him fast to a tree on the bank, with loose rein that he might crop his fill of the sweet spring herbage, and when the boat touched bank was in her and speedily aboard the ship.

Captain Tabor was leaning over the bulwarks, and his ruddy face was pale, and his look of devil-may-care gayety somewhat subdued.

When I gained the deck forward he came and grasped me by the arm, and led me into his own cabin, having first shouted forth to his mate an order to drop anchor and keep the ship in mid-stream.

"Now, in the name of all the fiends, what is afoot?" he cried out, though with a cautious cock of his eyes toward the deck, for English sailors are not black slaves when it comes to discussing matters of weight.

"There is a plot afoot against His Majesty King Charles, and you but yesterday, that being also a day on which it is unlawful to unload a ship, discharged a portion of your cargo, toward its furtherance and abetting," said I.

"Hell and damnation!" he cried out, "when I trust a woman's tongue again may I swing from my own yard-arms. What brought that fair-faced devil into it, anyway? Be there not men enough in this colony?"

"And you keep not a civil tongue in your head when you speak of Mistress Mary Cavendish; you will find of a surety that there be one man in this colony, sir," said I.

He laughed in that mocking fashion of his which incensed me

still further. Then he spoke civilly enough, and said that he meant no disrespect to one of the fairest ladies whom he had ever had the good fortune to see, but that it was so well known as to be no more slight in mentioning than the paint and powder wherewith a woman enhanced her beauty, that a woman's tongue could not be trusted like a man's, and that it were a pity that money, which were much better spent by her for pretty follies, should be put to such grim uses, and where were the gallants of Virginia that they suffered it, but did not rather empty their own purses?

I explained, being somewhat mollified, and also somewhat of his way of thinking, that men there were, but there was little gold since the Navigation Act. And I informed Captain Tabor how Mistress Mary Cavendish, having an estate not so heavily charged with expenses as some, and being her own mistress with regard to the disposal of its revenues, had the means which the men lacked.

"But what was the news which brought you thither, sir?" demanded Captain Tabor.

"You know of the plot —" I begun, but he broke in upon me fiercely.

"May the fiends take me, but what know I of a plot?" he cried.

"Can I not bring over gowns and kerchiefs and silken ribbons for a pretty maid without a plot? How knew you that? There is the woman's tongue again. But can I not bring over goods even of such sort; might I not with good reason suppose them to be for the defence of the cause of his most gracious Majesty King Charles against the savages, or any malcontents in his colonies? What plot, sirrah?"

"The plot for the cutting down of the young tobacco plants, Captain Tabor," said I.

His eyes blazed at me, while his face was pale and grim.

"How many know of the goods I discharged from *The Golden Horn* yesterday?" he asked.

"Three men, and I know not how many more, and two women," said I.

"Two women!" he groaned out. "Pestilence on these tide-waters which hold a ship like a trap! Two women!"

"But the concern is lest a third woman know," said I.

"If three women know, then God save us all, for their triple tongues will carry as far as the last trump!" cried Captain Tabor. Perturbed as he was, he never lost that air of reckless daring which compelled me to a sort of liking for him. "Out with the rest of it, sir," he said.

Then I told my story, to which he listened, scowling, yet with that ready laugh at his mouth. "'Tis a scurvy trick to serve a woman, both for her sake and the rest of us, to let her meddle with such matters," he said, "and so I told that cousin of hers, Master Drake, who came with her to give the order ere I sailed for England."

"Came any man save Ralph Drake with her then?" I asked.

"The saints forbid," he replied. "A secret is a secret only when in the keeping of one; with two it findeth legs, but with three it unfoldeth the swiftest wings of flight in all creation, and is everywhere with no alighting. Had three come to me with that mad order to bring powder and shot in the stead of silk stockings and garters and cambric shifts and kerchiefs, I would have clapped full sail on *The Golden Horn*, though —" he hesitated, then spoke in a whisper — "my mind is against tyranny, to speak you true, though I care not a farthing whether men pray on their knees or their feet, or in gowns or the fashion of Eden. And I care not if they pray at all, nor would I for the sake of that ever have forsaken, had I stood in my grandfather's shoes, the flesh-pots of old England for that howling wilderness of Plymouth. But for the sake of doing as I willed, and not as any other man, would I have sailed or swam the seas had they been blood instead of water. And so am I now with a due regard to the wind and the trim of my sails and the ears of talebearers, for a man hath but one head to lose with you of Virginia. But, the Lord, to make a little maid like that run the risk of imprisonment or worse, knew you aught of it, sir?"

I shook my head.

Captain Tabor laughed. "And yet she rode straight to the wharf with you yesterday," said he. "Lord, what hidden springs move a woman! I'll warrant, sir, had you known, you might have battened down the hatches fast enough on her will, convict though you be, and, faith, sir, but you look to me like one who is convict or master at his own choosing and not by the will of any other." So saying, he gave me a look so sharp that for a second I half surmised that he guessed my secret, but knew better at once, and said that our business was to deal not with what had been, but with what might be.

"Well," said he, "and what may that be, Master Wingfield, in your opinion? You surely do not mean to hold *The Golden Horn* in midstream with her cargo undischarged until the day of doom, lest yon old beldame offer up her fair granddaughter on the altar of her loyalty, with me and my hearties for kindling, to say naught of yourself and a few of the best gentlemen of Virginia. I forfeit my head if I set sail for England; naught is left for me that I see that shall save my neck but to turn pirate and king it over the high seas. Having swallowed a small morsel of my Puritan misgivings, what is to hinder my bolting the whole, like an exceeding bitter pill, to my complete purging of danger? What say you, Master Wingfield? Small reputation have you to lose, and sure thy reckoning with powers that be leaves thee large creditor. Will you sail with me? My first lieutenant shall you be, and we will share the booty."

He laughed, and I stared at him that he should stoop to jest, yet having a ready leap of comradeship toward him for it; then suddenly his mood changed. Close to me he edged, and began talking with a serious shrewdness which showed his mind brought fully to bear upon the situation. "You say, sir," said he, "that Mistress Mary Cavendish, in a spirit of youthful daring and levity, gave her grandmother a list of the goods which my Lady Culpeper ordered from England, and which even now is due?" I nodded.

"Know you by what ship?"

"The Earl of Fairfax," I replied, and recalled as I spoke a rumour that my Lord Culpeper designed his daughter Cate for the eldest son of the earl, and had so named his ship in honour of him.

"You say that the Earl of Fairfax is even now due?" said Captain Tabor.

I replied that she was hourly expected by what I had learned; then Captain Tabor, sitting loosely hunched with that utter abandon of all the muscles which one sees in some when they are undergoing a fierce strain of thought, remained silent for a space, his brows knitted. Then suddenly my shoulder tingled with the clap which he gave it, and the cabin rang and rang again with a laugh so loud and gay that it seemed a very note of the May day. "You are merry," I said, but I laughed myself, though somewhat doubtfully, when he unfolded his scheme to me, which was indeed both bold and humorous. He knew well the captain of the Earl of Fairfax, who had been shipmate with him.

"Many a lark ashore have we had together," said Calvin Tabor, "and, faith, but I know things about him now which compel him to my turn; the devil's mess have we both been in, but I need not use such means of persuasion, if I know honest Dick Watson." The scheme of which Captain Tabor delivered himself, with bursts of laughter enough to wake the ship, was, to speak briefly, that he should go with a boat, rowing against the current, by keeping close to bank and taking advantage of eddies, and meet the Earl of Fairfax before she reached Jamestown, board her, and persuade her captain to send the cases of my Lady Culpeper's goods under cover of night to *The Golden Horn*, whence he would unload them next morning, and Mistress Mary could show them to her grandmother, and then they were to be reshipped with all possible speed and secrecy, the Earl of Fairfax meanwhile laying at anchor at the mouth of the river, and then delivered to my Lady Culpeper.

There was but one doubt as to the success of this curious scheme in my mind, and that was that Mistress Mary might not easily lend herself to such deception. However, Captain Tabor, with a skill of devising concerning which I have often wondered whether it may be more common in the descendants of those who settled in New England, who were in such sore straits to get their own wills, than with us of Virginia, provided a way through that difficulty.

"'Tis full easy," said he. "You say that the maid's sister will say naught against it — and you?"

"I will say naught against her safety," said I. "What think you I care for any little quibbles of the truth when that be in question?"

"Well," said Captain Tabor, "then must you and Mistress Catherine Cavendish show the goods to the maid, and say naught as to the means by which you came by them; tell her they are landed from *The Golden Horn*, as indeed they will be; let her think aught she chooses, that they are indeed her own, purchased for her by her sister or her lovers, if she choose to think so, and bid her display them with no ado to Madam Cavendish, if she value the safety of the others who are concerned in this. Betwixt the mystery and the fright and the sight of the trinkets, if she be aught on the pattern of any other maid, show them she will, and hold her tongue till she be out of her grandmother's presence."

"It can be but tried," said I.

Then the captain sprang out on deck, and ordered a boat lowered, and presently had set me ashore, and was himself, with a half dozen sailors, fighting way downstream.

I found my horse on the bank where I had left him, and by him, waiting anxiously, Catherine Cavendish. She listened with deepening eyes while I told her Captain Tabor's scheme, and when I had done looked at me with her beautiful mouth set and her face as white as a white flower on a bush beside her. "Mary shall show the goods," said she. "Such a story will I tell her as will make her innocent of aught save bewilderment, and as for you and me, we are both of us ready to burn for a lie for the sake of her."

IX

I know not how Capt. Calvin Tabor managed his part to tranship those goods without discovery, but he had a shrewd head, and no doubt the captain of the Earl of Fairfax another, and by eight o'clock that May day *The Golden Horn* lay at her wharf discharging her cargo right lustily with such openness of zeal and shouts of encouragement and groans of labour 'twas enough to acquaint all the colony. And straightway to the great house they brought my Lady Culpeper's fallals, and clamped them in the hall where we were all at supper. Mistress Mary sprang to her feet, and ran to them and bent over them. "What are these?" she said, all in a quiver.

"The goods which you ordered, madam," spoke up one of the sailors, with a grin which he had copied from Captain Tabor, and pulled a forelock and ducked his head.

"The goods," said she, speaking faintly, for hers was rather the headlong course of enthusiasm than the secret windings of diplomacy.

"Art thou gone daft, sweetheart? The goods of which you gave the list this morning, which have but now come in on *The Golden Horn*," spoke up Catherine, sharply. I marvelled as I heard her whether it be ease or tenderness of conscience which can appease a woman with the letter and not the substance of the truth, for I am confident that her keeping to the outward show of honesty in her life was no small comfort to Catherine Cavendish.

Madam Cavendish was at table that night, though moving with grimaces from the stiffness of her rheumatic joints, and she ordered that the sailors be given cider, the which they drank with some haste, and were gone. Then Madam Cavendish asked Mistress Mary, with her wonderful keenness of gaze, which I never saw excelled, "Are those the goods which you ordered by *The Golden Horn*?" But I answered for her, knowing that Madam Cavendish would pardon such presumption from me. "Madam, those are the goods. I have it from Capt. Calvin Tabor himself." I spoke with no roundings nor glossings of subterfuge, having ever held that all the excuse for a lie was its boldness in a good cause, and believing in slaying a commandment like an enemy with a clean cut of the sword.

Mistress Mary gave a little gasp, and looked at me, and looked at her sister Catherine, and well I knew it was on the tip of her tongue to out with the whole to her grandmother. And so she would doubtless have done had not her wonderment and suspicion that maybe in some wise Catherine had conspired to buy for her in England the goods of which she had cheated herself, and the terror of doing harm to her sister and me. But never saw I a maid go so white and red and make the strife within her so evident.

We were well-nigh through supper when the goods arrived, and Madam Cavendish ordered some of the slaves to open the cases, which they did forthwith, and all my Lady Culpeper's finery was displayed.

Never saw I such a rich assortment, and calling to mind my Lady Culpeper's thin and sour visage, I wondered within myself whether such fine feathers might in her case suffice to make a fine bird, though some of them were for her daughter Cate, who was fair enough. Nothing would do but Mistress Mary, with her lovely face still strange to see with her consternation of puzzlement, should severally display every piece to her grandmother, and hold against her complexion the rich stuffs to see if the colours suited her. Madam Cavendish was pleased to express her satisfaction with them all, though with some demur at the extravagance. "'Tis rich enough a wardrobe for my Lady Culpeper," said she, at which innocent shrewdness I was driven to hard straits to keep my face grave, but Mistress Catherine was looking on with a countenance as calm as the moon which was just then rising.

Madam Cavendish was pleased especially with one gown of a sky colour, shot with silver threads, and ordered that Mistress Mary should wear it to the ball which was to be given at the governor's house the next night.

When I heard that I started, and Catherine shot a pale glance of consternation at me, but Mistress Mary flushed rosy-red with rebellion.

"I have no desire to attend my Lord Culpeper's ball, madam," said she.

"Lord Culpeper is the representative of his Majesty here in Virginia," said Madam Cavendish, with a high head, "and no granddaughter of mine absents herself with my approval. To the ball you go, madam, and in that sky-coloured gown, and no more words. Things have come to a pretty pass." So saying, she rose and, leaning heavily on her stick, with her black maid propping her, she went out. Then turned Mistress Mary imperiously to us and demanded to know the meaning of it all. "Whence came these goods?" said she to Catherine.

"On *The Golden Horn*, sweetheart; 'tis the list you gave this morning," replied Catherine, without a change in the fair resolve of her face.

"Pish!" cried Mary Cavendish. "The list I gave this morning was my Lady Culpeper's, and you know it. Whence came these?" and she spurned at a heap of the rich gleaming things with the toe of her tiny foot.

"I tell you, sweetheart, on *The Golden Horn*," replied Catherine. Then she turned to me in a rage. "The truth I will have," she cried out. "Whence came these goods?"

"On *The Golden Horn*, madam," I said.

She stamped her foot, and her voice rang so shrill that the black slaves, carrying out the dishes, rolled alarmed eyes at her. "Think you I will be treated like a child?" she cried out. "What means all this?"

Then close to her went Catherine, and flung an arm around her, and leaned her smooth, fair head against her sister's tossing golden one. "For the sake of those you love and who love thee, sweetheart," she whispered.

But Mistress Mary pushed her away and looked at her angrily. "Well, what am I to do for their sakes?" she demanded.

"Seek to know no more than this. The goods came on *The Golden Horn* but now, and 'tis the list you gave this morning."

"But it was not my list, and I deceived my grandmother, and I will go to her now and out with the truth. Think you I will have such a falsehood on my soul?"

Catherine leaned closer to her and whispered, and Mary gave a quick, wild glance at me, but I know not what she said. "I pray thee seek to know no more than that the goods came but now in a boat from *The Golden Horn*, and 'tis the list you gave this morning," said Catherine aloud.

"They are not mine by right, and well you know it." Then a thought struck me, and I said with emphasis, "Madam, yours by right they are and shall be, and I pray you to have no more concern in the matter."

Then so saying, I hastened out and went through the moonlight to the wharf to seek Captain Tabor and the captain of the Earl of Fairfax, who had come with his goods to see to their safety. Both men were pacing back and forth, smoking long pipes, and Captain Watson, of the Earl of Fairfax, a small and eager-spoken man, turned on me the minute I came within hearing. "Where be my Lady Culpeper's goods?" said he; "'tis time they were here and I on my way to the ship. Devil take me if I run such a risk again for any man."

Then I made my errand known. I had some fifty pounds saved

up from the wreck of my fortunes; 'twas a third more than the goods were worth. Would he but take it, pay the London merchant who had furnished them, and have the remainder for his trouble?

"Trouble, trouble!" he shouted out, "trouble! By all the foul fiends, man, what am I to say to my Lady Culpeper? Have you ever had speech with her that you propose such a game with her?"

Captain Tabor burst out with a loud guffaw of laughter. "You have not seen the maid for whom you run the risk, Dick," said he. "'Tis the fairest —"

"What care I for fair maids?" demanded the other. "Have I not a wife and seven little ones in old England? What think you a dimple or a bright eye hath of weight with me?"

"Time was, Dick," laughed Captain Tabor.

"Time that was no longer is," answered the other, crossly; then to me, "Send down my goods by some of those black fellows, and no more parleying, sir."

"But, sir," I said, "'twill be a good fifteen pound for Mistress Watson and the little ones when the merchant be paid."

"Go to," he growled out, "what will that avail if I be put in prison? What am I to say to my Lady Culpeper for the non-deliverment of her goods? Answer me that." Then came Captain Tabor to my aid with his merry shrewdness. "'Tis as easy as the nose on thy face, Dick," said he. "Say but to my lady that you have searched and the goods be not in the hold of the Earl of Fairfax, and must have miscarried, as faith they have, and say that next voyage you will deliver them and hold thyself responsible for the cost, as you well can afford with Master Wingfield's money."

"Hast ever heard my Lady Culpeper's tongue?" demanded the other. "'Tis easy to advise. Would you face her thyself without the goods in hand, Calvin Tabor?"

"Faith, and I'd face a dozen like her for fifteen pound," declared Captain Tabor. Then, with another great laugh. "I have it; send thy mate, send thy deaf mate, Jack Tarbox, man."

"But she will demand to see the captain."

"Faith, and the captain will be on board the Earl of Fairfax seeing to a leak which she hath sprung, and cannot leave her," said Tabor.

"But in two days' time the governor sails in my ship for England."

"Think ye the governor will concern himself about my lady's adornments when he be headed for England and out of reach of her complaints?"

gering young men, and after him came the aged morris dancers, only upheld from collapse in the mire by mutual upholdings, until they seemed like some monstrous animal moving with uncouth sprawls of legs as multifold as a centipede, and wavering drunkenly from one side of the road to the other, lurching into the dewy bushes, then recovering by the joint effort of the whole.

I stood well back to let them pass, being in that mood of self-importance, by reason of my love and the service rendered by it, that I could have seen the whole posse led to the whipping-block with a relish, when suddenly from their tipsy throats came a shout of such import that my heart stood still. "Down with the king!" hallooed one mad reveller, in a voice of such thickness that the whole sentence seemed one word; then the others took it up, until verily it seemed to me that their heads were not worth a farthing. Then, "Down with the governor! down with Lord Culpeper!" shouted that same thick voice of the man who was leading the wild crew like a bell-wether. He forged ahead, something more steady on his legs, but all the madder of his wits for that, with an arm around the waist of a buxom lass on either side, and all three dancing in time. Then all the rest echoed that shout of "Down with the governor!" Then out he burst again with, "Down, down with the tobacco, down with the tobacco!" But the volley of that echo was cut short by five horsemen galloping after the throng and scattering them to the right and left. Then a great voice of authority, set out with the strangest oaths which ever an imagination of evil compassed, called out to them to be still if they valued their heads, and cursed them all for drunken fools, and as he spoke he lashed with his whip from side to side, and his face gleamed with wrath like a demon's in the full light, and I saw he was Captain Noel Jaynes, and well understood how he had made a name for himself on the high seas. After him rode the brothers, Nicholas and Richard Barry, two great men, sticking to their saddles like rocks, with fair locks alike on the head of each flung out on the wind, and then came Ralph Drake rising in his stirrups and laughing wildly, and last Parson Downs, but only last because the road was blocked, for verily I thought his plunging horse would have all before him under his feet. They were all past me in a trice like a dream, the May revellers scattering and hastening forward with shrieks of terror and shouts of rage and peals of defiant laughter, and Captain Jaynes' voice, like a trumpet, overbearing everything, and shouts from the Barry brothers echoing him, and now and then coming the deep rumble of expostulations from the parson's great chest, and Ralph Drake's peals of horse-laughter, and I was left to consider what a tinderbox this Colony of Virginia was, and how ready to leap to flame at a spark even when seemingly most at peace, and to regard with more and more anxiety Mary Cavendish's part in this brewing tumult.

After the shouting and hallooing throng had passed I walked along slowly, reflecting, as I have said, when I saw in the road before me two advancing — a woman, and a man leading a horse by the bridle, and it was Mary Cavendish and Sir Humphrey Hyde.

And when I came up with them they stopped, and Humphrey addressed me rudely enough, but as one gentleman might another when he was angered with him, and not contemptuously, for that was never the lad's way with me. "Master Wingfield," he said, standing before me and holding his champing horse hard by the bits, "I pray you have the grace to explain this matter of the goods."

I saw that Mistress Mary had been acquainting him with what had passed and her puzzlement over it.

"There is naught to explain, Sir Humphrey," said I. "'Tis very simple: Mistress Mary hath the goods for which she sent to England."

"Master Wingfield, you know those are my Lady Culpeper's goods, and I have no right to them," cried Mary. But I bowed and said, "Madam, the goods are yours, and not Lady Culpeper's."

"But I — I lied when I gave the list to my grandmother," she cried out, half sobbing, for she was, after all, little more than a child tiptoed to womanhood by enthusiasm.

"Madam," said I, and I bowed again. "You mistake yourself; Mistress Mary Cavendish cannot lie, and the goods are in truth yours."

She and Sir Humphrey looked at each other; then Harry made a stride forward, and forcing back his horse with one hand, grasped me with the other. "Harry, Harry," he said in a whisper. "Tell me, for God's sake, what have you done."

"The goods are Mistress Mary Cavendish's," said I. They looked at me as I have seen folk look at a page of Virgil.

"Were they, after all, not my Lady Culpeper's?" asked Sir Humphrey.

"They are Mistress Mary Cavendish's," said I.

Mary turned suddenly to Sir Humphrey. "'Tis time you were gone now, Humphrey," she said, softly. "'Twas only last night you were here, and there is need of caution, and your mother —"

But Humphrey was loth to go. "'Tis not late," he said, "and I would know more of this matter."

"You will never know more of Master Wingfield, if that is what you wait for," she returned, with a half laugh, "and, Humphrey, your sister Cicely said but this morning that your mother was over curious. I pray you, go, and Master Wingfield will take me home. I pray you, go!"

Sir Humphrey took her hand and bent low over it, and murmured something; then, before he sprang to his saddle, he came close to me again. "Harry," he whispered, "she should not be in this business, and I would have not had it so could I have helped it, and, I pray you, have a care to her safety." This he spoke so low that Mary could not hear, and, moreover, she, with one of those sudden turns of hers that made her have as many faces of delight as a diamond in the sun, had thrown an arm around the neck of Sir Humphrey's mare, and was talking to her in such dulcet tones as her lovers would have died for the sake of hearing in their ears.

"Have no fears for her safety," I whispered back. "So far as the goods go, there is no more danger."

"What did you, Harry?"

"Sir Humphrey," I whispered back, while Mary's sweet voice in the mare's delicate ear sounded like a song, "sometimes an unguessed riddle hath less weight than a guessed one, and some fish of knowledge had best be left in the stream. I tell thee she is safe." So saying, I looked him full in his honest, boyish face, which was good to see, though sometime I wished, for the maid's sake, that it had more shrewdness of wit in it. Then he gave me a great grasp of the hand, and whispered something hoarsely. "Thou art a good fellow, Harry, in spite of, in spite of —" then he bent low over Mary's hand for the second time, and sprang to his saddle, and was off toward Jamestown on his white mare, flashing along the moonlit road like a whiter moonbeam.

Then Mary came close to me, and did what she had never before done since she was a child. She laid her little hand on my arm of her own accord. "Master Wingfield," said she, softly, "what about the goods?"

"The goods for which you sent to England are yours and in the great house," said I, and I heard my voice tremble.

She drew her hand away and stood looking at me, and her sweet forehead under her golden curls was all knitted with perplexity.

"You know, you know I — lied," she whispered like a guilty child.

"You cannot lie," I answered, "and the goods are yours."

"And not my Lady Culpeper's?"

"And not my Lady Culpeper's."

Mary continued looking at me, then all at once her forehead cleared.

"Catherine, 'twas Catherine," she cried out. "She said not, but well I know her; she would not own to it — the sweetheart. Sure a falsehood to hide a loving deed is the best truth of the world. 'Twas Catherine, 'twas Catherine, the sweetheart, the darling. She sent for naught for herself, and hath been saving for a year's time and maybe sold a ring or two. Somehow she discovered about the plot, what I had done. And she hath heard me say, that I know well, that I thought 'twas a noble list of Lady Culpeper's, and I wished I were a governor's wife or daughter, that I could have such fine things. I remember me well that I told her thus before ever *The Golden Horn* sailed for England, that time after Cicely Hyde slept with me and told me what she had from Cate Culpeper. A goodly portion of the goods were for Cate. 'Twas Catherine. Oh, the sweetheart, the darling! Was there ever sister like her?"

X

It was an industrious household at Drake Hill both as to men and women folk. The fields were full of ebony backs and plying arms of toil at sunrise, and the hum and whir of loom and spinning-wheels were to be heard in the negro cabins and the great house as soon as the birds.

Madam Judith Cavendish was a stern task-mistress, and especially for these latter duties. Had it not been for the stress of favour in which she held me, I question if my vocation as tutor to Mistress Mary would have had much scope for the last year, since her grandmother esteemed so highly the importance of a maid's being versed in all domestic arts, such as the spinning and weaving of flax and wool, and preserving and distilling and fine needlework. She set but small store by Latin and arithmetic for a maid, not even if she were naturally quick at them, as was Mistress Mary; and had it not been that she was bent upon keeping me in her service at Drake Hill, I doubt not that she would have clapped together the maid's books, whether or no, and set her to her wheel. As it was, a goodly part of every day was passed by her in such wise, but so fond was my pupil of her book that often I have seen her with it propped open, for her reference, on a chair at her side.

It was thus the next morning, the morning of the day of my Lord Culpeper's ball. It was a warm morning, and the doors and windows of the hall were set wide open, and all the spring wind and scent coming in and dimity curtains flying like flags, and the gold of Mistress Mary's hair tossing now and then in a stronger gust, and she and Catherine cramming down their flax baskets, lest the flax take wings to itself and fly away. Both Mary and Catherine were at their flax-wheels, but Madam Cavendish was in the loom-room with some of the black women. Mary had her Latin book open, as I have said before, on a chair at her side, but Catherine span with her fair face set to some steady course of thought, though she too was fond of books. Never a lesson had she taken of me, holding me in such scorn, but I questioned much at the time, and know now, that she was well acquainted with whatever knowledge her sister had got, having been taught by her mother and then keeping on by herself with her tasks. When I entered the hall, having been to Jamestown after breakfast and just returned, both maids looked up, and suddenly one of the wheels ceased its part in the duet, and Catherine was on her feet and her thread fallen whither it would. "Master Wingfield," said she, "I would speak with you."

"Madam, at your service," said I, and followed her, leading out on the green before the house. "What means this, what means this, sir?" she began when she was scarcely out of hearing of her sister.

"What did you about the goods? Did you, did you —?"

She gasped for further speech, and looked at me with such a haughtiness of scorn as never I had seen. It is hard for any man to be attacked in such wise by a woman, and be under the necessity of keeping his weapons sheathed, though he knoweth full well the exceeding convincing of them and their fine point to the case in hand. I bowed.

"Did you, did you —" she went on — "did you purchase those goods yourself for my sister? Did you?"

I bowed again. "Madam," said I, "whatever I have, and my poor flesh and blood and soul also, are at the service of not only your sister but her family."

I marvelled much as I spoke thus to see no flush of shameful consciousness overspread the maid's face, but none did, and she continued speaking with that sharpness of hers, both as to pale look and voice, which wounded like cold steel, which leaves an additional sting because of the frost in it. "Know you not, sir," said she, "that we cannot suffer a man in your position, a — a — to purchase my sister's wardrobe?" Then, before I knew what she was about to do, in went her hand to a broidered pocket which hung at her girdle, and out she drew a flashing store of rings and brooches, and one long necklace flashing with green stones. "Here, take these," she cried out. "I have no money, but such an insult I will not suffer, that my sister goes clad at your expense to the ball tonight. Take these; they are five times the value of the goods."

I would in that minute have given ten years of my life had Mistress Catherine Cavendish been a man and I could have felled her to the ground, and no man knowing what I believed I knew could have blamed me. The flashes of red and green from those rings and gewgaws which she held out seemed to pass my eyes to my very soul.

"Take them," she said. "Why do you not take them, sir?"

"I have no need of jewels, madam," I said, "and whatever the servant hath is his master's by right, and his master doth but take his own, and no discredit to him."

She fairly wrung her hands in her helpless wrath, and the gems glittered anew. "But, but," she stammered out, "know you the full result of this, Harry Wingfield? She, my sister Mary, thinks that I — I — sent to England for the goods for her; she knows that I have some acquaintance with what she hath done, and she — she is blessing me for it, and I cannot deny what she thinks. I — I — cannot tell her what you, you have done, lest, lest —" To my great astonishment she stopped short with such a flame of blushes as I had never seen on her face before, and I was at a loss to know what she might mean, but supposed that she considered that the shame of Mistress Mary's wearing finery which had been paid for out of a convict's purse would be more than she could put upon her, and yet that she dared not inform her, lest she refuse to wear the sky-blue robe to the governor's ball, and so anger Madam Cavendish.

"Madam," I said, "your sister is but blessing you for what you would have done, and wherefore need you fret?"

"God knows I would," she broke out, passionately. "Every jewel I possess, the very gown from my back, would I have sold to save her this, had I but known. Why did she not tell me, why did not she tell me? Oh, Harry, I pray you to take these jewels."

"I cannot take them, madam," I said. Yet such was her distress I was sorry for her, though I believed it to be rooted and grounded in falsity, and that she had no need to regard with such disapprobation her sister's being indebted to an English gentleman who gave her in all honour the best he had. Yet could I not yield and take those jewels, for more reasons than one; not only should I have lost the dear delight of having served Mary Cavendish, but I had a memory of wrong which would not suffer me to touch those rings, nor to allow that innocent maid to be benefited by them, since I cannot say what dark suspicions seized me when I looked at them.

"My God!" she said, "was ever such a web of falsehood as this? Here must I hear my sister's blessings upon me for what I have done, and I knowing all the time that 'twas you, and yet she must not know." Then again that flame of red overspread her face and neck to the meet of her muslin kerchief, and I knew not why.

"Madam," I said, "one deception opens the way for a whole flock," and I spoke with something of a double meaning, but she only cried out, with apparently no understanding of it, that things had come to a cruel pass, and back to the house she went; and I presently followed her to get my gun, having a mind to shoot a few wild fowl, since my pupil was at her wheel. And there the two sat, keeping up that gentle drone of industry which I have come to think of as a note of womanhood, like the hum of a bee or the purr of a cat or the call of a bird. They sat erect, the delicate napes of their necks showing above their muslin kerchiefs under their high twists of hair, for even Mary had her golden curls caught up that morning on account of the flax-lint, and from their fair, attentive faces nobody would have gathered what stress of mind both were in. Of a surety there must be a quieting and calming power in some of the feminine industries which be a boon to the soul.

But, as I passed through the hall, up looked Mary, and her beautiful face flashed out of peace into a sunlight of love and enthusiasm.

"Oh," she cried out, "oh, was there ever anyone like my sweetheart Catherine? To think what she hath done for me, to think, to think! And she, dear heart, loving the king! But better she loves her little sister, and will stand by her in her disloyalty, for the love of her. Was there ever any one like her, Master Wingfield?"

And I laughed, though maybe with some slight bitterness, for I was but human, and that outburst of loving gratitude toward another, and another whom I held in slight esteem, when it was I who had given the child my little all, and presently, when my term was expired, would have to return to England without a farthing betwixt me and starvation, and maybe working my way before the mast to get there at all, had a sting in it. 'Twas a strange thing that anything so noble and partaking of the divine as the love of an honest man for a woman should have any tincture of aught ignoble in it, and one is caused thereby to decry one's state of mortality, which seems as inseparable from selfish ends as the red wings of a rose from the thorny stem which binds it to earth. Truly the longer I live the more am I aware of the speck which mars the completeness of all in this world, and ever the desire for a better, and that longing which will not be appeased groweth in my soul, until methinks the very keenness of the appetite must prove the food.

"Was there ever one like her?" repeated Mary Cavendish, and as she spoke, up she sprang and ran to her sister and flung a fair arm around her neck, and drew her head to her bosom, and leaned her cheek against it, and then looked at me with a sidewise glance which made my heart leap, for curious meanings, of which the innocent thing had no reckoning, were in it.

I know not what I said. Truly not much, for the mockery of it all was past my power of dealing with and keeping my respect of self.

I got my fowling-piece from the peg on the wall, and was forth and ranging the wooded shores, with my eyes intent on the whirring flight of the birds, and my mind on that problem of the times which always hath, and doth, and always will, encounter a man who lives with any understanding of what is about him, but not always as sorely as in my case, who faced, as it were, an army of difficulties, bound hand and foot. But after a while the sport in which I was fairly skilled, and that sense of power which cometh to one from the proving of his superiority over the life and death of some weaker creation, and the salt air in my nostrils, gave me, as it were, a glimpse of a farther horizon than the present one of Virginia in 1682, and mine own little place in it. Then verily I could seem to see and scent like some keen hound a smoothness which should later come from the tangled web of circumstances, and a greatness which should encompass mine own smallness of perplexity.

When I was wending my way back to Drake Hill, with my gun over shoulder and some fine birds in hand, I met Sir Humphrey Hyde.

We were near Locust Creek, and the great house stood still and white in the sunlight, and there was no life around it except for the distant crawl of toil over the green of the tobacco fields and the great hum of the bees in the flowering honey locusts which gave, with the creek, the place its name. Sir Humphrey was coming from the direction of the house, riding slowly, stooping in the saddle as if with thought, and I guessed that he had been to see to the safety of the contraband goods. When he saw me he halted and shouted, in his hearty, boyish way, "Halloo, halloo, Harry, and what luck?" as if all there was of moment in the whole world, and Virginia in particular, was the shooting of birds on a May morning. But then his face clouded, and he spoke earnestly enough. "Harry, Harry," he said, in a whisper, though there was no life nearer than the bees, and they no bearers of secrets, except those of the flowers, "I pray thee, come back to the hall with me, and let us consult together."

I followed him back to the house, and he sprang from his saddle, had a shutter unhasped in a twinkling, knowing evidently the secret of it, and we were inside, standing amongst the litter of casks and cases in the great silent desertion of the hall of Locust Creek. Then he grasped me hard by both hands, and cried out, "Harry, Harry Wingfield, come to thee I must, for, convict though thou be, thou art a man with a head packed with wit, and Ralph Drake is half the time in his cups, and Parson Downs riding his own will at such a hard gallop that 'twill surprise me not if he leave his head behind, and as for Dick and Nick Barry, and Captain Dickson, and — and Major Robert Beverly, and all the others, what is it to them about this one matter which is more to me than the whole damned hell-broth?"

"You mean?" I said, and pointed to the litter on the hall floor.

"Yes," and then, with a great show of passion, "My God, Harry Wingfield, why, why did we gentlemen and cavaliers of Virginia allow a woman to be mixed in this matter? If, if — these goods be traced to her —"

"And, faith, and I see no reason why they should not be, with a whole colony in the secret of it," I said, coldly.

"Nay, none but me and Nick and Dick Barry, and the parson since yesterday, and Major Beverly and Capt. Noel Jaynes and you and the captain and sailors on *The Golden Horn*, who value their own necks. As God is my witness, none beside, Harry."

I could scarcely help laughing at the length of the list and the innocence of the lad. "Her sister Catherine, Sir Humphrey," said I.

"Hath she told her, Harry?"

"And the captain of the Earl of Fairfax."

"The governor's ship? Well, then, let us go through Jamestown proclaiming it with a horn," he gasped out, and made more of the two last than his own long list.

"Nay, the two last are as safe as we," said I. "Mistress Catherine holds her sister dearer than herself, and as for the captain of the governor's ship, lock a man's tongue with the key of his own interest if you wish it not to wag. But these goods must be moved from here."

"That is what I well know, Harry," he said, eagerly. "All night did I toss and study the matter. But where?"

"Not in any place on Madam Cavendish's plantation," I said, and did not say, as I might have, for 'twas the truth, that I had also tossed and studied, but as yet to no result.

"No, nor on mine, though I swear to thee, were I the only one to consider, I would have them there in a twinkling, but I cannot put my mother and sister in jeopardy even for —"

"Barry Upper Branch?"

"Nick and Dick swear they will not run the risk; that they have but too lately escaped with their lives, and are too close watched, and as for the parson, 'tis out of the question, and Ralph Drake hath no hiding place, and as for the others, they one and all refuse, and say this is the safest place in the colony, it being a household of women, and Madam Cavendish well known for her loyalty."

He looked at me and I at him, and again the old consideration, as I saw his handsome, gallant young face that perchance

Mary Cavendish might love him and do worse than to wed him, came over me.

"I will find a place for the goods," said I.

"You, Harry?"

"Yes, I," I said.

"But where, Harry?"

"Wait till the need for them come, lad." Then I added, for often in my perplexity the wish that the whole lot were at the bottom of the river had seized me, "There is need of them, I suppose?"

But Sir Humphrey said yes, with a great emphasis to that.

"There is sure to be fighting," he said, "and never were powder and shot so scarce. 'Tis well the Indians are quiet. This poor Colony of Virginia hath not enough powder to guard her borders, nor, were it not for her rich soil, enough of food to feed her children since the Navigation Act.

"Oh, God, Harry, if but Nathaniel Bacon had lived!"

"Amen," I said, and felt as I said it, that if indeed that hero were alive, this plot for the destroying of the young tobacco plants might be the earthquake which threw off a new empire; but as it were, remembering the men concerned, who had none of the stuff of Bacon in them, I wondered if it would prove aught more than a wedge in the scheme of liberty.

"There are those who would be ready to say that we gentlemen of Virginia, like Bacon, are all ready to shelter ourselves behind women's aprons," said Sir Humphrey Hyde, with a shamed glance at the goods, referring to that stationing of the ladies of the Berkeley faction, all arrayed in white aprons, on the earthworks before the advance of the sons and husbands and brothers in the Bacon uprising.

"And if you hear any man say that, shoot him dead, Sir Humphrey Hyde," I said, for, through liking not that story about Bacon, I was fiercer in defence of it.

"Faith, and I will, Harry," cried Sir Humphrey, "and Bacon was a greater man than the king, if I were to swing for it; but, Harry, you cannot by yourself move these. What will you do?"

But I begged him to say no more, and started toward the window, the door being fast locked as Mistress Mary had left it, when suddenly the boy stopped me and caught me by the hand, and begged me to tell him if I thought there might be any hope for him with Mary Cavendish, being moved to do so by her sending him away so peremptorily the night before, which had put him in sore doubt. "Tell me, Harry," he pleaded, and the great lad seemed like a child, with his honest outlook of blue eyes, "tell me what you think, I pray thee, Harry; look at me, and tell me, if you were a maid, what would you think of me?"

Loving Mary Cavendish as I did, and striving to look at him with her eyes, a sort of tenderness crept into my heart for this simple lover, who was as brave as he was simple, and I clapped a hand on his fair curls, for though he was so tall I was taller, and laughed and said, "If I were a maid, though 'tis a fancy to rack the brain, but, if I were a maid, I would love thee well, lad."

"My mother thinketh none like me, and so tells me every day, and says that I am like my father, who was the handsomest man in England; but then mothers be all so, and I know not how much of it to trust, and my sister Cicely loves Mary so well herself that she is jealous, and often tells me —" then the lad stopped and stared at me, and I at him, perplexed, not dreaming what was in his mind.

"Tells you what, Sir Humphrey?" said I.

"That, that — oh, confound it, Harry, there is no harm in saying it, for you as well as I know the folly of it, and that 'tis but the jealous fancy of a girl. Faith, but I think my sister Cicely is as much in love with Mary Cavendish as I. 'Tis but — my sister Cicely, when she will tease me, tells me 'tis not I but you that Mary Cavendish hath set her heart upon, Harry."

I felt myself growing pale at that, and I could not speak because of a curious stiffness of my lips, and I heard my heart beat like a clock in the deserted house. Sir Humphrey was looking at me with an anxiety which was sharpening into suspicion. "Harry," he said, "you do not think —"

"'Tis sheer folly, lad," I burst out then, "and let us have no more of it. 'Tis but the idle prating of a lovesick girl, who should have a lover, ere she try to steal a nest in the heart of one of her own sex. 'Tis folly, Sir Humphrey Hyde."

"So said I to Cicely," Sir Humphrey cried, eagerly, too interested in his own cause to heed my slighting words for his sister. "'Tis the rankest folly, I told her. Here is Harry Wingfield, old enough almost to be Mary's father, and beside, beside — oh, confound it, Harry," the generous lad burst out. "I would not like you for a rival, for you are a good half foot taller than I, and you have that about you which would make a woman run to you and think herself safe were all the Indians in Virginia up, and you are a dark man, and I have heard say they like that, but, but — oh, I say, Harry, 'tis a damned shame that you are here as you are, and not as a gentleman and a cavalier with the rest of us, for all the evidence to the contrary and all the government to the contrary, 'tis, 'tis the way you should be, and not a word of that charge do I believe. May the fiends take me if I do, Harry!" So saying, the lad looked at me, and verily the tears were in his blue eyes, and out he thrust his honest hand for me to grasp, which I did with more of comfort than I had had for many a day, though it was the hand of a rival, and the next minute forth he burst again: "Say, Harry, if it be true that thou art out of the running, and I believe it must be so, for how could? — say, Harry, think you there is any chance for me?"

"I know of no reason why there should not be, Sir Humphrey," I said.

"Only, only — that she is what she is, and I but myself. Oh, Harry, was there ever one like that girl? All the spirit of daring of a man she has, and yet is she full of all the sweet ways of a maid. Faith, she would draw sword one minute and tie a ribbon the next. She would have followed Bacon to the death, and sat up all night to broider herself a kerchief. Comrade and sweetheart both she is, and was there ever one like her for beauty? Harry, Harry, saw you ever such a beauty as Mary Cavendish?"

"No, and never will," cried I, so fervently and so echoing to the full his youthful enthusiasm that again that keen look flashed into his eyes. "Harry," he stammered out, "you do not — say, for God's sake, Harry, you are a man if you are a — a —, and every day have you seen that angel, and — and — Harry, may the devil take me if I would go against thee if she — you know I would not, Harry, for I remember well how you taught me to shoot, and, and — I love thee, Harry, not in such fool fashion as my sister loveth Mary, but I love thee, and never would I cross thee."

"Sir Humphrey," said I, "it is not what you would, nor what I would, nor what any other man would, but what be best for Mary Cavendish, and her true happiness of life, that is to consider, whether you love her, or I love her, or any other man love her."

"Faith, and a score do," he said, gloomily. "There be my Lord Estes and her cousin Ralph, and I know not how many more. Faith, I would not have her less fair, but sometimes I would that a few were colour blind. But 'tis different when it comes to thee, Harry. If she —"

"Sir Humphrey," I said, "were Mary Cavendish thy sister and I myself, and loving her and she me, and you having that affection which you say you have for me, would you yet give her to me in marriage and think it for her good?"

Then the poor lad coloured and stammered, and could not look me in the face, but it was enough. "Let there be no more talk betwixt you and me as to that matter, Sir Humphrey," I said.

"There is never now nor at any other time any question of marriage betwixt Mistress Mary Cavendish and her convict tutor, and if he perchance had been not colour blind and had learned to appraise her at her rare worth, the more had he been set against such. And all that he can do for thee, lad, he will do."

Sir Humphrey was easily pacified, having been accustomed from his babyhood to masterly soothing of his mother into her own ways of thought. Again, in spite of his great stature, he looked up at me like a very child. "Harry," he whispered, "heard you her ever say anything pleasant concerning me?"

"Many a time," I answered, quite seriously, though I was inwardly laughing, and could not for the life of me remember any especial favour which she had paid him in her speech. But I have ever held that a bold lover hath the best chance, and knowing that boldness depends upon assurance of favour, I set about giving it to Sir Humphrey, even at some small expense of truth.

"When, when, Harry?"

"Oh, many a time, Sir Humphrey."

"But what? I pray thee, tell me what she said, Harry."

"I have not charged my mind, lad."

"But think of something. I pray thee, think of something, Harry." He looked at me with such exceeding wistfulness that I was forced to cudgel my brains for something which, having a slight savour of truth, might be seasoned to pungency at fancy. "Often have I heard her say that she liked a fair man," I replied, and indeed I had, and believed her to have said it because I was dark, and seemingly inattentive to some new grace of hers as to the tying of her hair or fastening of her kerchief.

"Did she indeed say that, Harry, and do you think she had me in mind?" cried Sir Humphrey.

"Are you not a fair man?"

"Yes, yes, I am a fair man, am I not, Harry? What else? Sure you have heard her say more than that."

"I have heard her say she liked a hearty laugh, and one who counted not costs when his mind were set on aught, but rode straight for it though all the bars were up."

"That sure is I, Harry, unless my mother stand in the way. A man cannot bring his mother's head low, Harry, but sure if she forbid nor know not, as in this case of this tobacco plot, I stop for naught. Sure she meant me, then, Harry."

"And I have heard her say that she liked a young man, a man no older than she."

"Sure, sure she meant me by that, Harry, for I am the youngest of them all — not yet twenty. Oh, dear Harry, she had me in mind by that. Do you not think so?"

"I know of no one else whom she could have had in mind," I answered.

The lad was blushing with delight and confusion like a girl. He cast down his eyes before me; he stammered when he spoke. "Harry, if she but love me, I swear I could do as brave deeds as Bacon," he said. "I would die would she but carry about a lock of my hair on her bosom as she does his. I would, Harry. And you think I have some chance?"

My heart smote me lest I had misled him, for I knew with no certainty the maid's mind. "As much chance as any, and more than many, lad," I said, "and I will do what I can for thee."

"Harry," he said, then paused and blushed and twisted his great body about as modestly as a girl, "Harry."

"What, Sir Humphrey?"

"Once, once — I never told of it, and no one ever knew since I was alone, and it would have been boasting — but once — I — fought single-handed with that great Christopher Little, whom I met by chance when I was out in the woods, and 'twas two years since, and I, with scarce my full growth, and he pleading for mercy at the second round, with an eye like a blackberry and a nose like a gillyflower, and — and — Harry, you might tell her of it, and say not where you got the news, if you thought it no harm. And, Harry, you will mind the time when I killed the wolf with naught but an oak club for weapon, and she, maybe, hath not heard of that. And I should have been to the front with Bacon, boy as I was, had it not been for my mother — that you know well and could make her sure of. And, and — oh, confound it, Harry, little book wit have I in my head, and she is so clever as never was, and all I have to win her notice be in my hands and heels, for, Harry, you will remember the race I ran with Tom Talbot that Mayday; think you she knows of that? And — but she must know how I rode against Nick Barry last St. Andrew's, and, and — oh, Lord, Harry, what am I that she should think of me? But at all odds, whether it be me or you or any other man, see to it that these goods be moved and she not be drawn into this which is hatching, for it may be as big a blaze as Bacon started before we be done with it; but shall I not help thee, Harry, and when will you move them and where?"

"I want no help, lad," I said, and was indeed firmly set in my mind that he should know nothing about the disposal of the goods lest Mistress Mary come to grief through her love for him, and reasoning that ignorance was his best safeguard and hers.

We went forth from Locust Creek, I having promised that I would do all that I could to further his suit with Mary Cavendish, and when we reached the bend of the road, he having walked beside me, hitherto leading his horse, he was in his saddle and away, having first acquainted me anxiously with the fact that he was to wear that night to the governor's ball a suit of blue velvet with silver buttons, and asking me if I considered that it would become him in Mistress Mary's eyes. Then I went home to Drake Hill, passing along such a wonderful aisle of bloom of locust and peach and mulberry and honeysuckle and long trails of a purple vine of such a surprise of beauty as to make one incredible that he saw aright — bushes pluming white to the wind, and over all a medley of honey and almond and spicy scents seeming to penetrate the very soul, that I was set to reflecting in the midst of my sadness of renunciation of my love, and my anxiety for her if, after all, such roads of blessing which were set for our feet at every turn led not of a necessity to blessed ends, and if our course tended not to happiness, whether we knew it or not, and along whatever byways of sorrow.

XI

I have seen many beautiful things in my life, as happens to every one living in a world which hath little fault as to its appearance, if one can outlook the shadow which his own selfishness of sorrow and disappointment may cast before him; but it seemed that evening, when I saw Mary Cavendish dressed for the governor's ball, that she was the crown of all. I verily believe that never since the world was made, not even that beautiful first woman who comprehended in herself all those witcheries of her sex which have been ever since to our rapture and undoing, not even Eve when Adam first saw her in Paradise, nor Helen, nor Cleopatra, nor any of those women whose faces have made powers of them and given them niches in history, were as beautiful as Mary Cavendish that night. And I doubt if it were because she was beheld by the eyes of a lover. I verily believe that I saw aright, and gave her beauty no glamour because of my fondness for her, for not one whit more did I love her in that splendour than in her plainest gown. But, oh, when she stood before her grandmother and me and a concourse of slaves all in a ferment of awe and admiration, with flashings of white teeth and upheavals of eyes and flingings aloft of hands in half savage gesticulation, and courtesied and turned herself about in innocent delight at her own loveliness, and yet with the sweetest modesty and apology that she was knowing to it! That stuff which had been sent to my Lady Culpeper and which had been intercepted ere it reached her was of a most rich and wonderful kind. The blue of it was like the sky, and through it ran the gleam of silver in a flower pattern, and a great string of pearls gleamed on her bosom, and never was anything like that mixture of triumph in, and abashedness before, her own exceeding beauty and her perception of it in our eyes in her dear and lovely face. She looked at us and actually shrank a little, as if our admiration were something of an affront to her maiden modesty, and blushed, and then she laughed to cover it, and swept a courtesy in her circling shimmer of blue, and tossed her head and flirted a little fan, which looked like the wing of a butterfly, before her face.

"Well, how do you like me, madam?" said she to her grandmother, "and am I fine enough for the governor's ball?"

Madam Cavendish gazed at her with that rapture of admiration in a beloved object which can almost glorify age to youth. She called Mary to her and stroked the rich folds of her gown; she straightened a flutter of ribbon. "'Tis a fine stuff of the gown," she said, "and blue was always my colour. I was married in it. 'Tis fine enough for the governor's wife, or the queen for that matter." She pulled out a fold so that a long trail of silver flowers caught the light and gleamed like frost. No misgivings and no suspicions she had, and none, by that time, had Mary, believing as she did that her sister had bought all that bravery for her, and that it was hers by right, and only troubled by the necessity of secrecy with her grandmother lest she discover for what purpose her own money had been spent. But Catherine eyed her with such exceedingly worshipful love, admiration, and yet distress that even I pitied her. Catherine herself that night did no discredit to her beauty, her dress being, though it was an old one, as rich as Mary's, of her favourite green with a rose pattern broidered on the front of it, and a twist of green gauze in her fair hair, and that same necklace of green stones which she had shown me in the morning around her long throat, and her long, milky white arms hanging at her sides in the green folds of her gown, and that pale radiance of perfection in her every feature that made many call her the pearl of Virginia, though, as I have said before, she had no lovers. She and Mary were going to the ball, and a company of black servants with them. As for me, balls were out of the question for a convict tutor, and I knew it, and so did they. But suddenly, to my great amazement, Madam Cavendish turned to me: "And wherefore are you not dressed for the ball, Master Wingfield?" she said.

I stared at her, as did also Catherine and Mary, almost as if they suspected she had gone demented. "Madam," I stammered, scarce thinking I had understood her rightly.

"Why are you not dressed for the ball?" she repeated.

"Madam," I said, "pardon me, but you are well acquainted with the fact that I am not a welcome guest at the governor's ball."

"And wherefore?" cried she imperiously.

"Wherefore, madam?"

Mary and Catherine both looked palely at their grandmother, not knowing what had come to her.

"Madam," I said, "do you forget?"

"I forget not that you are the eldest son and heir of one of the best families in England, and as good a gentleman as the best of them," she cried out. "That I do not forget, and I would have you go to the ball with my granddaughters. Put on thy plum coloured velvet suit, Harry, and order thy horse saddled."

For the first time I seemed to understand that Madam Judith Cavendish had, in spite of her wonderful powers of body and mind, somewhat of the childishness of age, for as she looked at me the tears were in her stern eyes and a flush was on the ivory white of her face, and her tone had that querulousness in it which we associate with childhood which cannot have its own will.

"Madam," I said, gently, "you know that it is not possible for me to do as you wish, and also that my days of gayeties are past, though not to my regret, and that I am looking forward to an evening with my books, which, when a man gets beyond his youth, yield him often more pleasure than the society of his kind."

"But, Harry," she said piteously, and still like a child, "you are young, and I would not have —" Then imperiously again: "Get into thy plum coloured velvet suit, Master Wingfield, and accompany my granddaughters."

But then I affected not to hear her, under pretence of seeing that the sedan chairs were ready, and hallooed to the slaves with such zeal that Madam Cavendish's voice was drowned, though with no seeming rudeness, and Mary and Catherine came forth in their rustling spreads of blue and green, and the black bearers stood grinning whitely out of the darkness, for the moon was not up yet, and I aided them both into the chairs, and they were off. I stood a few moments watching the retreating flare of flambeaux, for runners carrying them were necessary on those rough roads when dark, and the breath of the dewy spring night fanned my face like a wing of peace, and I regretted nothing very much which had happened in this world, so that I could come between that beloved girl and the troubles starting up like poisonous weeds on her path.

But when I entered the hall Madam Cavendish, having sent away the slaves, even to the little wench who had been fanning her, with verily I believe no more of consciousness as to what was going on about her than a Jimson weed by the highway, called me to her in a voice so tremulous that I scarce knew it for hers.

"Harry, Harry," she said, "I pray thee, come here." Then, when I approached, hesitating, for I had a shrinking before some outburst of feminine earnestness, which has always intimidated me by its fire of helplessness and futility playing against some resolve of mine which I could not, on account of my masculine understanding of the requirements of circumstances, allow to melt, she reached up one hand like a little nervous claw of ivory, and caught me by the sleeve and pulled me down to a stool by her side. Then she looked at me, and such love and even adoration were in her face as I never saw surpassed in it, even when she regarded her granddaughter Mary, yet withal a cruel distress and self-upbraiding and wrath at herself and me. "Harry, Harry," she said, "I can bear no more of this." Then, to my consternation, up went her silken apron with a fling to her old face, and she was weeping under it as unrestrainedly as any child.

I did not know what to do nor say. "Madam," I ventured, finally, "if you distress yourself in such wise for my sake, 'tis needless, I assure, 'tis needless, and with as much truth as were you my own mother."

"Oh, Harry, Harry," she sobbed out, "know you not that is why I cannot bear it longer, because you yourself bear it with no complaint?" Then she sobbed and even wailed with that piteousness of the grief of age exceeding that of infancy, inasmuch as the weight of all past griefs of a lifetime go to swell it, and it is enhanced by memory as well as by the present and an unknown future. I knew not what to do, but laid a hand somewhat timidly on one of her thin silken arms, and strove to draw it gently from her face. "Madam Cavendish," I said, "indeed you mistake if you weep for me. At this moment I would change places with no man in Virginia."

"But I would have — I would have you!" she cried out, with the ardour of a girl, and down went her apron, and her face, like an aged mask of tragedy, not discoloured by her tears, as would have happened with the tender skin of a maid, confronted me. "I would have you the governor himself, Harry. I would have you — I would have —" Then she stopped and looked at me with a red showing through the yellow whiteness of her cheeks. "You know what I would have, and I know what you would have, and all the rest of my old life would I give could it be so, Harry," she said, and I saw that she knew of my love for her granddaughter Mary. Then suddenly she cried out, vehemently: "Not one word have I said to you about it since that dreadful time, Harry Wingfield, for shame and that pride as to my name, which is a fetter on the tongue, hath kept me still, but at last I will speak, for I can bear it no longer. Harry, Harry, I know that you are what you are, a convict and an exile, to shield Catherine, to shield a granddaughter of mine, who should be in your place. Harry Wingfield, I know that Catherine Cavendish is guilty of the crime for which you are in punishment, and, woe is me, such is my pride, such is my wicked pride, that I have let you suffer and said never one word."

I put her hand to my lips. "Madam," I said, "you mistake; I do not suffer. That which you think of as my suffering and my disgrace is my glory and happiness."

"Yes, and why, and why? Oh, Harry, 'tis that which is breaking my heart. 'Tis because you love Mary, 'tis because, I verily believe, you have loved her from the first minute you set eyes on her, though she was but a baby in arms. At first I thought it was Catherine, in spite of her fault, but now I know it was for the sake of Mary that you sacrificed yourself — for her sister, Harry, I know, I know, and I would to God that I could give you your heart's desire, for 'tis mine also!"

Then, so saying, this old woman, who had in her such a majesty of character and pride that it held folk aloof at a farther distance than loud swaggerings of importance of men high in office, drew down my head to her withered shoulder and touched my cheek with a hand of compassionate pity and blessing, as if I had been in truth her son, and caught her breath again and again with a sobbing sigh. All that I could say to comfort her I said, assuring her, as was indeed the truth, that no woman could justly estimate the view which a man might take of such a condition as mine, and how the power of service to love might be enough to content one, and he stand in no need of pity, but she was not much consoled. "Harry," she said, "Harry, thou art like a knight of olden times about whom a song was written, which I heard sung in my girlhood, and which used to bring the tears, though I was never too ready with them. Woe be to me that I, knowing what I know, have yet not the courage to sacrifice my pride and my unworthy granddaughter, and see you free. Oh, Harry, that thou shouldst sit at home when thou art fitted by birth and breeding to go with the best of them! Harry, I pray thee, put on thy plum coloured suit and go to the ball."

"Dear Madam Cavendish," I said, half laughing, for she seemed more and more like a child, "you know that it cannot be, and that I have no desire for balls."

"But I would have thee go, Harry."

"But I am not asked," I said.

"What matters that? 'Tis almost with open doors, since it is a farewell of my Lord Culpeper before sailing for England. Harry, go, and — a — and — I swear if any exception be taken to it, I — I — will tell the truth."

"Dear madam, it cannot be," I said, "and the truth is to be concealed not only for your sake, but for that of others."

Then she broke out in another paroxysm of childish wailing that never was such a wretched state of matters, such a wretched old woman handicapped from serving one by her love for another. "Harry, I cannot clear thee unless I convict my own granddaughter Catherine," she said, piteously, "and if I spared her not, neither her nor my pride, what of Mary? Catherine hath been like a mother to the child, and she loves her better than she loves me. 'Twould kill her, Harry. And, Harry, how can I give Mary to thee, and thou under this ban? Mary Cavendish cannot wed a convict."

"That she cannot and shall not," I said; "she shall wed a much worthier man and be happy, and sure 'tis her happiness that is the question."

But Madam Cavendish stared at me with unreasoning anger, not understanding, since she was a woman, and unreasoning as a woman will be in such matters. "If you love not my grand-daughter, Harry Wingfield," she cried out, "'tis not her grand-mother will fling her at your head. I will let you know, sir, that she could have her pick in the colony if she so chose, and it may be that she might not choose you, Master Harry Wingfield."

I laughed. "Madam Cavendish," I said, rising and bowing, "were I a king instead of a convict, then would I lay my crown at Mary Cavendish's feet; as it is, I can but pave, if I may, her way to happiness with my heart."

"Then you love her as I thought, Harry?"

"Madam," I said, "I love her to my honour and glory and never to my discontent, and I pray you to believe with a love that makes no account of selfish ends, and that I am happier at home with my books than many a cavalier who shall dance with her at the ball."

"But, Harry," she said, piteously, "I pray thee to go."

I laughed and shook my head, and went away to my own quarters and sat down to my books, but, at something past mid-night, Madam Cavendish sent for me in all haste. She had gone to bed, and I was ushered to her bedroom, and when I saw her thin length of age scarce rounding the coverlids, and her face frilled with white lace, and her lean neck stretching up from her pillows with the piteous outreaching of a bird, a great tenderness of com-passion for womanhood, both in youth and beauty and age and need, beyond which I can express, came over me. It surely seems to me the part of man to deal gently with them at all times, even when we suffer through them, for there is about them a mystery of helplessness and misunderstanding of themselves which should give us an exceeding patience. And it seems to me that, even in the cases of those women who are perhaps of greater wit and force of character than many a man, not one of them but hath her help-lessness of sex in her heart, however concealed by her majesty of carriage. So, when I saw Madam Cavendish, old and ill at ease in her mind because of me, and realised all at once how it was with her in spite of that clear head of hers and imperious way which had swayed to her will all about her for near eighty years, I went up to her, and, laying a gentle hand upon her head, laid it back upon the pillow, and touched her poor forehead, wrinkled with the cares and troubles of so many years, and felt all the pity in me uppermost. "'Tis near midnight, and you have not slept, madam," I said. "I pray you not to fret any longer about that which we can none of us mend, and which is but to be borne as the will of the Lord."

"Nay, nay, Harry," she cried out, with a pitiful strength of anger. "I doubt if it be the will of the Lord. I doubt if it be not the devil — Catherine, Catherine — Harry, my brain reels when I think that she should have done it — a paltry ring, and to let you —"

"It may be that she had not her wits," I said. "Such things have been, I have heard, and especially in the case of a woman with jewels. It may be that she knew not what she did, and in any case I pray you to think no more of it, dear madam." And all the time I spoke I was smoothing her old forehead under the flapping frills of her cap.

One black woman was there in the room, sitting in the shadow of the bed-curtains, fast asleep and making a strange purring noise like a cat as she slept.

Suddenly Madam Cavendish clutched hard at my hand. "Harry," she said, "I sent for you because I have lain here fretting lest Mary and Catherine get not home in safety with only the black people to guard them. I fear lest the Indians may be lurking about."

"Dear Madam Cavendish," I said, "you know that we stand in no more danger from the Indians."

"Nay," she persisted, "we can never tell what plans may be brewing in such savage brains. I pray thee, Harry, ride to meet them and see if they be safe."

I laughed, for the danger from Indians was long since past, but said readily enough that I would do as she wished, being, in fact, glad enough of a gallop in the moonlight, with the prospect of meeting Mary. So in a few minutes I was in the saddle and riding toward Jamestown. The night was very bright with the moon, and there was a great mist rising from the marshy lands, and such strangely pale and luminous developments in the distances of the meadows, marshalling and advancing and retreating, like companies of spectres, and lingering as if for consultation on the borders of the woods, with floating draperies caught in the boughs thereof, that one might have considered danger from others than Indians. And, indeed, I often caught the note of an owl, and once one flitted past my face and my horse shied at the evil bird, which is thought by the ignorant to be but a feathered cat and of ill omen, and indeed is considered by many who are wise to have presaged ill oftentimes, as in the cases of the deaths of the emperors Valentinian and Commodus. Be that as it may, I, having a pistol with me, shot at the bird, and, though I was as good a shot as any thereabouts, missed, and away it flew, with a great hoot as of laughter, which I am ready to swear I heard multiplied in a trice, as if the bird were joined by a whole company, and my horse shied again and would have bolted had I not held him tightly. Now, this which I am about to relate I am ready to swear did truly happen, though it may well be doubted. I had come within a short distance of Jamestown when I reached two houses of a small size, not far apart, not much removed from the fashion of the negro cabins, but inhabited by English folk. In the one dwelt a man who had been transported for a grievous crime, whether justly or not I cannot say, but his visage was such as to condemn him, and he was often in his cups and had spent many days in the stocks, and had made frequent acquaintance with the whipping-post, and with him dwelt his wife, an old dame with a tongue which had once earned her the ducking-stool in England. As I passed this house I saw over the door a great bunch of dill and vervain and white thorn, which is held to keep away witches from the threshold if gathered upon a May day. And I knew well the reason, for not many rods distant was the hut where dwelt one Margery Key, an ancient woman, who had been verily tied crosswise and thrown in a pond for witchcraft and been weighed against the church Bible, and had her body searched for witch-marks and the thatch of her house burned. I know not why she had not come to the stake withal, but instead she had fled to Virginia, where, witches being not so common, were treated with more leniency. It may have been that she had escaped the usual fate of those of her kind by being considered by some a white witch, and one who worked good instead of ill if approached rightly, though many considered that they who approached a white witch for the purpose of prof-iting by her advice or warning, were of equal guilt, and that it all led in the end to mischief. Be that as it may, this old dame Margery Key dwelt there alone in her little hut so over thatched and grown by vines, and scarce showing the shaggy slant of its roof above the bushes, that it resembled more the hole of some timid and wary animal than a human habitation. And if any visited her for consultation it was by night and secretly, and no one ever caught sight of her except now and then the nodding white frill of her cap in the green gloom of a window or the painful bend of her old back as she gathered sticks for her fire in the woods about. How she lived none knew. A little garden-patch she had, and a hive or two of bees, and a red cow, which many affirmed to have the eye of a demon, and there were those who said that her familiars stole bread for her from the plantation larders, and that often a prime ham was missed and a cut of venison, with no explanation, but who can say? Without doubt there are strange things in the earth, but we are all so in the midst of them, and even a part of their workings, that we can have no outside foothold to take fair sight thereof. Verily a man might as well strive to lift himself by his boot-straps over a stile.

But this much I will say, that, as I was riding along, cogitating something deeply in my mind as to the best disposal of the powder and the shot which Mary Cavendish had ordered from England, I, coming abreast of Margery Key's house, saw of a sudden a white cat, which many affirmed to be her familiar, spring from her door like a white arrow of speed and off down a wood-path, and my horse reared and plunged, and then, with my holding him of no avail, though I had a strong hand on the bridle, was after her with such a mad flight that I had hard work to keep the saddle. Pell-mell through the wood we went, I ducking my head before the mad lash of the branches and feeling the dew therefrom in my face like a drive of rain, until we came to a cleared space, then a great spread of tobacco fields, overlapping silver-white in the moonlight, and hamlet of negro cabins, and then Major Robert Beverly's house, standing a mass of shadow except for one moonlit wall, for all the family were gone to the governor's ball. Then, as I live, that white cat of Margery Key's led me in that mad chase around Beverly's house, and when I came to the north side of it I saw a candle gleam in a window and heard a baby's wail, and knew 'twas where his infant daughter was tended, and as we swept past out thrust a black head from the window, and a screech as savage as any wild cat's rent the peace of the night, and I believe that the child's black nurse took us, no doubt, for the devil himself. Then all the dogs howled and bayed, though not one approached us, and a great bat came fanning past, like a winged shadow, and again I heard the owl's hoot, and ever before us, like a white arrow, fled that white cat, and my horse followed in spite of me. Then, verily I speak the truth, though it may well be questioned, did that white cat lead us straight to the tomb which Major

Beverly had made upon his plantation at the death of his first wife, and in which she lay, and 'twas on a rising above the creek, and then the cat, with a wail which was like nothing I ever heard in this world, was away in a straight line toward the silver gleam of the creek, though every one knows well how cats hate water, and had disappeared. But, though to this I will not swear, I thought I saw a white gleam aloft, and heard a wail of a cat skyward along with the owl-hoots. And then my horse stood and trembled in such wise that I thought he would fall under me, and I dismounted and stroked his head and tried as best I could to soothe him, and we were all the time before the tomb, which was a large one. Then of a sudden it came to me that here was the hiding place for the powder and shot, for what safer hiding place can there be than the tomb of the first wife, when the second hath reigned but a short time, and is fair, and hath but just given her lord that little darling whose cries of appealing helplessness I could hear even there? So I gave the tomb door a pull, knowing that I should not, by so doing, disturb the slumbers of the poor lady within, and decided with myself that it would be easy enough to force it, and mounted and rode back as best I might to the road. And when I came to the little dwelling of Margery Key a thought struck me, and I rode close, though my horse shuddered as if with some strange fright of something which I could not see. I bent in my saddle and looked in the door, but naught could I see. Then I dismounted and tied my horse to a tree near by, and entered the house and looked about the sorry place as well as I could in the pale sift of moon-light, and — the old woman was not there. But one room there was, with a poor pallet in a corner and a chest against the wall and a stool, and a kettle in the fireplace, with a little pile of sticks and a great scattering of ashes, but no one there, and also, if I may be believed, *no broom*. All this I tell for what it may be worth to the credulity of them who hear; the facts be such as I have said. But whether believing it myself or not, yet knowing that that white cat, though it had been Margery Key in such guise, or her familiar imp on his way to join her at some revel whither she had ridden her broom, had done me good service, and, seeing the piteous small-ness of the pile of sticks on the hearth, and reflecting upon the dis-tressful bend of the old soul's back, whether she had sold herself to Satan or not, I lingered a minute to break down a goodly armful of brush in the wood outside and carry inside for the replenish-ment of her store. And as I came forth, having done so, I heard the door of the nearby house open, and saw two white faces peering out at me, and heard a woman's voice shriek shrilly that here was the devil seeking the witch, and though I called out to reassure them, the door clapped to with a bang like a pistol shot, and my horse danced about so that I could scarcely mount. Then I rode away, something wondering within myself, since I had been taken for the devil, how many others might have been, and whether men made their own devils and their own witches, instead of the Prince of Evil having a hand in it, and yet that happened which I have related, and I have told the truth.

XII

Such a blaze of light as was the governor's mansion house that night I never saw, and I heard the music of violins, and hautboys, and viola da gambas coming from within, and a silvery babble of women's tongues, with a deeper undertone of men's, and the tread of dancing feet, and the stamping of horses outside, with the whoas of the negro boys in attendance, and through the broad gleam of the moonlight came the flare and smoke of the torches. It seemed as if the whole colony was either dancing at the governor's ball or standing outside on tiptoe with interest. I sat waiting for some time, holding my restive horse as best I might, but there coming no cessation in the music, I dismounted, and seeing one of Madam Cavendish's black men, gave him the bridle to hold, and went up to the house and entered, though not in my plum coloured velvet, and, indeed, being not only in my ordinary clothes, but somewhat splashed with mire from my mad gallop through the woods. But I judged rightly that in so much of a crowd I should pass unnoticed both as to myself and my apparel. I stood in the great room near the door and watched the dance, and 'twas as brilliant a scene as ever I had seen anywhere even in England. The musicians in the gallery were sawing away for their lives on violins, and working breathlessly at the hautboys, and all that gay company of Virginia's best, spinning about in a country dance of old England. Such a brave show of velvet coats, and breeches, and flowered brocade waistcoats, and powdered wigs, and feathers, and laces, and ribbons, and rich flaunts of petticoats revealing in the whirl of the dance clocked hose on slender ankles, and high-heeled satin shoes, would have done no discredit to the court. But of them all, Mistress Mary Cavendish was the belle and the star. She was dancing with my Lord Estes when I entered, and such a goodly couple they were, that I heard many an exclamation of delight from the spectators, who stood thickly about the walls, the windows even being filled with faces of black and white servants. My Lord Estes was a handsome dark man, handsomer and older than Sir Humphrey Hyde, who, though dancing with the governor's daughter Cate, had, I could see, a rueful eye of watchfulness toward Mary Cavendish. As he and Cate Culpeper swung past me, Sir Humphrey's eyes fell on my face and he gave a start and blush, and presently, when the dance was over and his partner seated, came up to me with hand extended, as if I had been the noblest guest there. "Harry, Harry," he whispered eagerly, "she hath danced with me three times tonight, and hath promised again, and Harry, saw you ever any one so beautiful as she in that blue dress?"

I answered truthfully that I never had. Sir Humphrey, in his blue velvet suit with the silver buttons, with his rosy face and powdered wig, was one to look at twice and yet again, and I regarded him as always, with that liking for him and that fury of jealousy.

I looked at him and loved him as I might have loved my son, with such a sweet and brave honesty of simplicity he eyed me, and for the sake of Mary Cavendish, who might find his love for her precious, and I wished with all my heart that I might fling him to the floor where he stood; every nerve and muscle in me tingled with the restraint of the desire, for such an enhancement of a woman's beauty as was Mary Cavendish's that night, will do away with the best instincts of men, whether they will or not.

The next dance was the minuet, and Mary Cavendish danced it with my Lord Culpeper, the Governor of Virginia. The governor, though I liked him not, was a most personable man with much grace of manner, which had additional value from a certain harshness of feature which led one not to expect such suavity, and he was clad most richly in such a dazzle of gold broidery and fling of yellow laces, and glitter of buttons, as could not be surpassed.

My Lord was in fact clad much more richly than his wife and daughter, whose attire, though fair enough, was not of the freshest. It was my good luck to overhear my Lady Culpeper telling in no very honeyed tones, a gossip of hers, the lady of one of the burgesses, that her goods, for which she had sent to England, had miscarried, and were it not for the fact that there was a whisper of fever on the ship, she would have had the captain herself for a good rating, and had my Lord Culpeper not been for him, saying that the man was of an honest record, she would have had him set in the stocks for his remissness, that he had not seen to it that her goods were on board when the ship sailed. "And there goes poor Cate in her old murrey-coloured satin petticoat," said my lady with a bitter lengthening of her face, "and there is Mary Cavendish in a blue-flowered satin with silver, which is the very twin of the one I ordered for Cate, and which came in on the Cavendish ship."

"Well," said the other woman, who was long and lean, and had wedded late in life a man she would have scorned in her girlhood, and could not forgive the wrong she had done herself, and was filled with an inconsistency of spleen toward all younger and fairer than she, and who, moreover, was a born toad-eater for all in high places, "'tis fine feathers make fine birds, and were thy

Cate arrayed in that same gown in Mistress Cavendish's stead —"

"As I believe, she would not have had the dress had not Cate told Cicely Hyde, who is so intimate with Mary Cavendish," said my Lady Culpeper. "I had it from my lord's sister that 'twas the newest fashion in London. How else would the chit have heard of it, I pray?"

"How else, indeed?" asked the burgess's wife.

"And here my poor Cate must go in her old murrey-coloured petticoat," said my lady.

"But even thus, to one who looks at her and not at her attire, she outshines Mary Cavendish," said the other. That was, to my thinking, as flagrant hypocrisy as was ever heard, for if those two maids had been clad alike as beggars, Mary Cavendish would have carried off the palm, with no dissenting voice, though Cate Culpeper was fair enough to see, with her father's grace of manner, and his harshness of feature softened by her rose-bloom of youth.

Catherine Cavendish was dancing as the others, but seemingly with no heart in it, whereas her sister was all glowing with delight in the merriment of it, and her sense of her own beauty, and the admiration of all about her, and smiling as if the whole world, and at life itself, with the innocent radiance of a child.

As I stood watching her, I felt a touch on my arm, and looked, and there stood Mistress Cicely Hyde, and her brown face was so puckered with wrath and jealousy that I scarcely knew her. "Did not Mary's grandmother send you to escort her home, Master Wingfield?" said she in a sharp whisper, and I stared at her in amazement. "When the ball is over, Mistress Hyde," I said.

"'Tis time the ball was over now," said she. "'Tis folly to keep it up so late as this, and Mary hath not had a word for me since we came."

"But why do you not dance yourself, Mistress Hyde?"

"I care not to dance," said she pettishly, and with a glance of mingled wrath and admiration at Mary Cavendish that might have matched mine or her brother's, and I marvelled deeply at the waywardness of a maid's heart. But then came Ralph Drake, who had not drunken very deeply, being only flushed, and somewhat lost to discrimination, and disposed to dance with another since he could not have his cousin Mary, and he and Cicely went away together, and presently, when the minuet was over and another dance on, I saw them advancing in time, but always Cicely had that eye of watchful injury upon Mary.

It was late when the ball was done, but Mary would have stayed it out had it not been for Catherine, who almost swooned in the middle of a dance and had to be revived with aromatic vinegar, and lie for a while in my Lady Culpeper's bedchamber, with a black woman fanning her, until she was sufficiently recovered to go home. Mary did not espy me until, returning from her sister's side to order the sedan chairs, she jostled against me. Then such a blush of delight and relief came over her face as made my heart stand still with rapture and something like fear. "You here, you here, Harry?" she cried, and stammered and blushed again, and Sir Humphrey and Cicely, who were pressing up, looked at me jealously.

"I am here at your grandmother's request, Mistress Mary," I said.

Then my Lord Estes came elbowing me aside, and made no more of me than if I were a black slave, and hoarsely shouting for the sedan chairs and the bearers, and after him Ralph Drake and half a score of others, and all cursing at me for a convict tutor and thrusting at me. Then truly that temper of mine, which I have had some cause to lament, and yet I know not if it be aught I can help, it being seemingly as beyond the say of my own will as the recoil of a musket or the rebound of a ball, sent me forth into the midst of that gallant throng, and I would not say for certain, but at this late date I am inclined to believe that I saw Ralph Drake, who came in my way with a storm of curses, raising himself sorely from a pool of mud, which must have worked havoc with his velvets, and my Lord Estes struggling forth from a thorny rose bush at the gate, with much rending of precious laces. Then I, convict though I was, yet having, when authorised by the very conditions of my servitude, that resolution to have my way, that a king's army could not have stopped me, had the sedan chairs, and the bearers to the fore, and presently we were set forth on the homeward road, I riding alongside. All the road was white with moonlight, and when we came alongside Margery Key's house, as I live, that white cat shot through the door, and immediately after, I, looking back, saw the old dame herself standing therein, though it was near morning, and she quavered forth a blessing after me. "God bless thee, Master Wingfield, in life and death, and may the fish of the sea come to thy line, may the birds of the air minister to thee, and all that hath breath of life, whether it be noxious or guileless, do thy bidding. May even He who is nameless stand from the path of thy desire, and hold back from thy face the boughs of prevention whither thou wouldst go." This said old Margery Key in a strange, chantinglike tone, and withdrew, and a light flashed out in the next house, and the woman who dwelt therein screamed, and

Mistress Mary, thrusting forth her head from the chair, called me to come close.

As for Catherine, she was borne along as silently as though she slept, being, I doubt not, still exhausted with her swoon. When I came close to Mistress Mary's chair, forth came her little hand, shining with that preciousness of fairness beyond that of a pearl, and "Master Wingfield," said she in a whisper, lest she disturb Catherine, "what, what, I pray thee, was it the witch-woman said?"

I laughed. "She was calling down a blessing upon my head, Madam," I said.

"A blessing and not a curse?"

"As I understood it, though I know not why she should have blessed me."

"They say she is a white witch, and worketh good instead of harm, and yet —" said Mistress Mary, and her voice trembled, showing her fear, and I could see the negroes rolling eyes of wide alarm at me, for they were much affected by all hints of deviltry.

"I pray you, Madam, to have no fear," I said, and thought within myself that never should she know of what had happened on my way thither.

"They say that her good deeds work in the end to mischief," said Mary, "and, and — 'tis sure no good whatever can come from unlawful dealing with the powers of evil even in a good cause. I wish the witch-woman had neither cursed thee nor blessed thee, Harry."

I strove again to reassure her, and said, as verily I begun to believe, that the old dame's words whether of cursing or blessing were of no moment, but presently Mistress Mary declared herself afraid of riding alone shut within her sedan chair, and would alight, and have one of the slaves lead my horse, and walk with me, taking my arm the remainder of the way.

I had never known Mistress Mary Cavendish to honour me so before, and knew not to what to attribute it, whether to alarm as she said, or not. And I knew not whether to be enraptured or angered at my own rapture, or whether I should use or not that authority which I had over her, and which she could not, strive as best she could, gainsay, and bid her remain in her chair.

But being so sorely bewildered I did nothing, but let her have her way, and on toward Drake Hill we walked, she clinging to my arm, and seemingly holding me to a slow pace, and the slaves with the chairs, and my horse, forging ahead with ill-concealed zeal on account of that chanting proclamation of Margery Key, which, I will venture to say, was considered by every one of the poor fellows as a special curse directed toward him, instead of a blessing for me.

As we followed on that moonlight night, she and I alone, of a sudden I felt my youth and love arise to such an assailing of the joy of life, that I knew myself dragged as it were by it, and had no more choosing as to what I should not do. Verily it would be easier to lead an army of malcontents than one's own self. And something there was about the moonlight on that fair Virginian night, and the heaviness of the honey-scents, and the pressure of love and life on every side, in bush and vine and tree and nest, which seemed to overbear me and sweep me along as on the crest of some green tide of spring. Verily there are forces of this world which are beyond the overcoming of mortal man so long as he is encumbered by his mortality.

Mary Cavendish gathered up her blue and silver petticoats about her as closely as a blue flower-bell at nightfall, and stepped along daintily at my side, and the feel of her little hand on my arm seemed verily the only touch of material things which held me to this world. We came to a great pool of wet in our way, and suddenly I thought of her feet in her little satin shoes. "Madam, you will wet your feet if you walk through that pool in your satin shoes," I said, and my voice was so hoarse with tenderness that I would not have known it for my own, and I felt her arm tremble. "No," she said faintly. But without waiting for any permission, around her waist I put an arm, and had her raised in a twinkling from the ground, and bore her across the pool, she not struggling, but only whispering faintly when I set her down after it was well passed. "You — you should not have done that, Harry."

Then of a sudden, close she pressed her soft cheek against my shoulder as we walked, and whispered, as though she could keep silent no longer, and yet as if she swooned for shame in breaking silence: "Harry, Harry, I liked the way you thrust them aside when they were rude with you, to do me a service, and Harry, you are stronger, and — and — than them all."

Then I knew with such a shock of joy, that I wonder I lived, that the child loved me, but I knew at the same time as never I had known it before, my love for her.

"Mistress Mary," I said, "I but did my duty and my service, which you can always count upon, and I did no more than others would have done. Sir Humphrey Hyde —"

But she flung away from me at that with a sudden movement of amazement and indignation and hurt, which cut me to the quick. "Yes," she said, "yes, Master Wingfield, truly I believe that Sir Humphrey Hyde would do me any service that came in his way, and truly he is a brave lad. I have a great esteem for Humphrey — I have a greater esteem for Humphrey than for all the rest — and I care not if you know it, Master Wingfield."

So saying she called to the bearers of her chair, and would have a slave assist her to it instead of me, and rode in silence the rest of the way, I following, walking my horse, who pulled hard at his bits.

XIII

It was dawn before we were abed, but I for one had no sleep, being strained to such a pitch of rapture and pain by what I had discovered. The will I had not, to take the joy which I seemed to see before me like some brimming cup of the gods, but not yet, in the first surprise of knowing it offered me, the will to avoid the looking upon it, and the tasting of it in dreams. Over and over I said to myself, and every time with a new strengthening of resolution, that Mary Cavendish should not love me, and that in some way I would force her to obey me in that as in other things, never doubting that I could do so. Well I knew that she could not wed a convict, nor could I clear myself unless at the expense of her sister Catherine, and sure I was that she would not purchase love itself at such a cost as that. There remained nothing but to turn her fancy from me, and that seemed to me an easy task, she being but a child, and having, I reasoned, but little more than a childish first love for me, which, as every one knows, doth readily burn itself out by its excess of wick, and lack of substantial fuel. And yet, as I lay on my bed with the red dawn at the windows, and the birds calling outside, and the scent of the opening blossoms entering invisible, such pangs of joy and ecstasy beyond anything which I had ever known on earth overwhelmed me that I could not resist them. Knowing well that in the end I should prove my strength, for the time I gave myself to that advance of man before the spur of love, which I doubt not is after the same fashion as the unfolding of the flowers in the spring, and the nesting of the birds, and the movement of the world itself from season to season, and would be as uncontrollable were it not that a man is mightier even than that to which he owes his own existence, and hath the power of putting that which he loves before his own desire of it. But for the time, knowing well that I could at any time take up the reins to the bridling of myself, I let them hang loose, and over and over I whispered what Mary Cavendish had said, and over and over I felt that touch of delicate tenderness on my arm, and I built up such great castles that they touched the farthest skies of my fancy, and all the time braving the knowledge that I should myself dash them into ruins.

But when I looked out of my window that May morning, and saw that wonderful fair world, and that heaven of blue light with rosy and golden and green boughs blowing athwart it, and heard the whir of looms, the calls and laughs of human life, the coo of dove, the hum of bees, the trill of mock birds, outreaching all other heights of joy, the clangour of the sea-birds, and the tender rustle of the new-leaved branches in the wind, that love for me which I had seen in the heart of the woman I had loved since I could remember, seemed my own keynote of the meaning of life sounding in my ears above all other sounds of bane or blessing.

But the strength I had to act in discord with it, and thrust my joy from me, and I went to planning how I could best turn the child's fancy from myself to some one who would be for her best good. And yet I was not satisfied with Sir Humphrey Hyde, and wished that his wits were quicker, and wondered if years might improve them, and if perchance a man as honest might be found who had the keenness of ability to be the worst knave in the country. But the boy was brave, and I loved his love for Mary Cavendish, and I could think of no one to whom I would so readily trust her, and it seemed to me that perchance I might, by some praising of him, and swerving her thoughts to his track, lead her to think favourably of his suit. But a man makes many a mistake as to women, and one of the most frequent is that the hearts of them are like wax, to be moulded into this and that shape. That morning, when I met Mistress Mary at the breakfast table, she was pale and distraught, and not only did not speak to me nor look at me, but when I ventured to speak in praise of Sir Humphrey's gallant looks at the ball, she turned upon me so fiercely with encomiums of my Lord Estes, whom I knew to be not worthy of her, that I held my tongue. But when Sir Humphrey came riding up a little later, she greeted him with such warmth as at once put me to torture, and aroused that spirit of defence of her against myself which hath been the noblest thing in my poor life.

So I left them, Mistress Catherine at the flax-wheel, and Mary out in the garden with Sir Humphrey, gathering roses for the pot-pourri jars, and the distilling into rosewater, for little idleness was permitted at Drake Hill even after a ball. I got my horse, but as I started forth Madam Cavendish called — a stiffly resolute old figure standing in the great doorway, and I dismounted and went to her, leading my horse, which I had great ado to keep from nibbling the blossoms of a rose tree which grew over the porch. "Harry," she said in a whisper, "where is Mary?"

"In the garden with Sir Humphrey Hyde," I answered.

Then Madam Cavendish frowned. "And why is she not at her lessons?" she asked sternly.

"The lessons are set for the afternoon, and this morning she is gathering rose leaves, Madam," I answered; but that Madam Cavendish knew as well as I, having in truth so ordered the hours of the lessons.

"But," she said, hesitating, then she stopped, and looked at me with an angry indecision, and then at the garden, where the top of Mary's golden head was just visible above the pink mist of the roses, and Sir Humphrey's fair one bending over it. "Harry," she said, frowning, and yet with a piteous sort of appeal. "Why do you not go out into the garden and help to gather the rose leaves?" Then, before I could answer, as if angry with herself at her own folly, she called out to Mary's little black maid, Sukey, to bid her mistress come in from the garden and spin. But before the maid started I said low in Madam Cavendish's ear: "Madam, think you not that the sweet air of the garden is better for her after the ball, than the hot ball and the labour at the wheel?" And she gave one look at me, and called out to Sukey that she need not speak to her mistress, and went inside to her own work and left me to go my way. I was relieved in my mind that she did not ask me whither, since, if she had, I should have been driven to one of those broadsides of falsehood in a good cause for which I regret the necessity, but admit it, and if it be to my soul's hurt, I care not, so long as I save the other party by it.

I was bound for Barry Upper Branch, and rode thither as fast as I could, for I contemplated asking the Barry brothers to aid me in the removal of Mistress Mary's contraband goods, and was anxious to lose no more time about that than I could avoid.

I was set upon Major Robert Beverly's tomb as a most desirable hiding place for them, and knowing that there was a meeting of the Assembly that evening at the governor's, to discuss some matters in private before he sailed for England, Major Beverly being clerk, I thought that before the moon was up would be a favourable time for the removal, but I could not move the goods alone, remembering how those sturdy sailors tugged at them, and not deeming it well to get any aid from the slaves.

So I rode straight to Barry Upper Branch, and a handsome black woman in a flaunting gown, with a great display of beads, and an orange silk scarf twisted about her head, came to parley with me, and told me that both the brothers were away, and added that she thought I should find them at the tavern.

The tavern was a brick building abounding in sharp slants of roof, and dimmed in outline by a spreading cloud of new-leaved branches, and there was one great honey-locust which was a marvel to be seen, and hummed with bees with a mighty drone as of all the spinning-wheels in the country, and the sweetness of it blew down upon one passing under, like a wind of breath. And before the tavern were tied, stamping and shaking their heads for the early flies, many fine horses, and among them Parson Downs' and the Barry brothers', and from within the tavern came the sound of laughter in discordant shouts, and now and then a snatch of a song. Then a great hoarse rumble of voice would cap the rest, telling some loose story, then the laughter would follow — enough, it seemed, to make the roof shake — and all the time the hum of the bees in the honey-locust outside went on. Verily at that time in Virginia, with all the spirit of the people in a ferment of rebellion against the established order of things, being that same ferment which the ardour of Nathaniel Bacon had set in motion, and which, so far as I see now, was the beginning of an epoch of history, there was nothing after all, no plotting nor counterplotting, no fierce inveighing against authority, nor reckless carousing on the brinks of precipices, which could for a second stay the march of the mightiest force of all — the spring which had returned in its majesty of victory, for thousands of years, and love which had come before that.

I tied my horse with the others, with a tight halter, for he was apt to pick quarrels, having always a theory that such discomforts as flies or a long weariness of standing were in some fashion to be laid to the doors of other horses, and indeed made always of his own kind his special scapegoat of the dispensation of Providence. 'Tis little I know about that great mystery of the animal creation and its relation toward the human race, but verily I believe that that fine horse of mine, from his propensity for kicking and lashing out from his ironbound hoofs at whatever luckless steed came within his reach whenever the world went not to his liking, could not see an inch beyond the true horizon limit of the horse race, and attributed all that happened on earth, including man, to the agency of his own sort. Sure I was, from the backward glance of viciousness which he cast at the other stamping steeds as soon as I dismounted, that he concluded with no hesitation they had in some way led me to ride him thither instead of to his snug berth in the Cavendish stables, with his eager nose in his feed trough.

Before I entered the tavern, out burst Parson Downs, and caught hold of me, with a great shout of welcome. Half drunk he was, and yet with a marvellous steadiness on his legs, and a command of his voice which would have done him credit in the pulpit. It was said that this great parson could drink more fiery liquor and not betray it than any other man in the colony, and Nick Barry, who was something of a wag, said that the parson's wrestlings with spirits of another sort had rendered him powerful in his encounters with these also. Be that as it may, though I doubt not Parson Downs had drunk more than any man there, no sign of it was in his appearance, except that his boisterousness was something enhanced, and his hand on my shoulder fevered. "Good day, good day, Master Harry Wingfield," he shouted. "How goes the time with ye, sir? And, I say, Master Wingfield, what will you take for thy horse there? One I have which can beat him on any course you will pick, with all the creeks in the country to jump, and the devil himself to have a shy at, and even will I trade and give thee twenty pounds of tobacco to boot. 'Tis a higher horse than thine, Harry, and can take two strides to one of his; and mine hath four white feet, and thine but one, which, as every one knoweth well, is not enough. What say you, Harry?"

"Your reverence," I said, laughing, "the horse is not mine, as you know."

"Nay, Harry," he burst forth, "that we all know, and you know that we all know, is but a fable. Doth not Madam Cavendish treat you as a son, and are you not a convict in name only, so far as she is concerned? I say, Harry, you can ride my horse to the winning on Royal Oak Day, at the races. What think you, Harry?"

"Your reverence," I said, "I pray you to give me time," for well I knew there was no use in reasoning with the persistency to which frequent potations had given rise.

Up to my horse he went with that oversteadiness of the man in his cups, who moves with the stiffness of a tree walking, as if every lift of a heavy foot was the uplifting of a root fast in the ground, and went to stroking his head; when straightway, my horse either not liking his touch or the smell of his liquored breath, and judging as was his wont that the fault must by some means lie with his own race, straightway lashed out a vicious hind leg like a hammer, and came within an ace of the parson's own valuable horse — not the one which he proposed trading for mine — and the wind of the lash frighted the parson's horse, and he in his turn lashed out, and another horse at his side sprang aside; and straightway there was such a commotion in the tavern yard as never was, and slaves and white servants shouting, and forcing rearing horses to their regular standing, and I stroking my beast, and striving as best I could to bring his pure horse wits to comprehend the strong pressure and responsibility of humanity for the situation; and the Barry brothers and Captain Jaynes came running forth, Captain Jaynes swearing in such wise that it was beyond the understanding of any man unversed in that language of the high seas; and Nick Barry, laughing wildly, and Dick, glooming, as was the difference with the two brothers when in liquor. And the landlord, one John Halpin, stood in his tavern doorway with his eyebrows raised, but no other sign of consternation, knowing well enough that all this could not affect his custom, and being one of the most toughly leather-dried little men whom I have ever seen, and his face so hardened into its final lines of experience, that it had no power of changing under new ones. And behind him stood peering, some with wide eyes of terror, and some with ready laughs at nothing, the few other roisters in the tavern at that hour. 'Twas not the best time of day for the meeting of those choice spirits for the discussion of the other spirits which be raised, willy-nilly, from the grape and the grain, for the enhancing of the joy of life, and defiance of its miseries; but the Barrys and Captain Jaynes and the parson were nothing particular as to the time of day.

When the horses were something quieted, I, desiring not to unfold my errand in the tavern, got hold of Parson Downs by his mighty arm, and elbowed Dick Barry, who cursed at me for it, and cut short Captain Jaynes's last string of oaths, and hallooed to Nick Barry, and asked if I could have a word with them. Captain Jaynes, though, as I have said, being in the main curiously well disposed toward me, swore at first that he would be damned if he would stop better business to parley with a damned convict tutor; but the end of it was that he and the Barry brothers and Parson Downs and I stood together under that mighty humming locust tree, and I unfolded my scheme of moving the powder and shot from Locust Creek to Major Robert Beverly's tomb. Noel Jaynes stared at me a second, with his hard red face agape, and then he clapped me upon the shoulder, and shouted with laughter, and swore that it should be done, and that it was a burning hell shame that the goods had been put where they were to the risk of a maid of beauty like Mary Cavendish, and that he and the Barrys would be with me that very night before moonrise to move them.

Then the parson, who had a poetical turn, especially when in his cups, added, quite gravely, that no safer place could there be for powder than the tomb of love whose last sparks had died out in ashes; and Dick Barry cried with an oath that it would serve Robert Beverly rightly for his action against them in the Bacon rising, for though he was to the front with the oppressed people in this, his past foul treachery against them was not forgot, and well he remembered that when he was in hiding for his life —

But then his brother hushed him and said, with a shout of dry laughter, that the past was past, and no use in dwelling upon it, but that when it came to a safe hiding place for goods which were to set the kingdom in a blaze, and maybe hang the ringleaders, he knew of none better than the tomb of a first wife, which, when the second was in full power, was verily back of the farthest back door of a man's memory.

So it was arranged that the four were to meet me that very night after sunset and before moonrise, and move the goods, and I mounted and rode away, with Parson Downs shouting after me his proposition to trade horses, and even offering ten pounds to boot when he saw the splendid long pace of my thoroughbred flinging out his legs with that freest motion of anything in the world, unless it be the swift upward cleave of a bird when the fluttering of wing wherewith he hath gained his impetus hath ceased, and nothing except that invincible rising is seen.

XIV

The first man my eyes fell upon was Parson Downs, lolling in a chair by the fireless hearth, for there was no call for fire that May night. His bulk of body swept in a vast curve from his triple chin to the floor, and his great rosy face was so exaggerated with merriment and good cheer that it looked like one seen in the shining swell of a silver tankard. When Nick Barry finished a roaring song, he stamped and clapped and shouted applause till it set off the others with applause of it, and the place was a pandemonium. Then that same coloured woman who had parleyed with me the other day, and was that night glowing like a savage princess — as in truth she may have been, for she had a high look as of an unquenched spirit, in spite of her degradation of body and estate — went about with a free swinging motion of hips, bearing a tray filled with pewter mugs of strong spirits. Around this woman's neck glittered row on row of beads, and she wore a great flame-coloured turban, and long gold eardrops dangled to her shoulders against the glossy blackness of her cheeks, and bracelets tinkled on her polished arms, which were mighty shapely, though black. In faith, the wench, had she but possessed roses and lilies for her painting, instead of that duskiness as of the cheek of midnight, had been a beauty such as was seldom seen. Her dark face was instinct with mirth and jollity, and, withal, a fierce spark in the whitening roll of her eyes under her flame coloured turban made one think of a tiger-cat, and roused that knowledge of danger which adds a tingle to interest. A man could scarce take his eyes from her, though there were other women there and not uncomely ones. Another black wench there was, clad as gayly, but sunk in a languorous calm like a great cat, with Nick Barry, now his song was done, lolling against her, and two white women, one young and well favoured, and the other harshly handsome, both with their husbands present, and I doubt not decent women enough, though something violent of temper. As I entered, Mistress Allgood, one of them, begun a harangue at the top of a shrill voice, with her husband plucking vainly at her sleeve to temper her vehemence. Mistress Allgood was long and lean, and gaunt, with red fires in the hollows of her cheeks and a compelling flash of black eyes under straight frowning brows. "Gentlemen," said she — "be quiet, John Allgood, my speech I will have, since thou being a man hath not the tongue of one. I pray ye, gentlemen listen to my cause of complaint. Here my goodman and me did come to this oppressed colony of Virginia, seven years since, having together laid by fifty pound from the earnings of an inn called the Jolly Yeoman in Norfolkshire, in which for many years we had run long scores with little return, and we bought a small portion of land and planted tobacco, and set out trees. Then came the terror of the Indians, and Governor Berkeley, always in wait for the word of the king, and doing nothing, and once was our house burned, and we escaped barely with our lives, and then came Nat Bacon, and blessings upon him, for he made the beginning of a good work. And then did the soldiers riding to meet him, so trample down our tobacco fields with horse hoofs, that the leaves lay in a green pumice, and that crop lost. And then this Navigation Act, which I understand but little of except that it be to fill the king's pockets and empty ours, has made our crops of no avail, since we but sent the tobacco as a gift to the king, so little we have got in return. And look, look!" she shrieked, "I pray ye look, and sure this is the best I have, and me always going as well attired as any of my station in England. I pray ye look! Sure 'tis past mending, and the stitches and the cloth go together, as will the colony, unless somewhat be done in season to mend its state." So saying, up she flung her arm, and all the under side of the body of her gown was in rags, and up she flung the other, and that was in like case.

Then the other woman, who was a strapping lass, and had been a barmaid ere she came to Virginia in search of a husband, where she had found one Richard Longman afraid not to do her bidding and wed her, since he was as small and mild a man as ever was, joined in: "I say with Mistress Allgood," she shrieked out, and flung her own buxom arms aloft with such disclosures that a roar of laughter spread through the hall, and her husband blushed purple, and a protest gurgled in his throat. But at that his wife, who verily was a shrew, seized upon him by both of his little shoulders, and shook him until his face wagged like a rag baby with an utter limpness of helplessness, and shouted out, amid peals of laughter that seemed to shake the roof, that here was a pretty man, here forsooth was a pretty man. Here was her own husband, who let his own lawful wife go clad in such wise and lifted not a finger! Yes, lifted not a finger, and had to be dragged into the present doings by the very hair of his head by his wife, and that was not all. Yes, that was not all. Then, with that, up she flung one stout foot, and lo, a great hole was in the heel of her stocking, and the other, and then she flirted the hem of her petticoat into sight, and that was all of a fringe with rags. "Look, look!" she shrieked out. "I tell ye, Thomas Longman, I will have them look, and see to what a pass that cursed Navigation Act and the selling of the tobacco for naught, hath brought a decent woman. How long is it since I had a new petticoat? How long, I pray? Oh, Lord, had the men of this colony but the spirit of the women! Had but brave Nat Bacon lived!" With that, this woman, who had been perchance drinking too much beer for her head, though she was well used to it, burst into a storm of tears, and sprang to her feet, and cried out in a wild voice like a furious cat's: "Up with ye, I say! And why do ye stop and parley? And why do ye wait for my Lord Culpeper to sail? I trow the women be not afraid of the governor, if the men be! Up with ye, and this very night cut down the young tobacco plants, and cheat the king of England, who reigns but to rob his subjects. Who cares for the Governor of Virginia? Who cares for the king? Up with ye, I say!" With that she snatched a sword from a peg on the wall and swung it in a circle of flame around her head, and what with her glowing eyes and streaming black locks, and burning beauty of cheeks, and catlike shriek of voice, she was enough to have made the governor, and even the king himself, quail, had he been there, and all the time that mild husband of hers was plucking vainly at her gown. But the men only shouted with laughter, and presently the woman, with a savage glare at them, sank into her chair again, and Mistress Allgood went up to her, and the two whispered with handsome, fiercely wagging heads. Then entered another woman, after a clatter of horse's hoofs in the drive, and she had a presence that compelled all the men except one to their feet, though there was about her that foolishness which, in my mind, doth always hamper the extreme of enthusiasm. This woman, Madam Tabitha Story, was a widow of considerable property, owning a plantation and slaves, and she had, as was well known, gone mad with zeal in the cause of Nathaniel Bacon, and had furnished him with money, and would herself have fought for him had she been allowed. But Bacon, though no doubt with gratitude for her help, had, as I believe is the usual case with brave men, when set about with adoring women, but little liking for her. It was, in faith, a curious sight she presented as she entered that hall of Barry Upper Branch with the men rising and bowing low, and the other women eyeing her, half with defiant glares as of respectability on the defence, and half with admiration and comradeship, for she was to the far front in this rebellion as in the other. Madam Story was a woman so tall that she exceeded the height of many a man, and she was clad in black, and crowned with a great hat feathered with sable like a hearse, and her skin was of a whiteness more dazzling against the black than any colour. Her face had been handsome had it not been so elongated and strained out of its proper lines of beauty, and her forehead was of a wonderful height, a smooth expanse between bunches of black curls, and in the midst was set that curious patch which she had worn ever since Bacon's untimely death, it being, as I live, nothing more nor less than a mourning coach and four horses, cut so cunningly out of black paper that it was a marvel of skill.

She stared with scorn at the one black woman approaching her with the silver tray, then she turned and stared at Nick Barry, sitting half overcome with drink, lolling against the other. He cast a look of utter sheepishness at her, and then straightened himself, and rose like the other men, and Dick Barry motioned to both of the black women to withdraw, which they did, slinking out darkly, both with a fine rustle of silks. Then Madam Story saluted the other women, though somewhat stiffly, and Dick Barry, who was never lacking in a certain gloomy dignity, though they said him to be the worse of the two brothers, stepped forward. "Madam," he said, "I pray you to be seated." With that he led her with a courtly air to a great carved chair, in which his father had been used to sit, and she therein, somewhat mollified, her black length doubled on itself, and that mourning coach on her forehead was a wonderful sight.

Then arrived Major Robert Beverly and another notable man, one of the burgesses, whose name I do to this day conceal, in consequence of a vow to that effect, and then two more. Then Major Beverly, who was in fact running greater risks than almost any, inasmuch as he was Clerk of the Assembly, and was betraying more of trust, after he had saluted Madam Story conferred privately with Dick Barry, and my Lord Estes, and Parson Downs, with this effect. Dick Barry, with such a show of gallantry and seriousness as never was, prevailed upon the three ladies to forgive him his discourtesy, but hinted broadly that in an enterprise fraught with so much danger, it were best that none but the ruder sex should confer together, and they departed; Mistress Longman enjoining upon her husband to remain and deport himself like a man of spirit, and Mistress Allgood whispering with a sharp hiss into her goodman's alarmed ear, he nodding the while in token of assent.

But Madam Tabitha Story paused on the threshold ere she departed, standing back on her heels with a marvellous dignity, and waving one long, black-draped arm. "Gentlemen of Virginia," said she, in a voice of such solemnity as I had never heard excelled, "I beseech you to remember the example which that

hero who has departed set you. I beseech you to form your proceedings after the fashion of those of the immortal Bacon, and
remember that if the time comes when a woman's arm is needed
to strike for freedom, here is one at your service, while the heart
which moves it beats true to liberty and the great dead!"

Nick Barry was chuckling in a maudlin fashion when the door
closed behind her, and Parson Downs' great face was curving
upward with smiles like a wet new moon, but the rest were sober
enough in spite of some over indulgence, for in truth it was a grave
matter which they had met to decide, and might mean the loss of
life and liberty to one and all.

Major Robert Beverly turned sharply upon me as soon as the
women were gone, and accosted me civilly enough, though the
memory of my convict estate was in his tone. "Master Wingfield,"
said he, "may I inquire —" "Sir," I replied, for I had so made up my
mind, "I am with you in the cause, and will so swear, if my oath be
considered of sufficient moment."

I know not how proudly and bitterly I said that last, but Major
Beverly looked at me, and a kindly look came into his eyes.
"Master Wingfield," he said, "the word of any English gentleman
is sufficient," and I could have blessed him for it, and have ever
since had remorse for my taking advantage of his dark closet of an
old love for the hiding of the secret of the ammunition.

Then as we sat there, in a blue cloud of tobacco smoke,
through which the green bayberry candles gleamed faintly, and
which they could not overcome with their aromatic breath of
burning, the plot for the rooting up of the young crop was dis-
cussed in all its bearings.

I wondered somewhat to see Major Beverly, and still others of
the burgesses who presently arrived, placing their lives in jeopardy with men of such standing as some present. But a common
cause makes common confidence, and it might well have been,
hang one, hang all. Major Robert Beverly spoke at some length,
and his speech was, according to my mind, both wise and discreet,
though probably somewhat inflamed by his own circumstances.
The greatest store of tobacco of any one in the colony had Major
Robert Beverly, and a fair young wife who loved that which the
proceeds could buy. And as he spoke there was a great uproar outside, and the tramp of horses and jingle of swords and spurs, and a
whole troop of horse came riding into the grounds of Barry Upper
Branch. And some of those in the hall turned pale and looked
about for an exit, and some grasped their swords, and some
laughed knowingly, and Major Beverly strode to the door, and

behind him Parson Downs, and Capt. Noel Jaynes, and the Barry brothers, and some others, and I, pressing close, and there was a half whispered conference between Major Beverly and the leader of the horse. Then Major Beverly turned to us. "Gentlemen," he said, "I am assured that in case of a rising we have naught to fear from the militia, who are in like case with the other sufferers from the proceedings of the government, being about to be disbanded in arrears of their pay. Gentlemen, I am assured by Capt. Thomas Marvyn that his men are with us in heart and purpose, and though they may not help, unless the worse come to the worse, they will not hinder."

Then such a cheer went up from the conspirators in the hall of Barry Upper Branch, and the troop of horse outside, as it seemed, might have been heard across the sea which divided us from that tyranny which ruled us, and Nick Barry shouted to some of his black slaves, and presently every man of the soldiers was drinking cider made from the apples of Virginia, and with it, treason to the king and success to the rebels.

XV

I had not formed my plan of taking part in the coming insurrection without many misgivings lest I should by so doing bring harm upon the Cavendishes. But on discussing the matter in all its bearings with Major Robert Beverly, whom I had ever held to be a man of judgment, he assured me that in his opinion there could no possible ill result come to such a household of women, especially when the head of it was of such openly avowed royalist leanings. Unless, indeed, he admitted, the bringing over of the arms and the powder was to be traced to Mistress Mary Cavendish. This he said, not knowing the secret of his first wife's tomb, and I feeling, as indeed I was, an arch deceiver. But what other course is left open to any man, when he can shield the one he loves best in the whole world only at the expense of some one else? Can he do otherwise but let the other suffer, and even forfeit his sense of plain dealing? I have lived to be an old man, and verily nothing hath so grown in the light of my experience as the impossibility of serving love except at a loss, not only to others, but to oneself. But that truth of the greatest importance in the whole world hath also grown upon me, that love should be served at whatever cost. I cared not then, and I care not now, who suffered and who was wronged, if only that beloved one was saved.

I went home that night from Barry Upper Branch riding a horse which Dick Barry lent me, on learning that I had come thither without one, though not in what mad fashion, and Sir Humphrey rode with me until our roads parted. Much gaming was there that night after we left; we leaving the Barrys and my Lord Estes and Drake and Captain Jaynes and many others intent upon the dice, but Humphrey and I did not linger, I having naught to stake, and he having promised his mother not to play. "Sometimes I wish that I had not so promised my mother," he said, looking back at me over his great boyish shoulder as he rode ahead, "for sometimes I think 'tis part of the estate of a man to put up stakes at cards, and to win or lose as beseems a gentleman of Virginia and a cavalier. But, sure, Harry, a promise to a man's mother is not to be broke lightly, and indeed she doth ask me every night when I return late, and I shall see her face at the window when I ride in sight of the great house; but faith, Harry, I would love to win in something, if not in hearts, in a throw of the dice. For sure I am a man grown, and have never had my own will in aught that lies near my heart." With that he gave a great sigh, and I striving to cheer him, and indeed loving the lad, replied that he was but young, and there was still time ahead, and the will of one's heart required often but a short corner of turning. But he was angry again at me for that, and cried out I knew not for all I was loved in return, the heart of a certain maid as well as he who was despised, and spurred his horse and rode on ahead, and when we had come to the division of the road, saluted me shortly, and was gone, and the sound of his galloping died away in the distance, and I rode home alone meditating.

And when I reached Drake Hill a white curtain fluttered athwart a window, and I caught a gleam of a white arm pulling it to place, and knew that Mistress Mary had been watching for me — I can not say with what rapture and triumph and misgivings.

It was well toward morning, and indeed a faint pallor of dawn was in the east, and now and then a bird was waking. Not a slave on the plantation was astir, and the sounds of slumber were coming from the quarters. So I myself put my borrowed horse in stable, and then was seeking my own room, when, passing through the hall, a white figure started forth from a shadow and caught me by the arm, and it was Catherine Cavendish. She urged me forth to the porch, I being bewildered and knowing not how, nor indeed if it were wise, to resist her. But when we stood together there, in that hush of slumber only broken now and then by the waking love of a bird, and it seemed verily as if we two were alone in the whole world, a sense of the situation flashed upon me. I turned on my heel to reenter the house. "Madam," I said, "this will never do. If you remain here with me, your reputation —"

"What think you I care for my reputation?" she whispered. "What think you? Harry Wingfield, you cannot do this monstrous thing. You cannot be so lost to all honour as to let my sister — You cannot, and you a convict —"

Then, indeed, for the first time in my life and the last I answered a woman as if she were a man, and on an equal footing of antagonism with me. "Madam," I replied, "I will maintain my honour against your own." But she seemed to make no account of what I said. Indeed I have often wondered whether a woman, when she is in pursuit of any given end, can progress by other methods than an ant, which hath no power of circuitousness, and will climb over a tree with long labour and pain rather than skirt it, if it come in her way. Straight at her purpose she went. "Harry, Harry," she said, still in that sharp whisper, "you will not, you cannot — she is but a child."

Then, before I could reply, out ran Mary Cavendish herself, and was close at my side, turning an angry face upon her sister.

"Catherine," she cried out, "how dare you? I am no child. Think you that I do not know my own mind? How dare you? You shall not come between Harry and me! I am his before the whole world. I will not have it, Catherine!"

Then Catherine Cavendish, awakening such bewilderment and dismay in me as I had never felt, looked at her sister, and said in a voice which I can hear yet: "Have thy way then, sister; but 'tis over thy own sister's heart."

"What mean you?" Mary asked breathlessly.

"I love him!" said Catherine.

I felt the hot blood mount to my head, and I knew what shame was. I turned to retreat. I knew not what to do, but Mary's voice stopped me. It rang out clear and pitiless, with that pitilessness of a great love.

"And what is that to me, Catherine?" she cried out. "Sure it is but to thy shame if thou hast loved unsought and confessed unasked. And if I had ten thousand sisters, and they all in love with him, as well they might be, for there is no one like him in the whole world, over all their hearts would I go, rather than he should miss me for but a second, if he loved me. Think you that aught like that can make a difference? Think you that one heart can outweigh two, and the misery of one be of any account before that of three?"

Then suddenly she looked sharply at her sister and cried out angrily:

"Catherine Cavendish, I know what this means. 'Tis but another device to part us. You love him not. You have hated him from the first. You have hated him, and he is no more guilty than you be. 'Tis but a trick to turn me from him. Fie, think you that will avail? Think you that a sister's heart counts with a maid before her lover's? Little you know of love and lovers to think that."

Then to my great astonishment, since I had never seen such weakness in her before, Catherine flung up her hands before her face and burst into such a storm of wild weeping as never was, and fled into the house, and Mary and I stood alone together, but only for a second, for Mary, also casting a glance at me, then about her at the utter loneliness and silence of the world, fled in her turn. Then I went to my room, but not to sleep nor to think altogether of love, for my Lord Culpeper was to sail that day, and the next night was appointed for the beginning of the plant cutting.

XVI

I know not if my Lord Culpeper had any inkling of what was about to happen. Some were there who always considered him to be one who feathered his own nest with as little risk as might be, regardless of those over and under him, and one who saw when it behooved him to do so, and was blind when it served his own ends, even with the glare of a happening in his eyes. And many considered that he was in England when it seemed for his own best good without regard to the king or the colony, but that matters not, at this date. In truth his was a ticklish position, between two fires. If he remained in Virginia it was at great danger to himself, if he sided not with the insurgents; and on the other hand there was the certainty of his losing his governorship and his lands, and perhaps his head, if he went to tobacco cutting with the rest of us. He was without doubt better off on the high sea, which is a sort of neutral place of nature, beyond the reach for the time, of mobs or sceptres, unless one falls in with a black flag. At all events, off sailed my Lord Culpeper, leaving Sir Henry Chichely as Lieutenant-Governor, and verily he might as well have left a weather-cock as that well intentioned but pliable gentleman. Give him but a head wind over him and he would wax fierce to order, and well he served the government in the Bacon uprising, but leave him to his own will and back and forth he swung with great bluster but no stability. None of the colony, least of all the militia, stood in awe of Sir Henry Chichely, nor regarded him as more than a figurehead of authority when my Lord Culpeper had set sail.

The morning of the day after the sailing, the people of James-town whom one happened to meet on the road had a strange expression of countenance, and I doubt not that a man skilled in such matters could have read as truly the signs of an eruption of those forces of human passion in the hearts of men, as of an earthquake by the belching forth of smoke and fire from the mouth of a volcano. Everybody looked at his neighbour with either a glare of doubt and wariness, or with covert understanding, and some there were who had a pale seriousness of demeanour from having a full comprehension of the situation and of what might come of it, though not in the least drawing back on that account, and some were all flushed and glowing with eagerness and laughing from sheer delight in danger and daring, and some were like stolid beasts of the field watching the eye of a master, ready at its wink to leap forth to the strain of labour or fury. Many of these last were of our English labourers, whom I held in some sort of pity, and doubt as to whether it were just and merciful to draw them into such a stew kettle, for in truth many of them had not a pound of tobacco to lose by the Navigation Act, and no more interest in the uprising than had the muskets stacked in Major Robert Beverly's first wife's tomb. Yet, I pray, what can men do without tools, and have not tools some glory of their own which we take small account of, and yet which may be a recompense to them?

Nevertheless, I saw with some misgivings these honest fellows plodding their ways, ready to leap to their deaths maybe at the word of command, when it did not concern their own interests in the least, and especially when they had not that order of mind which enables a man to have a delight in glory and in serving those broad ends of humanity which include a man to his own loss.

Early that morning the news spread that Colonel Kemp of the Gloucester militia and a troop of horse and foot had been sent secretly against some plant-cutters in Gloucester County who had arisen before us, and had taken prisoners some twenty-two caught in the act. The news of the sending came first, I think, from Major Robert Beverly, the Clerk of the Assembly, who had withheld the knowledge for some time, inasmuch as he disliked the savour of treachery, but being in his cups that night before at Barry Upper Branch, out it came. 'Twas Dick Barry who told me. I fell in with him and Captain Jaynes on the Jamestown road that morning. "Colonel Kemp hath ridden against the rioters in Gloucester with foot and horse, by order of the general court, and Beverly hath been knowing to it all this time," he said gloomily. Then added that a man who served on two sides had no strength for either, and one who had raised his hand against Bacon had best been out of the present cause. But Captain Jaynes swore with one of his broadsides of mighty oaths that 'twas best as 'twas, since Beverly had some influence over the militia, and that he was safe enough not to turn traitor with his great store of tobacco at stake, and that should the court proceed to extremes with the Gloucester plant-cutters, such a flame would leap to life in Virginia as would choke England with the smoke of its burning.

We knew no more than the fact of the sending, but that afternoon came riding into Jamestown colonel Kemp with a small body of horse, having left the rest and the foot in Gloucester, there to suppress further disorder, and with him, bound to their saddles, some twenty-two prisoners, glaring about them with defiant faces and covered with dust and mire, and some with blood.

Something there was about that awful glow of red on face, on hand, or soaking through homespun sleeve or waistcoat, that was like the waving of a battle-flag or the call of a trumpet. Such a fury awoke in us who looked on, as never was, and the prisoners had been then and there torn from their horses and set free, had it not been for the consideration that undue precipitation might ruin the main cause. But the sight of human blood shed in a righteous cause is the spur of the brave, and goads him to action beyond all else. Quite silent we kept when that troop rode past us on their way to prison, though we were a gathering crowd not only of some of the best of Virginia, but some of her worst and most uncontrolled of indenture white slaves, and convicts, but something there must have been in our looks which gave heart to those who rode bound to their horses, for one and then another turned and looked back at us, and I trow got some hope.

However, before the night fairly fell, twenty of the prisoners, upon giving assurance of penitence, were discharged, and but two, the ringleaders, were committed and were in the prison. The twenty-two, being somewhat craven-hearted, and some of them indisposed by wounds, were on their ways homeward when we were afield.

We waited for the moon to be up, which was an hour later that night. I was all equipped in good season, and was stealing forth secretly, lest any see me, for I wished not to alarm the household, nor if possible to have any one aware of what I was about to do, that they might be acquit of blame through ignorance, when I was met in the threshold of an unused door by Mary Cavendish. And here will I say, while marvelling at it greatly, that the excitement of a great cause, which calls for all the enthusiasm and bravery of a man, doth, while it not for one moment alters the truth and constancy of his love, yet allay for the time his selfish thirst for it. While I was ready as ever to die for Mary Cavendish, and while the thought of her was as ever in my inmost soul, yet that effervescence of warlike spirit within me had rendered me not forgetful, but somewhat unwatchful of a word and a look of hers. And for the time being that sad question of our estates, which forbade more than our loves, had seemed to pale in importance before this matter of maybe the rising or falling of a new empire. Heart and soul was I in this cause, and gave myself the rein as I had longed to do for the cause of Nathaniel Bacon.

But Mary met me at the northern door, which opened directly on a locust thicket and was little used, and stood before me with her beautiful face as white as a lily but a brave light in her eyes.

"Where go you, Harry?" she whispered.

Then I, not knowing her fully, and fearing lest I disquiet her, answered evasively somewhat about hunting and Sir Humphrey. Some reply of that tenor was necessary, as I was, beside my knife for the tobacco cutting, armed to the teeth and booted to my middle. But there was no deceiving Mary Cavendish. She seized both my hands, and I trow for the minute, in that brave maiden soul of hers, the selfishness of our love passed as well as with me.

"I pray thee, Harry, cut down the tobacco on Laurel Creek first," she whispered, "as I would, were I a man. Oh! I would I were a man! Harry, promise me that thou wilt cut down first the tobacco on my plantation of Laurel Creek."

But I had made up my mind to touch neither that nor the tobacco on Drake Hill, lest in some way the women of the Cavendish family be implicated.

"There be enough, and more than enough, for tonight," I answered, and would have passed, but she would not let me.

"Harry," she cried, so loud that I feared for listening ears, "if you cut not down my tobacco, then will I myself! Harry, promise me!"

No love nor fear for me was in her eyes as she looked at me, only that enthusiasm for the cause of liberty, and I loved her better for it, if that could be. A man or woman who is but a bond slave to love and incapable of aught but the longing for it, is but a poor lover.

"I tell thee, Harry, cut down the plants on Laurel Creek!" she cried again, and I answered to appease her, not daring violent contradiction lest I rouse her to some desperate act, this wild, young maid with Nathaniel Bacon's hair in the locket against her heart, and as fiery blood as his in her veins, that it should come in good time, but that I was under the leadership of others and not my own.

"Then as soon as may be, Harry," she persisted, "for sure I should die of shame were my plants standing and the others cut, and Harry, sure it could not be at all, were it not for my fine gowns which the 'Golden Horn' brought over from England!"

With that she laughed, and stood aside to let me pass, but suddenly, as I touched her in the narrow way, her mood changed, and the woman in her came uppermost, though not to her shaking. But she caught hold of my right arm with her two little hands and pressed her fair cheek against my shoulder with that modest boldness of a maid when she is assured of love, and whispered: "Harry, if the militia is ordered out they say they will not fire, but — if thou be wounded, Harry, 'tis I will nurse thee, and no other, and —

Harry, cut all the plants that thou art able, before they come."

Then she let me go, and I went forth thinking that here was a helpmeet for a soldier in such times as these, and how I gloried in her because she held her love as one with glory. Round to the stable for my horse I stole, and it was very dark, with a soft smother of darkness because of a heavy mist, and the moon not up, and I had backed my horse out of his stall and was about to mount him, before I was aware of a dark figure lurking in shadow, and made out by the long sweep of the garments that it was a woman. I paused, and looked intently into the shadow, where she stood so silently that she might have deceived me had it not been for a flutter of her cloak in a stray wind.

"Who goes there?" I called out softly, but I knew well enough. 'Tis sometimes a stain on a man's manhood, the hatred he can bear to a woman who is continually between him and his will, and his keen apprehension of her as a sort of a cat under cover beside his path. So I knew well enough it was Catherine Cavendish, and indeed I marvelled that I had gotten thus far without meeting her. She stepped forward with no more ado when I accosted her, and spoke, but with great caution.

"What do you, Master Wingfield?" she whispered. "I go on my own business, an it please you, Madam," I answered something curtly, and I have since shamed myself with the memory of it, for she was a woman.

"It pleases me not, nor my grandmother, that one of her household should go forth on any errand of mystery at such a time as this, when whispers have reached us of another insurrection," she replied. "Master Wingfield, I demand to know, in the name of my Grandmother Cavendish, the purpose of your riding forth in such fashion?"

"And that, Madam, I refuse to tell you," I replied, bowing low. "You presume too greatly on your privileges," she burst out. "You think because my grandmother holds you in such strange favour that she seems to forget, to forget —"

"That I am a convict, Madam," I finished for her, with another low bow.

"Finish it as you will, Master Wingfield," she said haughtily, "but you think wrongly that she will countenance treason to the king in her own household, and 'tis treason that is brewing tonight."

"Madam," I whispered, "if you love your grandmother and value her safety, you will remain in ignorance of this."

Then she caught me by the arm, with such a nervous ardour

that never would I have known her for the Catherine Cavendish of late years.

"My God, Harry, you shall not go," she whispered. "I say you shall not! I — I — will go to my grandmother. I will have the militia out. Harry, I say you shall not go!"

But then my blood was up. "Madam," I said, "go I shall, and if you acquaint your grandmother, 'twill be to her possible undoing, and yours and your sister's, since the having one of the rioters in your own household will lay you open to suspicion. Then besides, your sister's bringing over of the arms may be traced to her if the matter be agitated."

Then truly the feminine soul of this woman leapt to the surface with no more ado.

"Oh, my God, Harry!" she cried out. "I care not for my grandmother, nor my sister, nor the king, nor Nathaniel Bacon, nor aught, nor aught — I fear, I fear — Oh, I fear lest thou be killed, Harry!"

"Lest my dead body be brought home to thy door, and the accusation of having furnished a traitor to the king be laid to thee, Madam?" I said, for not one whit believed I in her love for me. But she only sobbed in a distracted fashion.

"Fear not, Madam," I said, "if the militia be out, and I fall, it will go hard that I die before I have time to forswear myself yet again for the sake of thy family. But, I pray thee, keep to thyself for the sake of all."

With that I was in my saddle and rode away, for I had lingered, I feared, too long, and as God is my witness I had no faith that Catherine Cavendish did more than assume such interest in me for her own ends, for love, as I conceived it, was not thus.

I hastened on my way to Barry Upper Branch, where was the rendezvous, and on my way had to pass the house where dwelt that woman of strange repute, Margery Key, and it was naught but a solidity of shadow beside the road except for a glimmer of white from the breast of her cat in the doorway. But as I live, as I rode past, a voice came from that house, though how she knew me in that gloom I know not.

"Good speed to thee, Master Wingfield, and the fagots that thou didst gather for the despised and poor shall turn into blessings, like bars of silver. That which thou hast given, hast thou forever. Go on and fear not, and strike for liberty, and no harm shall come nigh thee." As she spoke I saw the bent back of the poor old crone in the doorway beside her cat, and partly because of her blessing, and partly because, as I said before, whether witch or not, she was aged and feeble, and ill fitted for such work, I leapt from my saddle and gathered her another armful of fagots, and laid them on her hearth. I left the old soul shedding such tears of gratitude over that slight service and calling down such childish blessings upon my head that I began to have little doubt that she was no witch, but only a poor and solitary old woman, which to my mind is the forlornest state of humanity. How a man fares without those of his own flesh and blood I can understand, since a man must needs have some comfort in his own endurance of hardships, but what a woman can do without chick or child, and no solace in her own dependency, I know not. Verily I know not that such be to blame if they turn to Satan himself for a protector, as they suspected Margery Key of doing.

I rode away from Margery Key's, having been delayed but a moment, and the quaver of her blessings was yet in my ears, when verily I did see that which I have never understood. As I live, there passed from the house of that ne'er-do-well next door, which was closed tightly as if to assure folk that all therein were sound asleep, a bright light like a torch, but no man carried it, and it crossed the road and was away over the meadows, and no man whom I saw carried it, and it waved in the wind like a torch streaming back, and I knew it for a corpse candle. And that same night the man who dwelt in that house was slain while pulling up the tobacco plants.

I rode fast, marvelling a little upon this strange sight, yet, though marvelling, not afraid, for things that I understand not, and that seem to savour of something outside the flesh, have always rather aroused me to rage as of one who was approached by other than the given rules of warfare rather than fear. I have always argued that an apparition should attack only his own kind, and hath no right to leave his own battlefield for ours, when we be at a disadvantage by our lack of understanding as to weapons. So if I had time I would have ridden after that corpse candle and gotten, if I could, a sight of the bearer had he been fiend or spook, but I knew that I had none to lose. So I rode on hard to Barry Upper Branch.

There was an air of mystery about the whole place that night, though it were hard to see the use of it. Whereas, generally speaking, there was a broad blazon of light from all the windows often to the revealing of strange sights within, the shutters were closed, and only by the lines of gold at top and bottom would one have known the house was lit at all. And whereas there were always to be seen horses standing openly before the porch, this night one knew there were any about only by the sound of their distant stamping. And yet this was the night when all mystery of plotting was to be resolved into the wind of action.

I entered and found a great company assembled in the hall, and all equipped with knives for the cutting of the tobacco plants, and arms, for the militia, as was afterwards proved, was an uncertain quantity. One minute the soldiers were for the government, when the promises as to their pay were specious, and the next, when the pay was not forthcoming, for the rioters, and there was no stability either for the one cause or the other in them.

There was a hushed greeting from one or two who stood nearest — Sir Humphrey Hyde among them — as I entered, then the work went on. Major Robert Beverly it was who was taking the lead of matters, though it was not fully known then or afterward, but sure it can do no harm at this late date to divulge the truth, for it was a glorious cause, and to the credit of a man's honour, if not to his purse, and his standing with the government.

Major Beverly stood at the head of the hall with a roll of parchment in his hand, wherefrom he read the names of those present, whom he was dividing into parties for the purpose of the plant-cutting, esteeming that the best plan to pursue rather than to march out openly in a great mob. Thus the whole company there assembled was divided into small parties, and each put under a leader, who was to give directions as to the commencement of the work of destruction.

My party was headed by Capt. Noel Jaynes, something to my discontent, for the hardest luck of choosing in the world to my mind is that of choosing a leader, for the leader is in himself a very gallstone. Never had it pleased me to follow any man's bidding, and in one way only could I comfort myself and retain my respect of self, and that was by the consideration that I followed by my own will, and so in one sense led myself.

When at last we set forth, some of us riding, and some on foot, with that old pirate captain to the front hunched to his saddle, for he never could sit a horse like a landsman, but clung to him as if he were a swaying mast, and worked his bridle like a wheel with the result of heavy lunges to right or left, I felt for the first time since I had come to Virginia like my old self.

We hurried along the moonlit road, then struck into a bridle-path, being bound for Major Robert Beverly's plantation, he being supposed to know naught of it, and indeed after his issuing of orders he had ridden to Jamestown, to see Sir Henry Chichely, and keep him quiet with a game at piquet, which he much affected.

As we rode along in silence, if any man spoke, Captain Jaynes quieted him with a great oath smothered in his chest, as if by a bed of feathers, and presently I became aware that there were more of us than when we started. We swarmed through the woods, our company being swelled invisibly from every side, and not only men but women were there. Both Mistress Allgood and Mistress Longman were pressing on with their petticoats tucked up, and to my great surprise both of the black women who lived at Barry Upper Branch. They slunk along far to the rear, with knives gleaming like white fire at their girdles, keeping well out of sight of the Barry brothers, who were both of our party, and looking for all the world like two female tigers of some savage jungle in search of prey, since both moved with a curious powerful crouch of secrecy as to her back and hips, and wary roll of fierce eyes.

When we were fairly in the open of Major Beverly's plantation some few torches were lit, and then I saw that we were indeed a good hundred strong, and of the party were that old graybeard who had played Maid Marion on Mayday, and many of the Morris dancers, and those lusty lads and lasses, and they had been at the cider this time as at the other, but all had their wits at their service.

Not a light was in Major Beverly's great house, not a stir in the slave quarters. One would have sworn they were all asleep or dead. But Captain Jaynes called a halt, and divided us into rank and file like a company of reapers, and to work we went on the great tobacco fields.

I trow it seemed a shame, as it ever does, to invoke that terrible force of the world which man controls, whether to his liberty or his slavery 'tis the question, and bring destruction upon all that fair inflorescence of life. But sometimes death and destruction are the means to life and immortality. Those great fields of Major Robert Beverly's lay before us in the full moonlight, overlapping with the lusty breadth of the new leaves gleaming with silver dew, and upon them we fell. We hacked and cut, we tore up by the roots. In a trice we were bedlam loosened — that is, the ruder part of us. Some of us worked with no less fury, but still with some sense of our own dignity as destroyers over destruction. But the rabble who had swelled our ranks were all on fire with rage, and wasted themselves as well as the tobacco. They filled the air with shouts and wild screams and peals of laughter. That fiercest joy of the world, the joy of destruction, was upon them, and sure it must have been one of the chiefest of the joys of primitive man, for all in a second it was as if the centuries of civilisation and Christianity had gone for naught, and the great gulf which lies back of us to the past had been leapt. One had doubted it not, had he seen those old men tearing up the tobacco plants, their mouths dribbling with a slow mutter of curses, for they had drunk much cider, and being aged, and none too well fed, it had more hold on them than on some of the others; and to see the women lost to all sense of decency, with their petticoats girded high on account of the dew, striding among the plants with high flings of stalwart legs, then slashing right and left with an uncertainty of fury which threatened not only themselves but their neighbours as well as the tobacco, and shrieking now and then, regardless of who might hear, "Down with the king!"

Often one cut a finger, but went on with blood flowing, and their hair begun to fly loose, and they smeared their faces with their cut hands, and as for the two black women, they pounced upon those green plants with fierce swashes of their gleaming knives, and though they could have sensed little about the true reason for it all, worked with a fury of savagery which needed no motive only its first impetus of motion.

Captain Jaynes rode hither and thither striving to keep the mob in order, and enjoining silence upon them, and now and then lashing out with his long riding whip, but he had set forces in motion which he could not stop. Fire and flood and wind and the passions of men, whether for love or rage, are beyond the leading of them who invoke them, being the instruments of the gods.

Sir Humphrey Hyde, who was beside me, slashing away at the plants, whispered: "My God, Harry, how far will this fire which we have kindled spread?" but not in fear so much as amazement.

And I, bringing down a great ring of the green leaves, replied, and felt as I spoke as if some other than I had my tongue and my voice:

"Maybe in the end, before it hath quite died out, to the destroying of tyranny and monarchy, and the clearing of the fields for a new government of equality and freedom."

But Sir Humphrey stared at me.

"Sure," he said, "it can do no more than to force the king to see that his colony hath grown from infancy to manhood, and hath an arm to be respected, and compel him to repeal the Navigation Act. What else, Harry?"

Then I, speaking again as if some other moved my tongue, replied that none could say what matter a little fire kindleth, but those that came after us might know the result of that which we that night begun.

But Sir Humphrey shook his head.

"If but Nat Bacon were alive!" he sighed. "No leader have we, Harry. Oh, Harry, if thou wert not a convict! Captain Jaynes is sure out of his element in defending the rights of the oppressed, and should be on his own quarterdeck with his cutlass in hand and his rapscallions around him, slaying and robbing, to be in full feather. Naught can he do here. Lord, hear those women shriek! Why did they let women come hither, Harry? Sure Nick Barry is in his cups. Not thus would matters have been were Bacon alive. The women would have been at home in their beds, and no man in liquor at work, for I trust not the militia. Would Captain Bacon were alive, as he would have been, had he not been foully done to death."

This he said believing, as did many, that Bacon's death was due to treachery and not fever, nor, as many of his enemies affirmed, from over indulgence in strong spirits, and I must say that I, remembering Bacon's greatness of enthusiasm and fixedness of purpose, was of the same belief.

As he spoke I seemed to see that dead hero as he would have looked in our midst with the moonlight shining on the stern whiteness of his face, and that look of high command in his eyes which none dared gainsay. And I answered again and again, as with an impulse not my own, "And maybe Bacon in truth leads us still, if not by his own chosen ways, to his own ends."

"Truly, Harry," Sir Humphrey agreed, "had it not been for Bacon, I doubt if we had been at this night's work."

All the time we talked, we advanced in our slashing swath up the field, and all the time that chorus of wild laughter and shrieks of disloyalty kept time with the swash of the knives, and all the time rose Captain Jaynes' storm of fruitless curses and commands, and now and then the stinging lash of his riding whip, and also Dick Barry's. As for Nick Barry, he lay overcome with sleep on a heap of the cut tobacco.

And all the time not a light shone in any of Major Robert Beverly's windows, and the slave quarters were as still as the tomb.

The store of ammunition in the tomb had been secretly removed and portioned out to the plant-cutters at nightfall.

It was no slight task for even a hundred to cut such a wealth of tobacco as Major Robert Beverly had planted, work as fast as they might, and proceed over the fields in a fierce crawl of destruction, like an army of locusts, and finally they begun to wax impatient. And finally up rose that termagant, Mistress Longman, straightening her back with a spring as if it were whalebone, showing us her face shameless with rage, and stained green with tobacco juice, and here and there red with blood, for she had slashed ruthlessly. She flung back her coarse tangle of hair, threw up her arms with a wild hurrahing motion, and screamed out in such a volume of shrillness that she overcapped all the rest of the tumult:

"To the stables, to the stables! Let out Major Beverly's horses, and let them trample down the tobacco."

Then such a cry echoed her that I trow it might have proceeded from a thousand throats instead of one hundred odd, and in spite of all that Captain Jaynes could do, seconded by some few of us gentlemen who rallied about him, but were helpless since we could not fire upon our coadjutors, that mob swept into Beverly's stables, and presently out leapt, plunging with terror, all his fine thoroughbreds, the mob riding them about the fields in wild career. And one of the maddest of the riders, sitting astride and flogging her steed with a locust branch, was Mistress Longman, while her husband vainly fled after her, beseeching her to stop, and those around were roaring with laughter.

Then some must let out the major's hogs, and they came rooting and tumbling with unwieldy gambols. And with this wild troop of animals, and the mob shrieking in a frenzy of delight, and now and then a woman in terror before the onslaught of a galloping horse, and now and then a whole group of cutters overset by a charging hog, and up and after him, and slaying him, and his squeals of agony, verily I had preferred a battlefield of a different sort. And all this time Major Robert Beverly's house stood still in the moonlight, and not a noise from the slave quarters, and the fields were all in a pumice of wasted plant life, and we were about to go farther when I heard again the cry of the little child coming from a chamber window. I trow they had given her some quieting potion or she had broken silence before.

With all our efforts the mob could not be persuaded to return Major Beverly's horses to his stables, which circumstance was afterward to the saving of his neck, since it was argued that he would not have abetted the using of his fine stud in such wise, some of the horses being recovered and some being lamed and cut.

So out of the Beverly plantation we swept; those on horseback at a gallop and those on foot tramping after, and above the tumult came that farthest-reaching cry of the world — the cry of a little child frantic with terror.

Then they were for going to another large plantation belonging to one Richard Forster, who had gone in Ralph Drake's party, when all of a sudden the horses of us who were leading swerved aside, and there was Mistress Mary Cavendish on her Merry Roger, and by her side, pulling vainly at her bridle, her sister Catherine.

XVII

Mary Cavendish raised her voice high until it seemed to me like a silver trumpet, and cried out with a wave of her white arm to them all: "On to Laurel Creek, I pray you! Oh, I pray you, good people, on to Laurel Creek, and cut down my tobacco for the sake of Virginia and the honour of the Colony."

It needed but a puff of any wind of human will to send that fiery mob leaping in a new direction. Straightway, they shouted with one accord: "To Laurel Creek, to Laurel Creek! Down with the tobacco, down with the governor, down with the king! To Laurel Creek!" and forged ahead, turning to the left instead of the right, as had been ordered, and Mary was swept along with them, and Catherine would have been crushed, had not a horseman, whom I did not recognise, caught her up on the saddle with him with a wonderful swing of a long, lithe arm, and then galloped after, and as for myself and Captain Jaynes, and Sir Humphrey, and others of the burgesses, whom I had best not call by name, we went too, since we might as well have tried to hold the current of the James River, as that headlong company.

But as soon as might be, I shouted out to Sir Humphrey above the din that our first duty must be to save Mary and Catherine. And he answered back in a hoarse shout, "Oh, for God's sake, ride fast, Harry, for should the militia come, what would happen to them?"

But I needed no urging. I know not whom I rode down, I trust not any, but I know not; I got before them all in some wise, Sir Humphrey following close behind, and Ralph Drake also, swearing that he knew not what possessed the jades to meddle in such matters, and shouting to the rabble to stop, but he might as well have shouted to the wind. And by that time there were more than a hundred of us, though whence they had come, I know not.

We gentlemen kept together in some wise, and gradually gained on Mary, who had had the start, and there were some seven of us, one of the Barrys, Sir Humphrey Hyde, Ralph Drake, Parson Downs, in such guise for a parson that no one would have known him, booted and spurred, and riding harder than any by virtue of his best horse in the Colony, myself, and two of the burgesses. We seven gaining on the rabble, in spite of the fact that many of them were mounted upon Major Robert Beverly's best horses, through their having less knowledge of horsemanship, closed around Mary Cavendish on Merry Roger, clearing the ground with long galloping bounds, and Catherine with the strange horseman was somewhat behind.

As we came up with Mary, she looked at us over her shoulder with a brightness of triumph and withal something of merriment, like a child successful in mischief, and laughed, and waved her hand in which, as I live, she held a sword which had long graced the hall at Drake Hill, and I believe she meditated cutting the tobacco herself.

Then a great cheer went up for her, in which we, in spite of our misgivings, joined. Something so wonderful and innocent there was in the fresh enthusiasm of the maid. Then again her sweet voice rang out:

"Down with the tobacco, gentlemen of Virginia, and down with all tyranny. Remember Nathaniel Bacon, remember Nathaniel Bacon!"

Then we all caught up that last cry of hers, and the air rang with "Remember Nathaniel Bacon!"

But as soon as might be, I rode close enough to speak with Mary Cavendish, and Sir Humphrey, who was on the other side, each with our jealousy lost sight of, in our concern for her.

"Child, thou must turn and go home," I said, and I fear my voice lost its firmness, for I was half mad with admiration, and love, and apprehension for her.

Then Sir Humphrey echoed me.

"The militia will be upon us presently," he shouted in her ear above the din. "Ride home as fast as you may."

She looked from one to the other of us, and laughed gayly and shook her head, and her golden curls flew to the wind, and she touched Merry Roger with her whip and he bounded ahead, and we had all we could do to keep pace, he being fresh. Then Parson Downs pelted to her side and besought her to turn, and so did Captain Jaynes, though he was half laughing with delight at her spirit, and his bright eyes viewed her in such wise that I could scarce keep my fingers from his throat. But Mary Cavendish would hear to none, and no way there was of turning her, lest we dragged her from her saddle.

Again I rode close and spoke so that no one beside her could hear.

"Go home, I pray you, if you love me," I said.

But she looked at me with a proud defiance, and such a spirit of a man that I marvelled at her.

"'Tis no time to talk of love, sir," said she. "When a people strike for liberty, they stop not for honey nor kisses."

Then she cried again, "Remember Nathaniel Bacon!" And

again that wild shout echoed her silver voice.

But then I spoke again, catching her bridle rein as I rode.

"Then go, if not because you love me, because I love thee," I said close to her ear with her golden hair blowing athwart my face.

"I obey not the man who loves me, but the man who weds me, and that you will not do, because you hold your pride dearer than love," said she.

"Nay, because I hold thee dearer than my love," said I.

"'Tis a false principle you act upon, and love is before all else, even that which may harm it, and thou knowest not the heart of a woman if thou dost love one, sir," said she. Then she gave a quick glance at my face, so close to hers in the midst of that hurrying throng, and her blue eyes gleamed into mine, and she said, with a bright blush over her cheeks and forehead and neck, but proudly as if she defied even her maiden shame in the cause of love, "But thou shalt yet know one, Harry."

Then, as if she had said too much, she pulled her bridle loose from my detaining hand with a quick jerk, and touched her horse, and we were on that hard gallop to Locust Creek.

Locust Creek was not a large plantation, but the fields of tobacco were well set, and it was some task to cut them. Captain Jaynes essayed to form the cutters into ranks, but with no avail, though he galloped back and forth, shouting like a madman. Every man set to work for himself, and it was again bedlam broke loose as at the other plantation. Then indeed for the first time I saw Mary Cavendish shrink a little, as if she were somewhat intimidated by the fire which she had lighted, and she resisted not, when Sir Humphrey, and her Cousin Ralph and I, urged her into the house. And as she entered, there was Catherine, having been brought thither by that stranger who had disappeared. And we shut the door upon both women, and then felt freer in our minds. Capt. Noel Jaynes swore 'twas a jade fit to lead an army, then inquired what in hell brought her thither, and why women were to the front in all our Virginian wars, whether they wore white aprons or not?

As he spoke Ralph Drake shouted out with a great laugh, that maybe 'twas for the purpose of carrying the men, and pointed, and there was one of the black wenches bringing Nick Barry, who else had fallen, upon her back to the field. Then she set him down in the tobacco and gave him a knife, and he went to cutting, having just enough wit to do that for which his mind had been headed, and naught else.

The mob took a fancy to that new cry of Mary Cavendish's,

and every now and then the field rang with it. "Remember Nathaniel Bacon, remember Nathaniel Bacon!" It had a curious effect, through starting in a distant quarter, where some of the fiercest of the workers were grouped, then coming nearer and nearer, till the whole field rang with that wide overspread of human voice, above the juicy slashing of the tobacco plants.

We had been at work some little time when a tall woman in black on a black horse came up at a steady amble, her horse being old. She dismounted near me and her horse went to nibbling the low-hanging boughs of a locust nearby, and the moon shone full on her face, and I saw she was the Widow Tabitha Story, with that curious patch on her forehead. Down to the tobacco she bent and went to work stiffly with unaccustomed hands to such work, and then again rang that cry of "Remember Nathaniel Bacon!" And when she heard that, up she reared herself, and raised such a shrill response of "Remember Nathaniel Bacon!" in a high-sobbing voice, as I never heard.

And after that for a minute the field seemed to fairly howl with that cry of following, and memory for the dead hero, always Madam Tabitha Story's voice in the lead, shrieking over it like a cat's.

"Lord, have mercy on us," said Parson Downs at my elbow. "She will have all England upon us, and wherefore could not the women have kept out of this stew?"

With that he went over to the widow and strove to quiet her, but she only shrieked with more fury, with Mistresses Longman and Allgood to aid her, and then — came in a mad rush upon us of horse and foot, the militia, under Capt. Robert Waller.

XVIII

I have seen the same effect when a stone was thrown into a boil of river rapids; an enhancement and marvellous entanglement of swiftness and fury, and spread of broken circles, which confused the sight at the time and the memory afterwards.

It was but a small body of horse and foot, which charged us whilst we were cutting the tobacco on the plantation of Laurel Creek, but it needed not a large one to put to rout a company so overbalanced by enthusiasm, and cider, and that marvellous greed of destruction. No more than seven gentlemen of us there were to make a stand, and not more than some twenty-five of the rabble to be depended upon.

As for me, the principal thought in my mind when the militia burst upon us, was the safety of Mary Cavendish. Straight to the door of the great house I rushed, and Sir Humphrey Hyde was with me. As for the other gentlemen, they were fighting here and there as they could, Captain Jaynes making efforts to keep the main body of the defenders at his back, but with little avail. I stood against the door of the house, resolved upon but one course — that my dead body should be the threshold over which they crossed to Mary Cavendish. It was but a pitiful resolve, for what could I do single handed, except for the boy Humphrey Hyde, against so many. But it was all, and a man can but give his all. I knew if the militia were to find Mary and Catherine Cavendish in that house, grave harm might come to them, if indeed it came not already without that. So I stood back against the door which I had previously tried, and found fast, and Sir Humphrey was with me. Then came a hush for a moment whilst the magistrate with Captain Waller, and others sitting on their horses around him, read the Riot Act, and bade us all disperse and repair to our homes, and verily I wonder, if ever there hath been in all the history of England such a farce and mummery as that same Riot Act, and if ever it were read with much effect when a riot were well under way.

Scarcely time they gave the worthy man to finish, and indeed his voice trembled as if he had the ague, and he seemed shrinking for shelter under his big wig, but they drowned out his last words with hisses, then there was a wild rush of the rabble and a cry of "Down with the tobacco!" and "A Bacon, A Bacon!" Then the militia charged, and there were the flashes of swords and partisans and the thunder of firearms.

I stood there, feeling like a deserter from the ranks, yet bound to keep the door of Laurel Creek, and I had a pistol in either hand

and so had Sir Humphrey Hyde, but for a minute nobody seemed to heed us. Then as I stood there, I felt the door behind me yield a bit and a hand was thrust out, and a voice whispered, "Harry, Harry, come in hither; we can hold the house against an army."

My heart leapt, for it was Mary, and, quicker than a flash, I had my mind made up. I turned upon Sir Humphrey and thrust him in before he knew it, through the opening of the door, and called out to him to bar and bolt as best he could inside, while I held the door. He, whether he would or not, was in the house, and seeing some of the soldiers riding our way with Captain Waller at their head, was forced to clap to the door, and shoot the bolts, but as he did so I heard a woman's shrill cry of agony ring out.

I stood there, and Captain Waller rode up with his soldiers, and flashing his sword before my face like a streak of fire, bade me surrender in the name of his Majesty, and stand aside. But I stood still with my two pistols levelled, and had him full within range. Captain Waller was a young man, and a brave one, and never to my dying day shall I forget that face which I had the power to still with death. He looked into the muzzles of my two pistols, and his rosy colour never wavered, and he shouted out again to me his command to surrender and stand aside in the name of the King, and I stood still and made no reply. I knew that I could take two lives and then struggle unarmed for perhaps a moment's space, and that all the time saved might be precious for those in the house. At all events, it was all that I could do for Mary Cavendish.

I held my pistols and watched his eyes, knowing well that all action through having its source in the brain of man, gives first evidence in the eyes. Then the time came when I saw his impulse to charge start in his eyes, and I fired, and he fell. Then I fired again, but wildly, for everything was in motion, and I know not whom I hit, if any one, then I felt my own right leg sink under me and I knew that I was hit. Then down on my knees I sank and put one arm through the great latch of the door, and thrust out with my knife with the free hand, and stout arms were at my shoulders striving to drag me away, but they might as well for a time have tried to drag a bar of steel from its fastenings. I thrust out here and there, and I trow my steel drew blood, and I suppose my own flowed, for presently I was kneeling in a widening circle of red. I cut those forcing hands from my arm, and others came. It was one against a multitude, for the rabble after hitting wild blows as often at their friends as at their enemies had broken and fled, except those who were taken prisoners. But the women stayed until the last and fought like wild cats, with the exception of Madam

Tabitha Story, who quietly got upon her old horse, and ambled away, and cut down her own tobacco until daybreak, pressing her slaves into service.

As for the other gentlemen, they were fighting as best they could, and all the time striving vainly to gather the mob into a firm body of resistance. None of them saw the plight I was in, nor indeed could have helped me had they done so, since there were but seven gentlemen of us in all, and some by this time wounded, and one dead.

I knelt there upon the ground before the door, slashing out as best I could with one hand, and they closed faster and thicker upon me, and at last I could no more. I felt a stinging pain in my right shoulder, and then for a minute my senses left me. But it was only for a moment.

When I came to myself I was lying bound with a soldier standing guard over me, though there was small need of it, and they were raining battering blows upon the door of Laurel Creek. Somehow they had conceived the idea that there was something of great import therein, by my mad and desperate defence. I know not what they thought, but gradually all the militia were centred at that point striving to force the door. As for the shutters, they were heavily barred, and offered no easier entrance. Indeed the whole house had been strengthened for defence against the Indians before the Bacon uprising, and was near as strong as a fort. It would have been well had we all entered and defended it, though we could not have held out for long, through not being provisioned.

At last Captain Jaynes and the other gentlemen begun to conceive the situation and I caught sight of them forcing their way toward me, and shouted to them with a failing voice, for I had lost much blood, to come nearer and assist me to hold the door. Then I saw Captain Jaynes sink in his saddle, and I caught a glimpse of a mighty retreat of plunging haunches of Parson Downs' horse, and indeed the gist of the blame for it all was afterward put upon the parson's great fiery horse, which it was claimed had run away with him first into the fight, then away from it, such foolish reasons do men love to give for the lapses of the clergy.

As for me, I believe in coming out with the truth about the clergy and laymen, and King and peasant, alike, whether it be Cain or King David, or Parson Downs or his Majesty King Charles the Second.

However, to do the parson justice, he did not fly until he saw the day was lost, and I trow did afterward better service to me than he might have done by staying. As for the burgesses, I know not whither nor when they had gone, for they had melted away like shadows, by reason of the great obloquy which would have attached to them, should men in their high office have been discovered in such work. Ralph Drake was left, who made a push toward me with a hoarse shout, and then he fell, though not severely wounded, and then the soldiers pressed closer. And then I felt again the door yield at my back, and before I knew it I was dragged inside, and, in spite of the pressure of the mob, the door was pushed to with incredible swiftness by Humphrey Hyde's great strength, and the bolt shot.

There I lay on the floor of the hall well-nigh spent, and Mary Cavendish was chafing my hands, bandaging my wounds with some linen got, I knew not whence, and Catherine was there, and all the time the great battering blows upon the door were kept up, and also on the window shutters, and the door began to shake.

Then I remembered something. There was behind the house a creek which was dry in midsummer, but often, as now, in spring-time, swollen with rains, and of sufficient depth and force to float a boat. And when it was possible it had been the custom to send stores of tobacco for lading on shipboard to England, by this short cut of the creek which discharged itself into the river below, and there was for that purpose a great boat in the cellar, and also a door and a little landing.

I, remembering this, whispered to Mary Cavendish with all the strength which I could muster.

"For God's sake," I cried, "go you to the cellar, the boat, the boat, the creek."

But Mary looked at me, and I can see her face now.

"Think you I did not know of that way?" she said, "and think you I would leave you here to die? No, let them come in and do their worst."

Then I turned to Catherine and pleaded with her as well as I could with those thundering blows upon the door, and I well-nigh fainting and my blood flowing fast, and she did not answer at all but looked at me.

Then I turned to Sir Humphrey Hyde. "For God's sake, lad," I cried, "if you love her, save her. Only a moment and they will be in here. Hear the door tremble, and then 'twill be arrest and imprisonment, and — I tell thee, lad, leave me, and save them."

"They can do as they choose," cried Mary. Then she turned to Sir Humphrey. "Take Catherine, and she will show you the way out by the creek," she said. "As for me, I remain here."

Catherine bent over me and tightened a bandage, but she did not speak. Sir Humphrey looked at me palely and doubtfully.

"Harry," he said, "I can carry thee to the boat and we can all escape in that way."

"Yes," I replied, "but if I escape through them, 'twill serve to convict them, and — and — besides, lad, I cannot be moved for the bleeding of my wounds, such a long way; and besides, it is at the best arrest for me, since I have been seen by the whole posse and have shot down Captain Waller. Whither could I fly, pray? Not back to England. Me they will take in custody in any case, and they will not shoot a wounded captive. My life is safe for the time being. Humphrey —" With that I beckoned him to lean over me, which he did, putting his ear close.

"Seize Mary by force and bear her away, lad," I whispered, "down cellar to the boat. Catherine will show thee the way."

"I cannot, Harry," he whispered back, and as I live the tears were in the boy's eyes. "I cannot leave thee, Harry."

"You must; there is no other way, if you would save her," I whispered back. "And what good can you do by staying? The four of us will be taken, for you can do nothing for me single handed. Captain Jaynes is killed — I saw him fall — and the parson has fled, and — and — I know not where be the others. For God's sake, lad, save her!"

Then Sir Humphrey with such a look at me as I never forgot, but have always loved him for, with no more ado, turned upon Mary Cavendish, and caught her, pinioning both arms, and lifted her as if she had been an infant, and Catherine would have gone to her rescue, but I caught at her hand, which was still at work on my bandage.

"Go you with them and show the way to the boat," I whispered. She set her mouth hard and looked at me. "I will not leave thee," she said.

"If you go not, then they will be lost," I cried out in desperation. For Mary was shrieking that she would not go, and I knew that Humphrey did not know the way, and could not find it and launch the boat in time with that struggling maid to encumber him, for already the door trembled as if to fall.

"I tell you they will not harm a wounded man," I cried. "If you leave me I am in no more worse case than now, and if you remain, think of your sister. You know what she hath done to abet the rebellion. 'Twill all come out if she be found here. Oh, Catherine, if you love her, I pray thee, go."

Then Catherine Cavendish did something which I did not

understand at the time, and perhaps never understood rightly. Close over me she bent, and her soft hair fell over my face and hers, hiding them, and she kissed me on my forehead, and she said low, but quite clearly, "Whatever thou hast done in the past, my scorn henceforth shall be for the deed, not for thee, for thou art a man."

Then to her feet she sprang and caught hold of Mary's struggling right arm, though it might as well have struggled in a vise as in Sir Humphrey Hyde's reluctant, but mighty grasp.

"Mary," she said, "listen to me. 'Tis the best way to save him, to leave him."

Then Mary rolled her piteous blue eyes at her over Sir Humphrey's shoulder from her gold tangle of hair.

"What mean you?" she cried. "I tell you, Catherine, I will never leave him!"

"If we remain, we shall all be in custody," replied Catherine in her clear voice, though her face was white as if she were dead, "and our estates may be forfeited, and we have no power to help him. And he must be taken in the end in any case. And if we be free, we can save him."

"I will not go without him," cried Mary. "Set me down, Humphrey, and take up Harry, and I will help thee carry him. Do as I tell thee, Humphrey."

"Harry will be taken in any case," replied Catherine, "and if you take him, you will be arrested with him, and then we can do nothing for him. I tell thee, sweet, the only way to save him is to leave him."

Then Mary gave one look at me.

"Harry, is this the truth they tell me?" she cried.

"As God is my witness, dear child," I replied. Then she twisted her white face around toward Sir Humphrey's, who stood pinioning her arms with a look himself as if he were dying.

"Let me loose, Humphrey," she said, "let me loose, then I swear I will go with you and Catherine."

Then Sir Humphrey loosed her, and straight to me she came and bent over me and kissed me. "Harry," she said in a whisper which was of that strange quality that it seemed to be unable to be heard by any in the whole world save us two, though it was clear enough — "I leave thee because thou tellest me that this is the only way to save thee, but I am thine for life and for death, and nothing shall ever come forever between thee and me, not even thine own self, nor the grave, nor all the wideness of life."

Then she rose and turned to Sir Humphrey and Catherine.

"I am ready," said she, and Sir Humphrey gave my hand one last wring, and said that he would stand by me. Then they fled and, as I lay there alone, I heard their footsteps on the cellar stairs, and presently the dip of the boat as she was launched, and heard it above all the din outside, so keen were my ears for aught that concerned her.

Then that sound and all others grew dim, for I was near swooning, and when the door fell with a mighty crash near me, it might have been the fall of a rose leaf on velvet, and I had small heed of the fierce faces which bent over me, yet the hands extended toward my wounds were tender enough. And I saw as in a dream, Capt. Robert Waller, with his arm tied up, and wondered dimly if we were both dead, for I verily believed that I had killed him, and I heard him say, and his voice sounded as if a sea rolled between us, "'Tis the convict tutor, Wingfield, who held the door, and unless I be much mistaken, he hath his death wound. Make a litter and lift him gently, and five of you search the house for whatever other rebels be hid herein."

And as I live, in the midst of my faintness, which made all sounds far away as from beyond the boundary of the flesh, and beyond the din of battle, which was still going on, though feebly, like a fire burning to its close, I heard the dip of oars on the creek, and knew that Mary Cavendish was safe.

A litter they fashioned from a lid of a chest while the search was going on, and I was lifted upon it with due regard to my wounds, which I thought a generous thing of Captain Waller, inasmuch as his own face was frowning with the pain of the wound which I had given him, but he was a brave man, and a brave man is ever a generous foe.

But when I was on the litter, breathing hard, yet with some consciousness, he bent close over me, and whispered "Sir, your wounds are bound up with strips torn from a woman's linen. I have a wife, and I know. Who was in hiding here, sir?"

My eyes flew wide open at that.

"No one," I gasped out. "No one as I live."

But he laughed, and bending still lower, whispered, "Have no fear as to that, Master Wingfield. Convict or not, you are a brave man, and that which you perchance gave your life to hide, shall be hidden for all Robert Waller."

So saying he gave the order to carry me forth with as little jolting as might be, and stationed himself at my side lest I come to harm from some over zealous soldier. But in truth the militia and the officers in those days were apparently of somewhat uncertain quantity as regarded their allegiance to the King or the Colony.

The sympathy of many of them was with the colonists who made a stand against tyranny, and they were half hearted, if whole-handed, for the King.

Just before they bore me across the threshold of Laurel Creek, those troopers who had been sent to search the house, clattered down the stair and swore that not so much as a mouse was in hiding there, then we all went forth.

Captain Waller, though walking somewhat weakly himself, kept close to my side. And he did not mount horse until we were out in the highway.

The grounds of Laurel Creek and the tobacco fields were a most lamentable sight, though I seemed to see everything as through a mist. Here and there one lay sprawled with limbs curled like a dead spider, or else flung out at a stiff length of agony. And Capt. Noel Jaynes lay dead with a better look on his gaunt old face in death than in life. In truth Capt. Noel Jaynes might almost have been taken for a good man as he lay there dead. And the outlaw who lived next door to Margery Key was doubled up where he fell in a sulky heap of death, and by his side wept his shrewish wife, shrilly lamenting as if she were scolding rather than grieving, and I trow in the midst of it all, the thought passed through my mind that it was well for that man that he was past hearing, for it seemed as if she took him to task for having died.

Of Dick Barry was no sign to be seen, but Nick lay not dead, but dead drunk, and over him was crouched one of those black women with a knife in her hand, and no one molested her, thinking him dead, but dead he was not, only drunk, and she was wounded herself, with the blood trickling from her head, unable to carry him from the field as she had brought him.

They carried me past them, and the black woman's eyes rolled up at us like a wild beast's in a jungle defending her mate, and I remember thinking, though dimly, as a man will do when he has lost much blood, that love was love, and perhaps showed forth the brighter and whiter, the viler and blacker the heart which held it, and then I knew no more for a space.

XIX

When I came to a consciousness of myself again, the first thing of which I laid hold with my mind as a means whereby to pull my recollections back to my former cognisance of matters was a broad shaft of sunlight streaming in through the west window of the prison in Jamestown. And all this sunbeam was horribly barred like the body of a wasp by the iron grating of the window, and had a fierce sting of heat in it, for it was warm though only May, and I was in a high fever by reason of my wounds. And another thing which served to hale me back to acquaintance with my fixed estate of life was a great swarm of flies which had entered at that same window, and were grievously tormenting me, and I was too weak to disperse them. All my wounds were dressed and bandaged and I was laid comfortably enough upon a pallet, but I was all alone except for the flies which settled upon me blackly with such an insistence of buzzing that that minor grievance seemed verily the greatest in the world, and for the time all else was forgot.

For some little time I did not think of Mary Cavendish, so hedged about was I as to my freedom of thought and love by my physical ills, for verily after a man has been out of consciousness with a wound, it is his body which first struggles back to existence, and his heart and soul have to follow as they may.

So I lay there knowing naught except the weary pain of my wounds, and that sense of stiffness which forbade me to move, and the fretful heat of that fierce west sunbeam, and the buzzing swarm of flies, for some little time before the memory of it all came to me.

Then indeed, though with great pain, I raised myself upon my elbow, and peered about my cell, and called aloud for some one to come, thinking some one must be within hearing, for the sounds of life were all about me: the tramp of horses on the road outside, the even fall of a workman's hammer, the sweet husky carol of a slave's song, and the laughter of children at play.

So I shouted and waited and shouted again, and no one came. There was in my cell not much beside my pallet, except a little stand which looked like one from Drake Hill, and on the stand was a china dish like one which I had often seen at Drake Hill, with some mess therein, what, I knew not, and a bottle of wine and some medicine vials and glasses. I was not ironed, and, indeed, there was no need of that, since I could not have moved.

Between the wound in my leg and various sword-cuts, and a

general soreness and stiffness as if I had been tumbled over a precipice, I was well-nigh as helpless as a week-old babe.

I called again, but no one came, and presently I quit and lay with the burning eye of the sun in my face and that pestilent buzz of flies in my ears, and my weakness and pain so increasing upon my consciousness, that I heeded them not so much. I shut my eyes and that torrid sunbeam burned red through my lids, and I wondered if they had found out aught concerning Mary Cavendish, and I wondered not so much what they would do with me, since I was so weak and spent with loss of blood that nothing that had to do with me seemed of much moment.

But as I lay there I presently heard the key turn in the lock, and one Joseph Wedge, the jailor, entered, and I saw the flutter of a woman's draperies behind him, but he shut the door upon her, and then without my ever knowing how he came there, was the surgeon, Martyn Jennings, and he was over me looking to my wounds, and letting a little more blood to decrease my fever, though I had already lost so much, and then, since I was so near swooning, giving me a glass of the Burgundy on the stand. And whilst that was clouding my brain, since my stomach was fasting, and I had lost so much blood, entered that woman whom I had espied, and she was not Mary, but Catherine Cavendish, and there was a gentleman with her who stood aloof, with his back toward me, gazing out of the window, and of that I was glad since he screened that flaming sunbeam from me, and I concerned myself no more about him.

But at Catherine I gazed, and motioned to her to bend over me, and whispered that the jailor might not hear, what had become of Mary. Then I saw the jailor had gone out, though I had not seen him go, and she making a sign to me that the gentleman at the window was not to be minded, went on to tell me what I thirsted to know; that she and Mary and Sir Humphrey had escaped that night with ease, and she and Mary had returned to Drake Hill before midnight, and had not been molested.

If Mary were suspected she knew not, but Sir Humphrey was then under arrest and was confined on board a ship in the harbour with Major Beverly, and his mother was daily sending billets to him to return home, and blaming him, and not his jailors, for his disobedience. She told me, furthermore, that it was Cicely Hyde who had led the militia to our assembly at Laurel Creek that night, and was now in a low fever through remorse, and though she told me not, I afterward knew why that mad maid had done such a thing — 'twas because of jealousy of me and Mary Cavendish, and she pulled down more upon her own head thereby than she wot of.

All this Catherine Cavendish told me in a manner which seemed strangely foreign to her, being gentle, and yet not so gentle as subdued, and her fair face was paler than ever, and when I looked at her and said not a word, and yet had a question in my eyes which she was at no loss to interpret, tears welled into her own, and she bent lower and whispered lest even the stranger at the window should hear, that Mary "sent her dear love, but, but —"

I raised myself with such energy at that that she was startled, and the gentleman at the window half turned.

"What have they done with her?" I cried. "If they dare —"

"Hush," said Catherine. "Our grandmother hath but locked her in her chamber, since she hath discovered her love for thee, and frowns upon it, not since thou art a convict, but since thou hast turned against the King. She says that no granddaughter of hers shall wed a rebel, be he convict or prince. But she is safe, Harry, and there will no harm come to her, and indeed I think that if they in authority have heard aught of what she hath done, they are minded to keep it quiet, and — and —"

Then to my exceeding bewilderment down on her knees beside me went that proud maid and begged my pardon for her scorn of me, saying that she knew me guiltless, and knew for what reason I had taken such obloquy upon myself.

Then the gentleman at the window turned when she appealed to him, and came near, and I saw who he was — my half brother, John Chelmsford.

XX

It was six years and more since I had seen my half brother, and I should scarcely have known him, for time had worked great changes in both his face and form. He was much stouter than I remembered him, and wore a ruddy point of beard at his chin, and a great wig, whereas I recalled him as smooth of face, with his own hair.

But he was a handsome man, as I saw even then, lying in so much pain and weakness, and he came and stood over me, and looked at me more kindly than I should have expected, and I could see something of our common mother in his blue eyes. He reached down his hand and shook the one of mine which I could muster strength to raise, and called me brother, and hoped that I found myself better, and gave me very many tender messages of our mother, and of his father likewise, which puzzled me exceedingly, until matters were explained. Colonel Chelmsford had parted with me when I left England with but scant courtesy, and as for my poor mother, I had not seen her at all, she being confined to her chamber with grief over my disgrace, and not one word had I received from them since that time. So when John Chelmsford said that our mother sent her dear love to her son Harry, and that nothing save her delicate health had prevented her from sailing to Virginia in the same ship to see the son from whom she had been so long parted, I gasped, and felt my head reel, and I called up my mother's face, and verily I felt the tears start in my eyes, but I was very weak.

Then forth from her pocket Catherine drew a ring, and it flashed green with a great emerald, and particoloured with brilliants, before my eyes, and I was well-nigh overcome by the sight of that and everything turned black before me, for it was my Lord Robert Ealing's great ring of exceeding value, for the theft of which I had been transported.

Straightway Catherine saw that it was too much for me, for she knelt down beside me and called John to give her a flask of sweet waters which stood on the table, and began bathing my forehead, the while my brother looked on with something of a jealous frown.

"'Twas thoughtless of me, Harry," she whispered, "but they say joy does not kill, and — and — dost thou know the ring?"

I nodded. It seemed to me that no jewels could ever be mined which I would know as I knew that green star of emerald and those encircling brilliants. That ring I knew to my cost.

"My Lord Ealing is dead," she said, "and thou knowest that he was a kinsman of the Chelmsfords, and after his funeral came this ring and a letter, and — and — thou art cleared, Harry. And — and — now I know why thou didst what thou did, Harry, 'twas — 'twas — to shield me." With that she burst into a great flood of tears, even throwing herself upon the floor of my cell in all her slim length, and not letting my brother John raise her, though he strove to do so.

"'Tis here, 'tis here I belong, John," she cried out wildly, "for you know not, you know not what injustice I have done this innocent man. Never can I make it good with my life."

It is here that I shall stop the course of my story to explain the whole matter of the ring, which at the time I was too weak and spent with pain to comprehend fully as Catherine Cavendish related it. It was a curious and at the same time a simple tale, as such tales are wont to be, and its very simplicity made it seem then, and seem now, well-nigh incredible. For it is the simple things of this world which are always most unbelievable, perhaps for this reason: that men after Eden and the Serpent, expect some subtlety of reasoning to account for all happenings, and always comes the suspicion that somewhat beside two and two go to make four.

My Lord Robert Ealing who had come to the ball at Cavendish Court that long last year, was a distant kinsman of our family, and unwedded, but a man who went through the world with a silly leer of willingness toward all womenkind. And 'twas this very trait, perhaps, which accounted for his remaining unwedded, although a lord, though the fact that his estates were incumbered may have had somewhat to do with it. Be that as it may, he lived alone, except for a few old servants, and was turned sixty, when, long after my transportation, he wedded his cook, who gave him three daughters and one son, to whom the estate went, but the ring and the letter came to the Chelmsfords. The letter, which I afterwards saw, was a most curious thing, both as to composition and spelling and chirography, for his lordship was no scholar. And since the letter is but short, I may perhaps as well give it entire. After this wise it ran, being addressed to Col. John Chelmsford, who was his cousin, though considerably younger.

"Dear Cousin. — (So wrote my Lord Ealing.) When this reaches you I shall be laid in silent tomb, where, perchance, I shall be more at peace than I have ever ben in a wurld, which either fitted me not, or I did not fit. At all odds there was a sore misfit betwixt us in some way. If it was the blam of the world, good ridance and parden, if it was my blam, let them which made me come to acount for't. I send herewith my great emruld ringg, with dimends which I suspect hath been the means of sending an inosent man into slavery. I had a mind some years agone to wed with Caterin Cavendish, and she bein a hard made to approche, having ever a stiff turn of the sholder toward me, though I knew not why, I was not willin to resk my sute by word of mouth, nor having never a gift in writin by letter. And so, knowin that mades like well such things, I bethought me of my emruld ring, and on the night of the ball, I being upstair in to lay off my hatt and cloak, stole privily into Catherin's chamber, she being a-dancin below, and I laid the ring on her dresing table, thinkin that she would see it when she entered, and know it for a love token.

"And then I went myself below, and Caterin, she would have none of me, and made up such a face of ice when I approached, that methought I had maybe wasted my emruld ring. So after a little up the stare I stole, and the ring was not where I had put it. Then thinkin that the ring had been stole, and I had neither that nor the made, I raised a great hue and cry, and demanded that a search be maid, and the ring was found on Master Wingfield, and he was therefor transported, and I had my ring again, and myself knew not the true fact of the case until a year agone. Then feeling that I had not much longer to live, I writ this, thinking that Master Wingfield was in a rich country, and not in sufferin, and a few months more would make not much odds to him. The facs of the case, cousin, I knew from Madam Cavendish's old servant woman Charlotte who came to my sister when the Cavendishs left for Virginia, having a fear of the sea, and later when my sister died, to my wife, and died but a year agone, and in her death-bed told me what she knew. She told me truly, that she did see Madam Cavendish on the night of the ball go into Caterin's chamber, and espying my emruld ring on her dressing-table, take it up and look at it with exceeding astonishment, and then lay it down not on the spot whereon I had left it, but on the prayer-book on the little stand beside her bed, and then go down stairs, frowning. Then this same Charlotte, having litle interest in life as to her own affairs, and forced to suck others, if she would keep her wits nourished, being watchful, saw me enter, and miss the ring, and heard the hue and cry which I raised. And then she, still watching, saw Master Harry Wingfield, who with others was searching the house for the lost treasure, stop as he was passing the open door of Caterin's chamber, because the green light of the emruld fixed his eyes, and rush in and secrete the ring upon his person. This Charlotte saw, and told Madam Cavendish, who bound her over to secrecy to save the honour of the family, believing that her own granddaughter Caterin was the thief. This epistle, cousin, is to prove to you that Caterin was no thief, but simply a cold maid, who hath no love for either hearts or gems, but of that I complain not, havin as I believe, wedded wisely, if not to please my famly, and three daughters and a son, hath my Betty given me, and most exceedin fine tarts hath she made, and puddens, and I die content, with this last writ to thee, cousin to clear Caterin Cavendish, and may be of an innosent gentleman likewise.

    "No more from thy cousin,
      "Ealing."

One strange feature was there about this letter, which the writer had not foreseen, while it cleared me well enough in the opinion of the family, to strangers it cleared me not at all, for who was to know for what reason I had entered Catherine's chamber, and took and secreted that ring of his lordship's? Strict silence had I maintained, and so had Madam Cavendish all these years, and naught in that letter would clear me before any court of law. Catherine being the only one whose innocence was made plain, I could now tell my story with no fear of doing her harm, but let those believe my part of it who would! Still I may say here, that I verily believe that I was at last cleared in the minds of all who knew me well, and for others I cared not. My term expired soon after that date, and though I chose to remain in Virginia and not return to England, yet my property was restored to me, for my half brother, John Chelmsford, when confronted by any gate of injustice leapt it like an English gentleman, with no ado. And yet after I heard that letter, I knew that I was a convict still, and knew that for some I would be until the end of the chapter, and when I grew a little stronger, that wild hope that now I might have Mary, dimmed within me, for how could I allow her to wed a man with a stain upon his honour? And even had I been pardoned, the fact of the pardon had seemed to prove my guilt.

It was three days after this, my brother and various others striving all the time, but with no effect, to secure my release, that Mary herself came to see me. Catherine, as I afterward discovered, had unlocked her chamber door and set her free while her grandmother slept, and the girl had mounted Merry Roger, and come straight to me, not caring who knew.

I heard the key grate in the lock, and turned my eyes, and

there she was: the blessing of my whole life, though I felt that I must not take it. Close to me she came and knelt, and leaned her cheek against mine, and stroked back my wild hair.

"Harry, Harry," she whispered, and all her dear face was tremulous with love and joy.

"Thou art no convict, Harry," she said. "Thou didst not steal the ring, but that I knew before, and I know not any better now, and I love thee no better now. And I would have been thine in any case."

"I am still a convict, sweetheart," I said, but I fear weakly.

"Harry," she cried out, "thou wilt not let that stand betwixt us now?"

"How can I let thee wed with a convict, if I love thee?" I said. "And know you not that this letter of my Lord Ealing's clears me not legally?"

"That I know," she answered frowning, "because thy brother hath consulted half the lawyers in England ere he came. I know that, my poor Harry, but what is that to us?"

"I cannot let thee wed a convict; a man with his honour stained, dear heart," I said.

Then she fixed her blue eyes upon mine with such a look as never I saw in mortal woman. She knew at that time what sentence had been fixed upon me for my share in the tobacco riot, but I did not know, and then and there she formed such a purpose, as sure no maid, however great her love for a man, formed before.

"Wait and see what manner of woman she is who loves thee, Harry," she said.

XXI

I lay in prison until the twenty-ninth day of May, Royal Oak Day. I know not quite how it came to pass, but none of my brother's efforts toward my release met with any success. I heard afterward some whispers as to the cause, being that so many of high degree were concerned in the riots, and that if I, a poor devil of a convict tutor, were let off too cheaply, why then the rest of them must be let loose only at a rope's end, and that it would never do to send me back to Drake Hill scot free, while Sir Humphrey Hyde and Major Robert Beverly and my Lord Estes, and others, were in durance, and some high in office in great danger of discovery. At all events, whatever may have been the reason, my release could not be effected, and in prison I lay for all those days, but with more comfort, since either Catherine or Mary — Mary I think it must have been — made a curtain for my window, which kept out that burning eye of the western sun, and also fashioned a gnat veil to overspread my pallet, so the flies could not get at me. I knew there were others in prison, but knew not that three of them were led forth to be hung, which might have been my fate, had I been a free man, nor knew that another was released on condition that he build a bridge over Dragon's Swamp. This last chance, my friends had striven sorely to get for me, but had not succeeded, though they had offered large sums, my brother being willing to tax the estate heavily. Some covert will there was at work against me, and it may be I could mention it, but I like not mentioning covert wills, but only such as be downright, and exercised openly in the faces of all men. I lay there not so uncomfortably, being aware of a great delight that the tobacco was cut, whether or no, as indeed it was on many plantations, and the King cheated out of great wealth.

This end of proceedings, with no Bacon to lead us, did not surprise nor disappoint me. Then, too, the fact that I was cleared of suspicion of theft in the eyes of her I loved and her family, at least, filled me with an ecstasy which sometimes awoke me from slumber like a pain. And though I was quite resolved not to let that beloved maid fling away herself upon me, unless my innocence was proven world-wide, and to shield her at all costs to myself, yet sometimes the hope that in after years I might be able to wed her and not injure her, started up within me. She came to see me whenever she could steal away, Madam Cavendish being still in that state of hatred against me, for my participation in the riot, though otherwise disposed enough to give her consent to our marriage on the spot. And every day came my brother John and Catherine, and now and then Parson Downs. And the parson used to bring me choice spirits in his pocket, and tobacco, though I could touch only the latter for fear of inflaming my wounds, and he used to sit and read me some of Will Shakespeare's Plays, which he bore under his cassock, and a prayer-book openly in hand, that being the only touch of hypocrisy which ever I saw about Parson Downs.

"Lord, Harry, thou dost not want prayers," he would say, "but rather being fallen as thou art, in an evil sink of human happenings, somewhat about them, and none hath so mastered the furthest roots of men's hearts as Will Shakespeare. 'Tis him and a pipe thou needst, lad." So saying, down he would sit himself betwixt me and the fiery western window, and I got to believe more in his Christianity, than ever I had done when I had heard him hold forth from the pulpit.

'Twas from him I knew the sad penalty which they fixed upon for me, for the 29th of May, that being Royal Oak Day, when they celebrated the Restoration in England, and more or less in the colonies, and on which a great junketing had been arranged, with races, and wrestling, and various sports.

Parson Downs came to me the afternoon of the 28th, and sat gazing at me with a melancholy air, nor offered to read Will Shakespeare, though he filled my pipe and pressed hard upon me a cup of Burgundy.

"'Twill give thee heart, Harry," he said, "and surely now thy wounds be so far healed, 'twill not inflame them, and in any case, why should good spirit inflame wounds? Faith, and I believe not in so much bleeding and so little stimulating. I'll be damned, Harry, if I see what is left to inflame in thee, not a hint of colour in thy long face. Stands it not to reason, that if no blood be left in thee for the wounds to work upon, they must even take thy vitals? But I am no physician. However, smoke hard as thou canst, poor Harry, if thou wilt not drink, for I have something to tell thee, and there is that about our good tobacco of Virginia — now we have rescued it, betwixt you and me, from royal freebooters — which is soothing to the nerves and tending to allay evil anticipations."

Then, as I lay puffing away something feebly at my pipe, still with enjoyment, he unfolded his evil news to me. It seemed that my brother had commissioned him so to do.

"'Tis a shame, Harry," he said, "and I will assure thee that all that could be done hath been, and if now there were less on guard, and a place where thou couldst hide with safety, the fleetest horse in the Colony is outside, if thou wert strong enough to sit him. And so thou escaped, I would care not if never I saw him again, though I paid a pretty penny for him and love him better than ever I loved any woman, since he springs to order and stands without hitching, and with never a word of nagging in my ears to make me pay penance for the service. What a man with a good horse, and good wine, and good tobacco, wanteth a wife for, passeth my understanding, but I know thou art young, and the maid is a fair one. Faith, and she was in such sore affliction this morning because of thee, Harry, as might well console any man. Had she been Bacon's widow, she had not wedded again, but gone widow to her death. Thou shouldst have seen her, lad, when I ventured to strive to comfort her with the reflection that her suffering in thy behalf was not so grievous as was Bacon's wife's for his death, for thou art to have thy life, my poor Harry, and no great hurt, though it may be somewhat wearisome if the sun be hot. But Mistress Mary Cavendish flew out at me in such wise, though she hath known all along to what fate thou wert probably destined, and said such harsh things of poor Madam Bacon, that I was minded to retreat. Keep Mary Cavendish's love, when she be wedded to thee, Harry, for there is little compromise with her for faults, unless she loveth, and she hath found out that Cicely Hyde betrayed the plans of the plant-cutters, and for her and Madam Bacon her sweet tongue was like a fiery lash, and Catherine was as bad, though silent. Catherine, unless I be greatly mistaken, will wed thy brother John, but unless I be more greatly mistaken, she loveth thee, and now, my poor Harry, wouldst know what they will do to thee tomorrow?"

I nodded my head.

"They will even set thee in the stocks, Harry, at the new field, before all the people at the sports," said Parson Downs.

XXII

I truly think that if Parson Downs had informed me that I was to be put to the rack or lose my head it would not have so cut me to the heart. Something there was about a gentleman of England being set in the stocks which detracted not only from the dignity of the punishment, but that of the offence. I would not have believed they would have done that to me, and can hardly believe it now. Such a punishment had never entered into my imagination, I being a gentleman born and bred, and my crime being a grave one, whereas the stocks were commonly regarded for the common folk, who had committed petty offences, such as swearing or Sabbath-breaking. I could not for some time realise it, and lay staring at Parson Downs, while he tried to force the Burgundy upon me and stared in alarm at my paleness.

"Why, confound it, Harry," he cried, "I tell thee, lad, do not look so. Hadst thou killed Rob Waller instead of wounding him, it would have been thy life instead of thy pride thou hadst forfeited."

"I wish to God I had!" I burst out, yet dully, for still I only half realised it all.

"Nay, Harry," declared the parson, "thy life is of more moment than thy pride, and as to that, what will it hurt thee to sit in the stocks an hour or so for such a cause? 'Twill be forgot in a week's time. I pray thee have some Burgundy, Harry, 'twill put some life into thee."

"'Twill never be forgot by me," said I, and indeed it never has been, and I know not why it seemed then, and seems now, of a finer sting of bitterness than my transportation for theft.

Presently I, growing fully alive to the state of the matters, wrought up myself into such a fever of wrath and remonstrance that it was a wonder that my wounds did not open. I swore that submit to such an indignity I would not, that all the authorities in the Colony should not force me to sit in the stocks, that I would have my life first, and I looked about wildly for my own sword or pistols, and seeing them not, besought the parson for his. He strove in vain to comfort me. I was weakened by my wounds, and there was, I suppose, something of fever still lingering in my veins for all the bleeding, and for a space I was like a madman at the thought of the ignominy to which they would put me. I besought that the lieutenant-governor should be summoned and be petitioned to make my offence a capital one. I strove to rise from my couch, and the vague thought of finding a weapon and committing some crime so grave that the stocks would be out of the question as a punishment for it, was in my fevered brain.

"As well go to a branch of a locust-tree blown by the May wind with honey for all seeking noses, as to Chichely," said Parson Downs. "And as for the burgesses, they are afraid of their own necks, and some of us there be would rather have thee sit in stocks than lose thy life, for we hold thy life dear, Harry, and some punishment it must be for thee, for thou didst shoot a King's officer, though with a damned poor aim, Harry."

Then I said again, with my heart like a drum in my ears, that I wished it had been better, though naught I had against Robert Waller, and as I learned afterward he had striven all he dared for my release, but the militia, being under some suspicion themselves, had to act with caution in those days.

Presently, while the parson was yet with me, my brother John came in, and verily, for the first time, I realised that we were of one blood. Down on his knees beside me he went.

"Oh, my God, Harry," he cried, "I have done all that I could for thee, and vengeance I will have of some for this, and they shall suffer for it, that I promise thee. To fix such a penalty as this upon one of our blood!"

"John," I whispered, grasping his hand hard, "I pray thee —"

But he guessed my meaning. "Nay, Harry," he cried, "better this, for if I went back to our mother and told her that thou wert dead, after her long slight of thee and the long wrong we have all done thee, it would be a sorer fate for her than the stocks for thee."

But I pleaded with him by the common blood in our veins to save me from this ignominy, and my fever increased, and he knew not how to quiet me. Then in came Catherine Cavendish, and what she said had some weight with me.

"For shame!" she said, standing over me, with her face as white as death, but with resolution in her eyes, "for shame, Harry Wingfield! Full easy it is to be brave on the battlefield, but it takes a hero to quail not when his vanity be assailed. Have not as good men as thou, and better, sat in the stocks? And think you that it will make any difference to us, except as we suffer with you? And 'tis harder for my poor sister than for thee, but she makes no complaint, nor sheds a tear, but goes about with her face like the dead, and such a look in her eyes as never I saw there before. And she told me to say to thee that she could not come today, but that she would make amends, and that thou hadst no cause to overworry, and I know not what she meant, but this much I do know, a brave man is a brave man whether it be the scaffold or the stocks, and — and — thou hast gotten thyself into a fever, Harry."

With that she bade my brother John get some cool water from the jailer, and she bathed my head and arranged my bandages with that same skill which she had showed at the time when I was bruised by the mad horse, and my brother looked on as if only half pleased, yet full of pity. And Catherine, as she bathed my head, told me how Major Beverly and Sir Humphrey were yet confined on shipboard, and Dick Barry was in the prison not far from me, and Nick and Ralph Drake were in hiding, but my Lord Estes was scot-free on account of his relationship to Governor Culpeper and had been to Drake Hill, but Mary would not see him. And she said, furthermore, that her grandmother did not know that I was to be set in the stocks, and they dared not tell her, as she was grown so feeble since the riot — at one time inveighing against me for my disloyalty, and saying that I should never have Mary, though I was cleared of my disgrace and no more a convict, and at another time weeping like a child over her poor Harry, who had already suffered so much and was now in prison.

Catherine in that way, which none but a woman hath, since it pertains both to love and authority, brought me to my senses, and I grew both brave and shamed at the same time, and yet after she had gone, never was anything like the sting of that ignominy which was prepared for me on the morrow. Many a time had I seen men in the stocks, and passed them by with no ridicule, for that, it seemed to me, belonged to the same class of folk as the culprits, but with a sort of contempt which held them as less than men and below pity even. The thought that some day I, too, was to sit there, had never entered my head. I looked at my two feet upholding the coverlid, and pictured to myself how they would look protruding from the boards of the stocks. I recalled the faces of all I had ever seen therein, and wondered whether I would look like this or that one. I remembered seeing them pelted by mischievous boys, and as the dusk thickened, it seemed alive with jeering faces and my ears rang with jibes. I said to myself that now Mary Cavendish was farther from me than ever before. Some dignity of wretchedness there might be in the fate of a convict condemned unjustly, but none in the fate of a man who sat in the stocks for all the people to gaze and laugh at.

I said to myself that that cruelest fate of any — to be made ridiculous in the eyes of love — was come to me, and love henceforth was over and gone. And thinking so, those grinning and jibing faces multiplied, and the air rang with laughter, and I trow I was in a high fever all night.

XXIII

The sports and races of Royal Oak Day were to be held on the "New Field" (so called), adjoining the plantation of Barry Upper Branch. The stocks had been moved from their usual station to this place to remind the people in the midst of their gayety that the displeasure of the King was a thing to be dreaded, and that they were not their own masters, even when they made merry.

On the morning of that day came my brother John's man-servant to shave and dress me, and the physician to attend to my wounds. It was a marvel that I was able to undergo the ordeal, and indeed, my brother had striven hard to urge my wounds as a reason for my being released. But such a naturally strong constitution had I, or else so faithfully had the physician tended me, with such copious lettings of blood and purges, that except for an exceeding weakness, I was quite myself. Still I wondered, after I had been shaven and put into my clothes, which hung somewhat loosely upon me, as I sat on a bench by the window, however I was to reach the New Field.

It was a hot and close day, with all the heaviness of sweetness of the spring settling upon the earth, and my knees had knocked together when my brother's man-servant and the physician, one on each side of me, led me from the bed to the bench.

So very weak was I that morning, after my feverish night, that, although the physician had let a little more blood to counteract it, I verily seemed almost to forget the stocks and what I was to undergo of disgrace and ignominy, being principally glad that the window was to the west, and that burning sun which had so fretted me, shut out.

The physician, long since dead, and an old man at that date, was exceeding silent, eyeing everybody with an anxious corrugation of brows over sharp eyes, and he had always a nervous clutch of his hands to accompany the glance, as if for lancets or the necks of medicine-flasks, never leaving a patient, unless he had killed or cured. He had visited me with as much faithfulness as if I had been the governor, and yet with no kindness, and I know not to this day, whether he was for or against the King, or bled both sides impartially. He looked at me with no compassion, and I might, from his manner, as well have been going to be set on a throne as in the stocks, but he counted my pulse-beats, and then bled me.

My brother John's man, however, whom he had brought from England, and whom I had known as a boy, and sometimes stolen away to hunt with, he being one of the village lads, shaved me as if it had been for my execution, and often I, somewhat dazed by the loss of blood, looking at him, saw the great tears trickling down his cheeks. A soft hearted man he was, who had met with sore troubles, having lost his family, a wife and three little ones, after which he returned to England and entered my brother's service, though he had been brought up independently, being the son of an innkeeper.

Something there was about this gentle, downcast man, adding the weight of my sorrow to his own, which would have aroused me to courage, if, as I said before, I had not been in such a state of body, that for the time my consciousness of what was to come was clouded.

There I sat on my bench, leaning stiffly back against the prison wall, a strange buzzing in my ears, and I scarcely knew nor sensed it when Parson Downs entered hurriedly, and leant over me, whispering that if I would, and could, my chance to escape was outside.

"The fleetest horse in the Colony," said he, "and, Harry, I have seen Dick Barry, and if thou canst but ride to the turn of the road, thou wilt be met by Black Betty and guided to a safe place; and the jailer hath drank over much Burgundy to which I treated him, and — and if thou canst, Harry —"

Then he stopped and looked at me and turned angrily to the physician who was packing up his lancets and vials to depart. "My God, sir," he cried, "do you kill or cure? You have not bled him again? Lord, Lord, had I but a lancet and a purge for the spirit as you for the flesh, there would be not only no sin but no souls left in the Colony! You have not bled him again, sir?"

But Martyn Jennings paid no more heed to him than if he had been a part of the prison wall, and, indeed, I doubt if he ever heeded any one who had not need of either his nostrums or his lancet, and after a last look at my bandages he went away.

Then Parson Downs and my brother's man looked at each other.

"It is of no use, sir," said the man, whose name was Will Wickett. "Poor Master Wingfield cannot ride a horse; he is far too weak." And with that verily the tears rolled down his cheeks, so womanish had he grown by reason of the sore trials to which he had been put.

"Faith, and I believe he would fall off at the first motion of the horse," agreed Parson Downs with a great scowl. I looked at, and listened to them both, with a curious feeling that they were talking about some one else, such was my weakness and giddiness from that last bloodletting.

Then Parson Downs, with an exclamation which might have sounded oddly enough if heard from the pulpit, but which may, after all, have done honour to his heart, fetched out a flask of brandy from his pocket, and bade Will Wickett find a mug somewhere, which he did speedily, and he gave me a drink which put new life into me, though it was still out of the question for me to ride that fiery horse which stood pawing outside the prison. And just here I would like to say that I never forgot, nor ceased to be grateful for the kindly interest in me, and the risk which the parson was disposed to take for my sake that day. A great risk indeed it would have been, and would doubtless have cost him his living, had I ridden across country on that famous horse of his; but he seemed not to think of that, but shook his head sadly after I had swallowed the brandy, and then my brother John came in and he turned to him.

"A fine plan for escape I had with the jailer drunk and the sentries blinded by my last winnings at cards, but Harry is too weak to ride," he said.

Then I, being somewhat restored by the brandy, mustered up strength enough to have a mind and speak it, and declared that I would not in any case avail myself of his aid to escape, since I should only bring trouble upon him who aided me, and should in the end be caught. And just as I spoke came a company of soldiers to escort me to the stocks, and the chance, for what it was worth, was over.

This much however had my brother gained for me, since I was manifestly unable to walk or ride: one of the Cavendish chairs which they had brought from England, was at the prison door, and some of our black men for bearers, half blubbering at the errand upon which they were bound.

Somebody had rigged a curtain of thin silk for the chair, so that I, when I was set therein, had great privacy, though I knew by the sounds that I was attended by the motley crowd which usually is in following at such affairs, beside the little troop of horse which was my escort, and my brother and Parson Downs riding on either side. Parson Downs, though some might reckon him as being somewhat contumelious in his manner of leaving the tobacco cutting, yet was not so when there was anything to be gained by his service. He was moreover quit of any blame by his office of spiritual adviser, though it was not customary for a criminal to be attended to the stocks by a clergyman, but only to the scaffold. But, as I began to gather some strength through that fiery draught which I had swallowed, and the fresh air, it verily seemed to me, though I had done with any vain complaints and was of a mind to bear my ignominy with as much bravery as though it were death, that it was as much of an occasion for spiritual consolation. I could not believe — when we were arrived at the New Field, and I was assisted from my chair in the midst of that hooting and jeering throng, which even the soldiers and the threatening gestures of the parson and my brother served but little to restrain — that I was myself, and still more so, when I was at last seated in that shameful instrument, the stocks.

Ever since that time I have wondered whether mankind hath any bodily ills which are not dependent upon the mind for their existence, and are so curable by some sore stress of it. For verily, though my wounds were not healed, and though I had not left my bed for a long time, and my seat was both rough and hard, and my feet were rudely piniooned between the boards, and the sun was blistering with that damp blister which frets the soul as well as the flesh, I seemed to sense nothing, except the shame and disgrace of my estate. As for my bodily ailments, they might have been cured, for aught I knew of them. To this time, when I lay me down to sleep after a harder day's work than ordinary, I can see and hear the jeers of that rude crowd around the stocks. Truly, after all, a man's vanity is his point of vantage, and I wonder greatly if that be not the true meaning of the vulnerable spot in Achilles's heel. Some slight dignity, though I had not so understood it, I had maintained in the midst of my misfortunes. To be a convict of one's free will, to protect the maid of one's love from grief, was one thing, but to sit in the stocks, exposed to the jibes of a common crowd, was another. And more than aught else, I felt the sting of the comedy in it. To sit there with my two feet straight out, soles to the people, through those rude holes in the boards, and all at liberty to gaze and laugh at me, was infinitely worse than to welter in my blood upon the scaffold. How many times, as I sat there, it came to me that if it had been the scaffold, Mary Cavendish could at least have held my memory in some respect; as it was, she could but laugh. Full easy it may be for any man with the courage of a man to figure in tragedy, but try him in comedy, if you would prove his mettle.

Shortly after I arrived there in the New Field, which was a wide, open space, the sports began, and I saw them all as in a dream, or worse than a dream, a nightmare. First came Parson Downs, whispering to me that as long as he could do me no good, and was in sore need of money, and, moreover, since he would by so doing divert somewhat the public attention from me, he would enter the race which was shortly to come off for a prize of five pounds.

Then came a great challenge of drums, and the parson was in his saddle and the horses off on the three-mile course, my eyes following them into the dust-clouded distance, and seeing the parson come riding in ahead to the winning post, with that curious uncertainty as to the reality, which had been upon me all the morning. That is, of the uncertainty of aught save my shameful abiding in the stocks.

As I said before, it was a hot day, and all around the field waved fruit boughs nearly past their bloom, with the green of new leaves overcoming the white and red, and the air was heavy with honey-sweet, and, as steady as a clock-tick through all the roaring of the merrymakers, came the hum of the bees and the calls of the birds. A great flag was streaming thirty feet high, and the gay dresses of the women who had congregated to see the sports were like a flower garden, and the waistcoats of the men were as brilliant as the breasts of birds, and nearly everybody wore the green oak-sprig which celebrated the Restoration.

Then again, the horses, after the challenge of the drums, sped around the three-mile course, and attention was diverted somewhat from me. There had been mischievous boys enough for my torment, had it not been for my brother John, who stood beside the stocks, his face white and his hand at his sword. Many a grinning urchin drew near with a stone in hand and looked at him, and looked again, then slunk away, and made as if he had no intention of throwing aught at me. After the horse racing came music of drums, trumpets, and hautboys, and then in spite of my brother, the crowd pressed close about me, and many scurrilous things were said and many grinning faces thrust in mine, and thinking of it now, I would that I had them all in open battlefield, for how can a man fight ridicule? Verily it is like duelling with a man of feathers. Quite still I sat, but felt that dignity and severity of bearing but made me more vulnerable to ridicule. Utterly weaponless I was against such odds.

I was glad enough when the drums challenged again for a race of boys, who were to run one hundred and twelve yards for a hat. Everybody turned from me to see that, and I watched wearily the straining backs and elbows of the little fellows, and the shouts of encouragement and of triumph when the winner came in smote my ears as through water, with curious shocks of sound.

Then ten fiddlers played for a prize, and while they played, the people gathered around me again, for races more than music have the ability to divert the minds of English folk; but they left me again, when there was a wrestling for a pair of silver knee-buckles. I remember to this day with a curious dizziness of recollection, the straining of those two stout wrestlers over the field, each forcing the other with all his might, and each scarce yielding a foot, and finally ending the strife in the same spot as where begun. I can see now those knotted arms and writhing necks of strength, and hear those quick pants of breath, and again it seems as then, a picture passing before my awful reality of shame. Then two young men danced for a pair of shoes, and the crowd gathered around them, and I was quite deserted, and could scarcely see for the throng the rhythmic flings of heels and tosses of heads. But when that sport was over, and the winner dancing merrily away in his new shoes, the crowd gathered about me again, and in spite of my brother, clods of mud began to fly, and urchins to tweak at my two extended feet.

Then that happened, which verily never happened before nor since in Virginia, and can never happen again, because a maid like Mary Cavendish can never live again.

Slow pacing into the New Field in that same blue and silver gown which she had worn to the governor's ball, with a wonderful plumed hat on her head, and no mask, and her golden hair flowing free, behind her Catherine and Cicely Hyde, like two bridesmaids, came my love, Mary Cavendish.

And while I shrank back, thinking that here was the worst sting of all, like the sting of death, that she should see me thus, straight up to the stocks she came, and gathering her blue and silver gown about her, made her way in to my side, and sat there, thrusting her two tiny feet, in their dainty shoes, through the apertures next mine, for the stocks were made to accommodate two criminals.

And then I looked at her, and would have besought her to go, but the words died on my lips, for in that minute I knew what love was, and how it could triumph over, not only the tragedy, but that which is more cruel, the comedy of life. Surely no face of woman was ever like Mary Cavendish's, as she sat there beside me, with such an exaltation of love, which made it like the face of an angel. Not one word she said, but looked at me, and I knew that after that she was mine forever, in spite of my love, which would fain shield her from me lest I be for her harm, and I realised that love, when it is at its best, is past the consideration of any harm, being sufficient unto itself for its own bliss and glory.

But presently, I, looking at her, felt my strength failing me again, and her face grew dim, and she drew my head to her shoulder and sat so facing the multitude, and such a shout went up as never was.

And first it was half derision, and Catherine and Cicely Hyde stood near us like bridesmaids, and my brother John kept his place. Then came Madam Judith Cavendish in a chair, and she was borne close to us through the throng and was looking forth with the tears running over her old cheeks, and extending her hands as if in blessing, and she never after made any opposition to our union. Then came blustering up Parson Downs and Ralph Drake, who afterward wedded Cicely Hyde, and the two Barrys who had braved leaving hiding, and the two black wenches who dwelt with them, one with a great white bandage swathing her head, and Sir Humphrey Hyde, who had just been released, and who, while I think of it, wedded a most amiable daughter of one of the burgesses within a year. And Madam Tabitha Storey, with that mourning patch upon her forehead, was there, and Margery Key, with — marvellous to relate in that crowd — the white cat following at heel, and Mistresses Allgood and Longman with their husbands in tow. All these, with others whom I will not mention, who were friendly, gathered around me, the while Mary Cavendish sat there beside me, and again that half derisive shout of the multitude went up.

But in a trice it all changed, for the temper of a mob is as subject to unexplained changes as the wind, and it was a great shout of sympathy and triumph instead of derision. Then they tore off the oak-sprigs with which they had bedecked themselves in honour of the day, and by so doing showed disloyalty to the King, and the militia making no resistance, and indeed, I have always suspected, secretly rejoicing at it, they had me released in a twinkling, and foremost among those who wrenched open the stocks was Capt. Calvin Tabor. Then Mary Cavendish and I stood together there before them all.

It was all many years ago, but never hath my love for her dimmed, and it shall live after Jamestown is again in ashes, when the sea-birds are calling over the sunset-waste, when the reeds are tall in the gardens, when even the tombs are crumbling, and maybe hers and mine among them, when the sea-gates are down and the water washing over the sites of the homes of the cavaliers. For I have learned that the blazon of love is the only one which holds good forever through all the wilderness of history, and the path of love is the only one which those that may come after us can safely follow unto the end of the world.

THE END

www.ingramcontent.com/pod-product-compliance
Lightning Source LLC
Chambersburg PA
CBHW030514260626
47157CB00005B/1742